John Holden

A wizard's wanderings from China to Peru

John Holden

A wizard's wanderings from China to Peru

ISBN/EAN: 9783337197407

Printed in Europe, USA, Canada, Australia, Japan

Cover: Foto ©Andreas Hilbeck / pixelio.de

More available books at **www.hansebooks.com**

A WIZARD'S WANDERINGS

FROM

CHINA TO PERU.

BY

JOHN WATKINS HOLDEN, F.S.Sc. (Lond.),

THE BOHEMIAN MAGICIAN.

LONDON :

DEAN & SON, 160A, FLEET STREET. E.C.

1886

INTRODUCTION.

———

ALEXANDRE DUMAS, *père*, laid down the dictum that 'prefaces were for failures.' However that may be, I fear it is not possible to dispense with one here, as, though I am pretty well known in the professional world, I fear the general reading public on first glancing at these pages would naturally ask: 'Who the dickens is Dr. Holden?' Well, if you please, I was born very young on the 1st February, 1844, at the good old city of Worcester, and christened there on the following Palm Sunday, which might possibly account for my early love of 'Palming, or Sleight-of-hand!' As my youthful record is on a par almost with that of the hero in 'A Bad Boy's Diary,' I think I had better charitably draw the line here and pass it over.

At sixteen, I found myself under fire, fighting under a foreign flag for some quixotic craze they called Liberty, with two other Englishmen only, instead of returning to England and entering Her Majesty's Navy, as my *pater*, who was Lord Lieutenant of his county and Member of Parliament, had intended me to do. Estranged from my family, I determined to be independent of everybody, and thus early commenced my Bohemian life.

It was whilst travelling through Morocco that I first gave any serious thoughts to the 'Magic Art.' At Castillejos, my travelling companion, a Hungarian Count, and myself, arranged to join a famous conjurer, one Sed Hamlah, and make the grand tour through some outlandish parts of Africa, calling ourselves the 'Cold Hot Iron Doctors.' The natives believe in burning the part afflicted with pain to effect a cure, so we simply took with us a stock of lunar caustic and, shall I add 'brass.' Through Morocco, Algeria, Tunis, Tripoli, Egypt Proper, Nubia, Darfur, &c., we travelled, meeting with adventures such as I fancy few other Englishmen have gone through. This gave me an excellent insight into the mysteries of Oriental Magic, and an acquisition of many strange and incomprehensible wonders, which I have since worked up to suit our Occidental ideas. I often think to myself, could the late poor old Sed Hamlah get leave to come up from the 'Shades' for a night, he would hardly recognise many of his old tricks in the guise I present them to my Mayfair patrons !

Having learnt all I required in the East, I next thought it necessary to be able to address an audience, not only in the Queen's English, but from an elocutionary point of view as well. An opening offering itself, I engaged with 'Drake's Diorama of India,' as Lecturer and Cicerone and very soon made my mark. Mr. Drake is still on the road, and, I am sure, he will be pleased to hear that some of the most agreeable memories of the past are associated with the several tours made under his direction. In these days of bogus managers it is quite a relief to speak with unqualified praise of the honourable and conscientious manner, Mr. Drake ever behaved to his Company when on tour. It was now time to try the anxieties and routine of an Acting Manager's life ; so, after a short experience with Mr. Simontin, of Dublin, Dr. Corry, of Belfast, and the late Mr. Hodges, of the Aberdeen Theatre Royal, I became Acting Manager of the 'London Opera Company,' which gave me a good insight into the taking of theatres, advertising, billing, &c. It also gave me an opportunity of addressing larger and more fashionable audiences, as, Gibus in hand, and left hand on heart, I would come before the curtain and ask 'the indulgence of the audience for the Prima or Seconda Donna (as the case might be), who was suffering from a severe cold, &c., &c., &c.'

All this time, however, no chance offered itself of appearing as a Wizard ; besides which, it was necessary I should take a course of lessons in 'palming,' and obtain the latest European magical novelties. I was introduced to Professor Hellis, of Notting Hill, one of the most elegant Palmers of the day, as many of my readers may remember who ever saw his performances at the old Polytechnic, in its palmy days. This gentlemen gave me (for a consideration) a course of lessons invaluable to me, and most deeply do I feel indebted to him for the same. Under the kind and cordial auspices of Professor Hellis, I finished my course of instruction in the Mysteries of the Magic Art—I feel that I am but discharging in a trifling degree my debt of gratitude to that kind-hearted man in acknowledging my obligations to him. But who of his professional contemporaries ever applied to him for aid, or counsel, that did not experience the most prompt, generous, and effectual assistance ? Having, in course of time, learnt the most requisite information, the time was now ripe, I thought, to make a first appearance. This was done at the Hope Hall, Liverpool, in the summer of 1877, and a few months afterwards an engagement was obtained at the Royal Polytechnic Institution, Regent Street, and

in a rather amusing manner. An appointment was made, and I had
to appear before the Directors at mid-day, in the room at the top of
the building, and to then and there show them what I was capable of
doing. Ten minutes or so before that hour, I knocked at the door,
which was ajar (pardon the paradox) and receiving no reply, looked
in, and noticed the room empty. A brilliant idea suddenly seized me.

Taking several coins I wrapped them up in some bright coloured
paper and quietly hid them behind a clock, or almanack, or something
at the extreme end of the room, and then closed the door and cleared
out of the building altogether, waiting outside in Regent Street, until
I saw the worthy Directors, and their most courteous Secretary, Mr.
J. Howell, enter the Institution, and wind their way up aloft. Leisurely
following, and allowing them time to be seated, I knocked at the door
and was told to come in.   'We don't want you to make any display,
or speech, but merely give us a specimen, Dr. Holden, of what you can
accomplish,' said one of the Directors.

'Well, gentlemen, it is somewhat difficult, *sans* preparation you
know, but if you will allow me I will introduce a marvellous Oriental
feat viz. the '*Vanishing* of Money' a trick, by-the-bye, they are adepts at
in the far East.   In this case, however, I shall get my money back
again, so the latter part will be more Occidental than Oriental perhaps.
You observe, gentlemen, I take three coins, and roll them up in this
little piece of bright coloured paper, I tuck up my sleeves, so that
nothing passes *that* way, and in my bare hands and arms I vanish
these coins so.' Here I apparently made them smaller and smaller,
and then at length vanished them altogether, showing the backs and
fronts of both hands. 'Now, gentlemen, comes the most remarkable
feature of this trick, I shall command that my coins re-appear—let us
see—where shall we say? Ah! there behind that clock, or whatever
it is, at the other side of the room! Pass ; kindly see if they are there.'
Of course they were ; I had already placed them there, but the elderly
gentleman who got up from his seat to look for them, seemed perfectly
convinced that by no earthly laws of well-known Polytechnic science
could such a miracle occur, and the look they all gave when he brought
from behind (whatever they were hid), the coins rolled up in the bright
coloured paper, will never be forgotten by the author of the hoax.

Whether the Directors thought one of their number was a confederate or not, it is difficult to surmise; at all events it was the means of
getting me an engagement there, and opening on Boxing Day, 1877, I
made a very favourable impression. The *Times* of December 27th,
remarking—'The *Prestidigitateur* at the Polytechnic is Dr. Holden,
and his skill in sleight of hand is not unworthy of the dignified title
which he bears.' The *Daily News* remarks—' Dr. Holden's conjuring
is very good indeed.' The *Railway Record*, of December 29th.—
'Evidently a great acquisition amongst our London entertainers, so

exquisitely finished are his performances, and so enchanting the *débon-naire* air which he infuses into them; whilst the *Sunday Times* summed up with 'Dr. Holden gives his marvellous entertainment of Legerdemain, and performs many feats which seem to baffle description.'

Having travelled nearly all the world over, I thought it now my best policy to settle down in London and make a name there, more especially so, as performing, in 1878 at the Granville, Ramsgate, Mr Mitchell, Jun., of the Royal Library, Old Bond Street, London, happening to be present at one of my representations there, very kindly and considerately recommended me to his father, who at once placed me on his books, and obtained some high class engagements, T.R.H. The Duke and Duchess of Teck, and the daughters of H.R.H. the Princess of Wales, being my first patrons. Then the Brazilian Ambassador, Earl Dudley, Duke and Duchess of Norfolk, at Arundel Castle, Lord Londesborough and many others of note. On May 24th, 1879 through Mr. Mitchell's influence a Royal command took me to Balmoral Castle, where I had the great honour of appearing before Her Most Gracious Majesty the Queen-Empress, the late lamented Prince Leopold, the Princess Beatrice, and, for a second time, the daughters of the Princess of Wales, T.R.H. Princesses Victoria and Maud.

Several times during the performance Her Majesty had some kind word of encouragement to give me, and at the conclusion she personally complimented me, remarking that my performance was 'so different to anything I have seen before, and the usual style of conjuring.' Her Majesty was no doubt thinking of Anderson, the 'Wizard of the North,' who had appeared there some fifteen years previously, or possibly a longer period even than that. This was a red-letter day for me, as the announcement appeared in the Court Circular and all the other papers copied. But success, I soon found, begets envy, and my professional contemporaries, instead of looking at the honour in the light I looked at it, viz., as an exceptional honour to the Magical Profession, thought fit to sneer and pass some cutting remarks, but that, I might have expected.

On December 1st, 1880, the anniversary of H.R.H. the Princess of Wales' birthday, another Royal command took me down to Sandringham, where I performed in presence of the most aristocratic audience I ever had hoped to appear before. It included T.R.H. the Prince and Princess of Wales, the Duke of Cambridge, Lord Hartington, Lord and Lady Claud Hamilton. The Duchess of Manchester and a number of other distinguished visitors. The Prince of Wales personally complimented me on my success, and in less than three months afterwards, viz. on February 21st, 1881, I appeared again before their Royal Highnesses and suite, at Marlborough House, with far greater *éclat* even than at Sandringham. Success was now assured, engagements rolled in from all parts. I was induced to accept the appointment as 'Entrepreneur of Magic' to the largest firm in London, and for two years or more, with the aid of a staff of competent deputies, satisfactorily fulfilled a vast number of private engagements in town and country, with occasional tours of short duration to the Continent, Channel Islands, Scotland, and Ireland. In Dublin, October, 1882, I appeared at the Ancient Concert Rooms, Great Brunswick Street, afterwards visiting Kingstown, Bray, Gorey, Wexford, and Cork, where I appeared at the Royal Opera House. The greatest honour I consider I ever received, was in Scotland, on April 4th, 1883, when I passed my third degree in Freemasonry and was made a Master Mason the one ambition of my life, and before which, all other honours I have received (and they are legion), sink and 'pale their ineffectual fires.' At the Alexandra Palace I appeared year after year to large audiences, and this summer I completed a month's engagement at the Crystal Palace, Sydenham, in the Entertainment Court there, a room admirably adapted for magical performances. The crowded audiences I performed to spoke well for the able and experienced management this popular place is now under, thanks to the energy of Captain Henshaw Russell.

It seems indeed marvellous what one can accomplish in so short a period by personal energy alone. It shows one what perseverance and determination will do if properly applied. During this period I have given my whole mind and soul to the Magic Art, and have thought of nothing else. Experiment after experiment have I conceived, and it may well be said, 'Alone he did it,' for I never allow anyone on the stage with me, nor do I take an assistant about with me. In August, 1884, an unlooked for honour was accorded, viz., the making me a 'Foundation Fellow of the Society of Science, Letters and Art, of London.' I fancy I have now said quite enough about myself.

Bacon says: 'Long speeches are flat things, and carry little weight.' So are long prefaces. The Spartans have been praised as the most eloquent of the races of Greece—and why? Simply because laconic brevity was their peculiar forte.

Let us to the point, at once, and call a spade a spade. Just as good wine needs no bush, so truth asks but few words, without periphrases or reservations. Speech was well compared by Themistocles to a piece of tapestry gradually unrolled, whereas thoughts unspoken lie in packs. But in choosing a carpet men do not look at a mile of it, but only at as much of it as contains a fair type of the pattern. The rest should be kept for other occasions It was stated the other day, by an eminent Professor, in the course of a lecture, that 'Cato did not begin to learn the Greek language until he was eighty-four years of age.' Young England of to-day are telling their fathers that they are anxious to follow the example of Cato! If more time were devoted to the living languages at our public schools than to the dead languages and political economy, it would do far more good to the rising generation !

In these pages I shall endeavour to give a truthful, concise description of what came under my notice during a Professional Tour as a Public Entertainer, all the world over. As, however, this is not a Diary of a Magician's Wanderings, I shall touch on the professional part of it but lightly, as I am fully aware the subject is not to everyone's taste, whilst pleasant, light geographical facts cannot but commend themselves to all.

'It is for wandering in it that the world was made so wide,' wrote Goethe, and over this same world I am now going to take you. Was it not the Emperor Hadrian, who, to keep fresh his recollections of travels in Greece, built at his magnificent villa, at Tivoli, *fac similes* of the glorious Temples of Pœcilè, and Lycëum, planting by their side the Grove of an Academy, and carrying the stream of an ideal Penëus thorough the pleasant Vale of an imitative Temple? Now Hadrian, with all the imperial power of Rome, would have been totally unable to enjoy the '*embarras de richesse*' of foreign travel, which we, in the Nineteeenth Century, are able to indulge in, if only we possess sufficient capital. The remarks I shall have the honour of making in these pages may possibly construct a humbler Tivoli, and, together, (may I hope) we shall enjoy the pleasures experienced of old by the Greek traveller in the Villa of Hadrian?

16, Hastings Street, London, W.C., 1886.

CONTENTS.

CHAPTER I.

COMMENCEMENT OF THE TOUR—ADIEU TO LONDON—ADVICE
WITH REGARD TO GOING OUT TO INDIA—DESCRIPTION OF
THE BEST ROUTE—THE ORIENTAL NAVIGATION COMPANY—
DEPARTURE FROM DOVER .. .. ,. I

CHAPTER II.

ARRIVAL AT PARIS—PARIS AND THE PARISIANS—BON' MOT
OF THE EMPRESS EUGENIE—THE RUE ROYALE—THE SIEGE
OF PARIS—THE COMMUNISTS 5

CHAPTER III.

OFF TO NORWAY—HAMMERFEST—THE MIDNIGHT SUN—DEN-
MARK — COPENHAGEN — SWEDEN — LINNÆUS — EMPLOY-
MENTS OF WOMEN AT STOCKHOLM 8

CHAPTER IV.

RUSSIA—PETER THE GREAT—CATHERINE THE SECOND—ST.
PETERSBURG—THE RHINE—GERMANY AND THE GERMANS.. II

CHAPTER V.

SPAIN—DESCRIPTION OF MADRID—SEVILLE—BARCELONA—
GENERAL REMARKS ON SPAIN—A SPANISH BULL-FIGHT .. 13

CHAPTER VI.

CROSSING THE ALPS—ARRIVAL IN ITALY—VENICE—GONDOLAS
AND GONDOLIERS—THE BRIDGE OF SIGHS—MILAN—ROME
—HUMOROUS REMARKS OF AN AMERICAN TOURIST—THE
BAY OF NAPLES—VESUVIUS—HERCULANEUM AND POMPEII
—BRINDISI 16

CHAPTER VII.

A TRIP TO AUSTRALIA—MELBOURNE—SYDNEY—AUSTRALIAN
WINES—HONOLULU—THE CAROLINE ISLANDS 24

PAGE

CHAPTER VIII.

A TRIP TO INDIA—BOMBAY—INDIAN RAILWAYS—BENARES—
THE GANGES — DELHI — THE BUDDHISTS — HYDERABAD—
THE AUTHOR'S PROFESSIONAL SUCCESS AT THAT FAMOUS
CITY—EUROPEAN REQUISITES FOR THE INDIAN CLIMATE—
MORNING AND NIGHT IN INDIA—THE 'LOGANS' OR ROCKING-
STONES—THE MOSQUES OF AHMEDABAD—HINDOO CHIL-
DREN—INDIAN PILGRIMS   33

CHAPTER IX.

ARRIVAL AT CEYLON—GENERAL DESCRIPTION OF THE ISLAND
—DESCRIPTION OF BANKOK, THE CAPITAL OF SIAM—THE
WHITE ELEPHANT—SUNDAY MORNING'S DIVINE SERVICE AT
SEA—THE MAHARAJAH OF JOHORE   45

CHAPTER X.

A VOYAGE TO CHINA—PEKIN—THE OPIUM-SMOKER—THE
CHINESE AND THE BRITISH—CHINESE PROVERBS—LEGEND
OF THE ORIGIN OF THE FAN—THE JOSS-HOUSE   51

CHAPTER XI.

SHANGHAI—FISH AND FOWL IN CHINA—CHINESE JUNKS—
CHINESE IMITATIONS—INVETERATE GAMBLERS   55

CHAPTER XII.

A TRIP TO JAPAN—YOKOHAMA—TOKIO—YEDDO—JAPANESE
WINDOW-GARDENING—THE LANGUAGE OF FLOWERS—HOW
TO KEEP YOURSELF COOL IN HOT CLIMATES—THE AINOS OF
JAPAN—MANNERS AND CUSTOMS OF THE JAPANESE   ..   57

CHAPTER XIII.

CROSSING THE PACIFIC—SAN FRANCISCO—THE CHINESE IN
CALIFORNIA — GIANT TREES OF CALIFORNIA — OGDEN —
SPLENDID SCENERY IN AMERICA   64

CHAPTER XIV.

DESCRIPTION OF NEW YORK—THE BROADWAY—THE FALLS OF
NIAGARA—THE TERRAPIN TOWER—A VISIT TO THE FALLS
—THE LAKES   70

PAGE

CHAPTER XV.

A VOYAGE TO MADEIRA—DESCRIPTION OF FUNCHAL—OUR FELLOW-VOYAGERS—A CRUISE IN SEARCH OF HEALTH— REMINISCENCES OF HOME—OUR BRITISH SAILORS   72

CHAPTER XVI.

THE APPROACH TO TABLE BAY—SOUTH AFRICAN SCENERY— THE LION'S HEAD—TABLE MOUNTAIN—ARRIVAL OF AN AMERICAN WHALE SHIP—THE PHANTOM SHIP OF VANDER- DECKEN—STRANGE TRADITIONS—SPECIAL FEATURES OF CAPE TOWN   85

CHAPTER XVII.

WITCHCRAFT' IN SOUTH AFRICA—AN IMPOSTOR—STRANGE PREDICTIONS—THE AMAXOSA—HOW THEY WERE DUPED— CETEWAYO'S WITCH-DOCTORS—HOW CETEWAYO'S HIDING- PLACE WAS DISCOVERED — KIMBERLEY — THE DIAMOND FIELDS OF SOUTH AFRICA   96

CHAPTER XVIII.

'THE DARK CONTINENT'—STANLEY AND LIVINGSTONE— LORD WOLSELEY — GORDON — KHARTOUM — A SAIL DOWN THE NILE—REMINISCENCES OF PAST AGES—UJIJI—THE SIMOON—THE SPHINX—THE PYRAMIDS   101

CHAPTER XIX.

PALESTINE — THE HOLY SEPULCHRE — THE TALMUD — THE MISHNAH—DEAN STANLEY'S BOOK ON THE HOLY LAND— THE CEDARS OF LEBANON—BETHLEHEM—DISTINGUISHED MODERN JEWISH MUSICIANS..   106

CHAPTER XX.

THE ARABS AND THEIR HORSES—ARABIAN AND TURKISH CUSTOMS—THE BEARD—SOME STRANGE ADVENTURES OF THE AUTHOR—OUT AND ABOUT—THE AUTHOR'S 'BOHEMIAN NOTES'   113

CHAPTER XXI.

SUMMONED TO BALMORAL — AN ENTERTAINMENT GIVEN BEFORE THE QUEEN — A MAGICAL DISTRIBUTION — THE SILK CLOTH—THE BOUQUET—THE ROYAL PROGRAMME OF THE AUTHOR'S PERFORMANCE BEFORE HER MAJESTY— GENERAL REMARKS ON SCOTLAND   120

CHAPTER XXII.

LIFE IN SCOTLAND — PORT GLASGOW — LOCH LOMOND—
TOURISTS TO THE SCOTTISH LAKES—GENERAL REMARKS ON
SCOTLAND 129

CHAPTER XXIII.

NECROMANCY—ROGER BACON—THE ELIXIR OF LIFE—SUPER-
STITIOUS IDEAS—THE CHINESE — SUPERSTITIONS ABOUT
BIRDS—THE SWALLOW—KINDNESS TO ANIMALS A NOBLE
QUALITY 133

CHAPTER XXIV.

'SPIRITUALISM'—MEDIA — DR. RADCLIFFE—SHAKESPEARE'S
'MACBETH' — IMPOSTURES — SEANCES — EXPOSURES OF
'SPIRITUALISM' BY SIR GEORGE SITWELL AND HERR CARL
VON BUCH 138

CHAPTER XXV.

'FORTUNE-TELLING' BY CARDS—A SPANISH SUPERSTITION—
'THOUGHT-READING' — ITS FALLACY AND ABSURDITY —
A FEW COMMON-SENSE OBSERVATIONS—CURIOUS INSTANCES
WITH REGARD TO THE SO-CALLED 'SECOND SIGHT' .. 146

CHAPTER XXVI.

THE 'ART OF MAGIC'—NOT EASILY ATTAINED—EXPLANATION
OF SOME INTERESTING EXPERIMENTS—THE OLD STYLE OF
CONJURING OUT OF DATE—THE DEMON COIN—THE WIZARD'S
POCKET-HANDKERCHIEF — HINTS ON CONJURING—THE
'TRICK OF TRICKS'—THE GREAT INDIAN SAND TRICK—
THE ENCHANTED SEGAR 155

CHAPTER XXVII.

SUPERSTITIONS WITH REGARD TO WEATHER—THE LEGEND
OF ST. SWITHIN 159

CHAPTER XXVIII.

'SPIRITUALISM'—AN EXPOSE OF THE IMPOSTURE—HEAR
BOTH SIDES OF THE QUESTION—A REMARKABLE INCIDENT
WITH REGARD TO SO-CALLED 'SPIRITUALISM'—'THE FLOAT-
ING TABLE'—'SPIRIT-RAPPING'—THE SPIRITUALIST MUSI-
CAL BOX—'INVISIBLE WRITING' 163

A WIZARD'S WANDERINGS

CHINA TO PERU.

———

CHAPTER I.

COMMENCEMENT OF THE TOUR—ADIEU TO LONDON—ADVICE WITH
REGARD TO GOING OUT TO INDIA—DESCRIPTION OF THE BEST
ROUTE—THE ORIENTAL NAVIGATION COMPANY—DEPARTURE
FROM DOVER.

'Not to laugh when nature prompts, is but a knavish, hypocritical
way of making a mask of one's face.'—*Pope.*

LET us suppose, then, that our preparations are completed, that
our luggage is at the depôt, our purse well-filled, our money-belt
also, and that we are going to start on our contemplated tour.
Now that we are about to bid adieu to London, the place actually
rises several degrees in our estimation. The 'silvery Thames'
looks less pea-soupy than we ever noticed it before, and, for the
first time in our lives, we actually notice architectural beauties
about old Somerset House, which was, once upon a time, a
palace, but was levelled to the ground by the Protector Somerset,
in 1549. After his execution, three years later, Somerset House,
his residence, became Crown property. It was built from the
designs of Sir William Chambers, 1775. Go where you may in
this tight little island, if you come across an old-fashioned bed-
room, the chances are: 'Queen Elizabeth slept here.' She slept
several times in Somerset House.

There was a touch of the courtier as well as of the wit in
Sydney Smith's reply to the lady, who, arguing that it was always

high tide at London Bridge, at twelve o'clock, appealing to him with, 'Now, Mr. Smith, is it not so?' 'It used not to be so, I believe, formerly, but perhaps the Lord Mayor and aldermen have altered it lately.'

One hundred men could not carry the amount of the National Debt of England counted out in ten pound Bank of England notes, notwithstanding the lightness of the paper they are printed on.

Great Britain has, at present, no fewer than fifty colonies, in different parts of the world; so a man has a choice before him, where to settle down in, if, in these days of depression, he could only manage to get there. Looking at the vast numbers of un-employed hanging about the London streets, willing to work, but unable to find the same, how fervently have I, over and over again, wished I had the loan of Aladdin's lamp, that I might put a few hundred golden sovereigns in each of their pockets, and dis-patch them *high presto* over to Canada, where they, perhaps, might improve their condition.

Considering that Englishmen have invaded every country in the world for commercial and industrial purposes, it is unreason-able and ungenerous on their part to complain about the migration of foreign labourers hither. But for the influx of foreigners in times past, England would not have secured her manufacturing supremacy. It must not be forgotten that some of our most profitable industries were taught us by foreigners. Nor does the influence which foreigners have exerted in the development of British manufactures belong exclusively to the period of 'ancient history.' Our chief manufacture, namely, that of iron and steel, still owes much to them. Both of our two new centres of this great industry—Middlesborough and Barrow-in-Furness—have been, practically, the creation of foreigners, the late Mr. Bolckow having been the founder of the former, and Mr. H. W. Schneider, if not the founder of the latter, at least the discoverer of the rich deposits of hæmatite ore to which its prosperity has been due. Again, the value of the services which another foreigner—the late Sir William Siemens—rendered, not only to the iron and steel manufacture, but to various other British industries, cannot be adequately estimated. In art and science, as well as in industry, we have been laid under a heavy debt of gratitude to foreigners. The grand cathedrals of which we boast were largely the work of foreign stonemasons, and one of the greatest names in English scientific literature, is that of a naturalised foreigner, Sir William Herschel, from whom a late Lord Chancellor claims descent. We owe even our House of

Commons to a foreigner. It is manifestly unreasonable, there-fore, to denounce foreigners as intruders upon British soil. Still it is unfortunate that in one great industry, namely, seamanship, foreigners should preponderate over Englishmen.

In deciding upon the best time of year to go out to India or 'gorgeous East,' the points to be considered are :—firstly, the season in England at time of departure ; secondly, the best season in which to pass down the Red Sea, so as to avoid as much as possible the suffering consequent upon the heat during that part of the journey ; and, thirdly, the season upon arrival in India. The great object, of course, is to make the immediate change of climate to the traveller as inconsiderable as possible.

The Red Sea is hot all the year round. The best time for any person to leave England for either of the Presidencies, is September or October. Anyone going out to India for the first time will feel the heat less than old stagers, especially in the Red Hot Sea.

The Brindisi route has the advantage of being, at least, the shortest and quickest. Brindisi is 1,300 miles from Calais, so you have only 800 miles sea voyage to Alexandria, and a pleasant trip through the Tyrol and Italy. If you leave, suppose on Monday, at 5 a.m., and after one of the most delightful trips perhaps in the world, passing by the mountains of Argosella, the Island of Claudia, and the Isle of Candia, you can reach Alexandria on Thursday. Leave Suez on Friday, arriving at Aden in six days. From Aden to Ceylon, it would take nine days, four days more to Madras, four days to Calcutta.

At Messrs. Green and Co.'s, Managers of the ' Orient,' and the Pacific Steam Navigation Company, Fenchurch Street, London, we take our Ocean ticket, also one for Naples, where their magni-ficent steamer will call nine days after leaving Gravesend. We book for Sydney, Australia, 12,065 by Red Sea route, or 13,580 miles *via* Cape Town route.

I like the former route best, as the accommodation on board is as near perfection as possible. A pleasant little tour is before us through Europe, with a knowledge that, bar accident, dusty, and tired, sick of continental cookery and imposition, we find at Naples a haven of rest on board—a British steamer one might well be proud of.

Let us then suppose we have run past Kent with its charming, comfortable-looking, homely scenery, with not a square yard of land running to waste, fields well looked after, contented-looking peasantry (if it is not hop-picking time), and a take-it-altogether-generally-speaking-solvent-general-appearance of things in general.

We bid adieu to the white cliffs of Old England, and sniff with unction the ozone as the spray washes over the deck of the *Calais-Douvres.*

'Tremendous motion felt and rueful throes.'—*Milton.*

All our cares are placed on the shelf, we mean to enjoy ourselves, let the natives swindle us as they like. We have been to the Scottish Highlands ere now, have we not? Well, after that ordeal, we ought to be able to stand anything! In a very few hours time we arrive at Paris. There is something about Paris very attractive. Like the loadstone it draws.

CHAPTER II.

ARRIVAL AT PARIS—PARIS AND THE PARISIAN—BON MOT OF THE
EMPRESS EUGENIE—THE RUE ROVALE—THE SIEGE OF PARIS—
THE COMMUNISTS.

IT is essentially a show city, all is insincere and got up for effect.
A Frenchman does not know what he wants, and he won't be
satisfied until he gets it. Voltaire, whose wit like a Malay
Kreese, carried poison on its blade, turned his satire on his own
countrymen, whom he epigrammatically described as : *Moitié singe,
moitié tigre.*

The Frenchman, who has got a dash of German blood in his
veins, is active in mind and body, has neither time nor per-
tinacity to be inquisitive ; he has general views, but changes them
every moment ; is quick to anger, ambitious and egotistical, but
none so readily takes or makes a joke.

Count Bulow cleverly describes the three nations, French,
English, and German. 'Some years ago a prize was offered
for the best drawing of a camel. A French artist, as soon as he
heard of it, rushed to the Jardin des Plantes, and in a week had
finished a beautiful imaginative picture. The Englishman took
a week to consider, and then went to Arabia, whence he returned
in six months with an accurate and bold sketch of the subject.
The German shut himself up in his atelier and endeavoured to
elaborate a camel from the depths of his moral consciousness,
and he is still at work.'

Jean Jacques Rousseau remarked : ' Oh, Paris ! Paris ! Paris !
A mass of houses ; an abyss of. ills ! If all the griefs and crimes
which those houses enclose were to appear on their exteriors from
every stone would ooze a tear or a drop of blood.' If you give a
Frenchman a sovereign he wants change. *On dit* an Englishman is never happy except when he is miserable. A Scotchman
never at home except when he is abroad ; and an Irishman never
at peace except when he is at war. Of course we should have a
look in at the Café Chantant to hear the latest favourite. When

5

charming and pschutt song.   L'Alcazar was crowded nightly, and all Paris, high and low, had gone wild about her.

> 'Swans sing before they die; 'twere no bad thing
>   Should certain persons die before they sing.'—*Coleridge*.

did not apply to this music-hall artiste for a wonder, I thought. I once heard a bon mot not easily forgotten. 'Il réflechi,' said the Empress Eugénie to the late Emperor, admiring a beautiful looking-glass he had just presented her with. 'Which is more than you do,' he replied. 'Il est poli,' quietly answered the Empress, 'which is more than you are.'

As we stroll down the Rue Royale, admiring the well displayed contents of the different shop windows, we cannot help thinking of the miserable Communists of 1871, who, in this very street, bribed the firemen to fill their engines with petroleum, and play on six burning houses in which twenty-seven persons perished.   I happened to be shut up in Paris during the Siege of 1870, and should think many to their dying days will remember the kindness of our compatriot, Dr. Evans, who saved the Empress from the mob, and afterwards spent something like £48,000 amongst the wounded Frenchmen.

In Paris the women are always thirty, or sixty, a woman of forty does not exist.

In the Royal Library there is a Chinese chart of the heavens, made about 600 B.C. in which 1460 stars are correctly inserted.

Louis Philippe once remarked to Madame Grisi, the wife of M. Mario, as she stood fondling her two young children :. 'Ah, madame, are those then some of your little Grisettes?' 'No, Sire, was the quick reply, perfect in every requirement of the pun, 'no Sire, these are my little Marionettes!'

As no doubt my readers are aware, the Louvre and Tuileries are situated on the right bank of the Seine, between it and the Rue de Rivoli. The two piles were completed and harmonised under the second Empire, and occupied with their enclosures an area of nearly sixty acres, forming one single palace of supreme splendour, grandeur and magnitude. The Louvre consists of an old and new Louvre. During the reign of the Commune, not only did the devouring element threaten to destroy the inestimable treasures of the Louvre, but one day a number of men carrying slow matches and led by a man (if you can call him a man) named Napias Piquat, made all the preparations to set fire to several parts of the Museum of the Louvre, and two of the guardians were shot.

This Napias Piquat threatened to make the whole building one great conflagration. He was taken and shot.

On Sunday, May 21st, a concert was held in the Salle des Maréchaux, which extended the whole depth of the Palace and the height of two floors; it was one of the most splendid and gorgeously decorated halls in Paris. On the walls were ranged the busts and figures of marshals and generals of the Empire; the ceiling was exquisitely carved and painted.

It is almost impossible to describe the Communists. These reckless madmen and fools, deaf to reason, bent on every form of wickedness and excess, made Paris, once so gay, their frightened slave, crouching to earth under their dreaded and loathsome tyranny. The aspect of Paris after the suppression of the *émute* was sad in the extreme, Paris sad, motionless and waste—filled with dead, dying and wounded. Consternation in every breast—solitude in every street !

First came the Siege with famine, separation and poverty, then the insurrection of Mont-matre ! Cannonading day and night— ceaseless musketry—mothers in tears—sons pursued—wounded wherever you happened to look. It was of a character savage and barbarous in the extreme—nothing was respected. God—pro- perty—person or religion. Human, or divine laws were set at defiance. Who can wonder that the retribution should be other than terrible ? The glowing fires of burning Paris illuminated the Prussian camp at St. Denis !

O Commune of Paris ! That the bloodless revolution of Sep- tember should end in fire and sword, in rapine and murder under the eyes of the Victor ! Paris left to do what the Prussian hordes had left undone made it a seething cauldron. A diaboli- cal genius presided over their work of destruction ; individuals wearing the fireman's uniform were seen to throw combustible liquids by means of engines and pails on the burning pile, instead of trying to extinguish the flames, and if anybody attempted to arrest the conflagration, he was fired at by those demons in their wild revenge.

Let us now suppose we are like 'Sir Boyle Roache's bird,' and pay a flying visit due North. Travelling on the Continent is not like travelling here in England. Red Tape shows itself every- where. The boasted French politeness is but a 'beautiful myth,' still the novelty of the thing makes it endurable, and we try and fancy we are enjoying railway rides over Europe. The train service is certainly improving year by year, and well it may do. Let us then start right off, due North.

CHAPTER III.

OFF TO· NORWAY—HAMMERFEST—THE MIDNIGHT SUN—DEN-
MARK—COPENHAGEN—SWEDEN—LINNÆUS—EMPLOYMENTS OF
WOMEN AT STOCKHOLM.

DURING the dog-days commend me to Norway. The less luggage we take the better, a portmanteau and a bundle of rods, sticks, &c., ought to suffice. With such light encumbrances it is possible to spend a month or six weeks very comfortably travelling over-land across the Hardunger, the Fillie, or the Dovre Fjelds for instance, or even farther north, if time and weather permit. Roughly, 4s. 6d. to 5s. a day, secures the best accommodation the roadside station-houses have to offer, and abundance of wholesome, if not very varied food, while the expenses of travelling by cariole may be taken at something over 2s. per Norwegian mile, one Norwegian mile being equal to seven English. With the help of a phrase book all necessary conversation with the natives may be carried on, and the language is not at all difficult to acquire.

The chief requisites for comfortable travelling are a disposition to treat the peasants considerately with a little of their own serious politeness, and a well replenished bag of small change, a commo-dity very scarce 'up country.' So, after a visit to Hammerfest, where, of course, we buy shoes and bone spoons of the Laps, after stealing a glance at the red midnight sun on the threshold of the dim and mysterious Arctic circle, we bid adieu to Norway with regret.

Denmark's most ancient inhabitants were Cimbri and Teutones, who were driven out by the Jutes or Goths. Denmark's name is supposed to be derived from *Dan*, the founder of the Danish Monarchy, and *Mark*, a 'German word signifying country.'

Copenhagen has been bombarded by our fleet several times. The last time was in September, 1807, when it surrendered to Admiral Gambier and Lord Cathcart.

Hans Christian Andersen, the poet and teller of fairy tales, was a Dane. You have of course, read 'The Ugly Duckling'; if not by all means do so.

8

Copenhagen was built by Waldemar the First, 1157, and became the capital in 1443. The University was founded in 1479 In 1794 the palace, valued at four millions, was destroyed by fire, and 100 persons lost their lives. The following year the Arsenal, Admiralty, and fifty streets were destroyed by fire.

A very enjoyable couple of days can be spent here.

Sweden's ancient inhabitants were the Fins, now the modern inhabitants of Finland. The internal state of the kingdom is little known previous to the 11th century. The entire population in 1871 was only 4,204,117 or about that of London. Here the women work like slaves, it's simply disgraceful. Stockholm is built on *hoimen* or islands, and was fortified by Berger Jarl about 1254. Here the Swedish nobility were massacred by Christian the Second in 1520.

In these pleasant parts, you meet with that charming ideal, a pretty, high-spirited, educated young woman, who is able to darn a stocking, mend her own frock, command a regiment of pots and kettles, feed the pigs, milk the cow. During the dog-days, there are many worse places to visit than Sweden. This is becoming a very popular tour, especially to anyone fond of fishing and roughing it. The steamers plying between the two countries are comfortable, and the table not at all bad.

On mention of Sweden, one name above all others, must be uppermost in our minds, viz., that of *Linnæus*, the naturalist. Karl von Linné was born at Rashult, in the province of Smaland, May 13th, 1707.

The writer is not altogether unacquainted with woman's work in Europe. He has seen her around the pit-mouth, at the forge—in male attire it is true—hundreds of them in 'merrie England,' over and over again, and that quite recently. In 'sunny France' he has seen them filling blast furnaces and tending coke ovens. Daily has he watched her bearing the heat and burden of the day in the fields of the 'Fatherland,' and in Austria—Hungary, doing the work of man and beast on the farm and in the mine. He has seen women emerge from the coal pits of 'busy Belgium' where little girls and young women graduate under-ground as hewers of coal, and drawers of carts, for it is no uncommon thing on the Continent to hitch women and dogs together, that manufacturing may be done cheaply. Aged, bent and sun-burnt, he has seen women with ropes over shoulders, toiling on the banks of canals and dykes in picturesque Holland.

Having seen all this he was yet surprised to find in a city so beautiful and seemingly so rich and prosperous as Stockholm,

women still more debased. In Stockholm she is almost exclusively employed as hod-carrier and bricklayer's assistant. She
carries brick, mixes mortar, and, in short, does all the heavy work
about the building. At the dinner hour you see groups of women
sitting on the piles of wood and stones eating their frugal repast.
They are paid for a day of hard work of this toil, lasting twelve
hours, the munificent sum of one kroner, equivalent to 1s. 1¾d.
Women sweep the streets, haul the rubbish, attend to the parks,
do the gardening, and row the numerous ferries which abound at
Stockholm.

CHAPTER IV.

OUR next look is at Russia, which was originally known as the eastern part of ancient Sarmatia. Its name is derived from the Roxolani, a Salvonic tribe. Rurick, a Varangian chief, appears to have been the first to establish a government in 862. His descendants ruled amid many vicissitudes till 1598. The progress of the Russian power under Peter the Great, and Catherine the Second, is unequalled for rapidity in the history of the world.

The Russian language, though not devoid of elegance is, to a foreigner, of very difficult pronunciation; the number of letters and diphthongs being forty-two. The supposed population of the Empire is 82,159,630. Russia's estimated revenue is £34,500,000; and her expenditure £37,850,000, according to the last Russian budget.

Amber in great quantities is found here, the dredgers being more successful after a violent storm, which has no doubt disturbed the bottom of the bay along the shore, and exposed the pieces of amber to the action of the dredges. Amber is, as no doubt you are aware, a resinous exudation from ancient forests, possibly submerged thousands of years ago.

St. Petersburg, the modern capital, was founded by Peter the Great, 27 May, 1703. He built a small hut for himself and some wooden hovels. In 1710, the Count Golovkin built the first house of brick; and the next year, the Emperor, with his own hands, laid the foundation of a house of the same material. The seat of the empire was transferred from Moscow to this place, in 1711. Beds of turf exist in Russia covering 70,000 square miles, which would furnish sufficient material to provide all Russia with light for ten thousand years.

The first Russian newspaper was published and edited by Peter the Great himself, in 1703.

The area of Russia is almost exactly similar in extent to that

11

of the moon, with this difference, however : Whilst the area of the moon is a fixed quantity, that of Russia is continually increasing.

The inhabitants of Black Russia are nearly all flatfooted, which makes the soldiers drawn from those particular parts incapable of long and rapid marches.   In our own army, no flat-footed man is admitted.

Having had enough of Northern Europe, we find it quite a relief to visit, in imagination, Germany, which has few more attractive places of interest than the noble Rhine, which is about 800 miles in length, and rises in the Swiss Canton of the Grisons.

If you speak the language—well and good—you will be delighted with all you see and hear.   Mark Twain is of opinion that any gifted person ought to learn English in 30 hours, French in 30 days, and German in 30 years.   The great fault, in my humble opinion, of a German is, that he cannot understand a joke unless it be a very practical one, and herein he resembles the matter-of-fact Lowland Scot, and the English peasant.

There are two million widows in Germany. It is said : ' Some of the husbands are in heaven, but the majority are in this country.'

Ratisbon Cathedral is worth a visit.   The city is on the Danube, in Bavaria, near Munich, and was made a free imperial city about 1200.   Several Diets have been held here.   It was made an Archbishopric in 1806. ' Tears cannot restore her, therefore, I weep,' is on a wife's tombstone here, and attracts our attention as we wander through this handsome edifice.   A German proverb says : ' A German will do as much work as three Russians, an Englishman as much as three Germans, and an American as much as three Englishmen.'   On one monument we noticed here :

> ' Underneath this stone doth lie,
> As much virtue as could die ;
> Which in its life did vigour give,
> To as much beauty as could live.'

The above is a free translation.

CHAPTER V.

SPAIN is a land of singular contrasts. I have frequently been in Italy at the most flowery time of the year, but anything like the gorgeous display of the Flower Fair at Barcelona, I have never witnessed, and yet, for days and days, you may travel through this country, over arid, uninteresting, dull plains, with not a bit of vegetation to enliven the scene. Even at the smallest inns, the attendants use fans to keep those horrid flies away from the traveller. Thirty-six hours' rail journey by mail train from Paris brings you to Madrid.

The climate is a serious drawback in a place where the daily official report constantly gives a variation of temperature from 6° to 19°, and few days in the year the dreaded east wind does not blow.

As in most southern towns, the middle of the day is the only real quiet time. When the sun reigns supreme the streets are deserted, blinds are closed, and the inhabitants retire to shady rooms and *patios*, to enjoy their siesta in darkness.

The first thing in the morning you hear the tinkling of bells of herds of sheep and asses, brought in by picturesque-looking brigands in peaked hats, leathern jackets, and long crooks or goads, so dear to Velasquez and Murillo. Cows being rare in the arid plains that surround Madrid, the milk of sheep and asses is used instead. Go where you will in Spain, it is bound almost to be a Saint's day. Saints' days are the rule, the ordinary days the exception. The utter absence of small birds in most rural places, seems very strange. Only near men's habitations, do you hear the song of the birds. For a city like Seville of only 100,000 inhabitants, it is amazing what a number of idle citizens there are abroad 'worshipping the rising sun,' and hoping that something will turn up to-morrow to their advantage. You see no anxious faces 'running to catch the first train'; no bustling and hustling

18

each other, trying who shall be first at the office or the mart. 'Why hurry? there is plenty of time to-morrow.'

Barcelona possesses one of the most magnificent specimens of Gothic architecture I know of in its Cathedral. In this country so rich and beautiful are the churches, that one wishes they could be turned inside out under the bright, clean sky.

Some old-fashioned dames still cling to the traditional *Mantilla de tira*, which is a scarf of rich black silk bordered with lace ; this fastened to the hair and wrapped round her shoulders is very graceful. The *Mantilla* is far more popular than the bonnet. In their tastes here they are decidedly national, and hate any foreign innovation. The scene in the Prado, and along the Alcala is very gay. The Andalusian horses are beautifully shaped and step well in light conveyances, but have not enough weight for large barouches and landaus.

The carriages and servants also lack the finish and perfection of detail that distinguish a good English, or French turn-out. But if the carriages fall short of perfection, their fair occupants bear away the palm of beauty from every other city. It would be impossible to find anywhere so many pretty, or rather beautiful women, as may be seen every day during the season driving in the Prado.

The Spaniards, whatever their faults, are at heart an essentially chivalrous people. Spain is now like a young man on his entrance into life, making his experiences and sowing his wild oats. In these oats are many weeds, and severe will be the suffering ere they can be eradicated, but there is a good and rich soil below, and in the Spanish character there is a nobility of nature, and a sincerity and earnestness of purpose that will bear good fruit some day. Spanish pride, however, will never endure the indignity of having a foreigner seated on the throne of old Castile.

I remember once hearing Castelar, the famous popular orator, speak in the House of Deputies. I did not know a word he said, but for all that it was a great treat, for he was without a doubt a second Demosthenes. Oratory in Spain is very much practised, and a fine Spanish speech is noble and inspiring. The speakers are in general dignified and impressive, only occasionally permitting themselves to burst forth with a vehemence that is the more startling from their previous calmness. Of course we have a look at a 'Bull Fight'. The wooden paling is quite eight feet high that surrounds the arena. On this paling is a ledge upon which the *chulo* can place his foot to enable him to spring over the barrier, should the infuriated bull pursue him too closely, and nobody is allowed to remain in the space between it and the first row of seats. The entrance of the *chulos*, banderillos, and three *espadas* is a pretty sight. The stake they offer to public amusement is no less than life. Each *espada* carries a long sharp sword with a crimson flag on his left arm. They wear their hair very long, either twisted up, or in a net. Lastly come the *picadores* on horseback. I use the word advisedly! their eyes are mercifully bandaged. When it gets too tame, you hear cries of, '*Banderillas, banderillas*,' ' fuega, fuega,' resounds on every side till the barbed sticks with the crackers on them to stick in the flesh of the infuriated bull, are brought out. How vividly such a scene as a modern 'Bull Fight' brings before one the descriptions of the gladiatorial fights in the Colosseum. It is gratifying to know that amongst ladies of the higher classes, the amusement is looked upon with disfavour. In Madrid very few ladies are ever present, young girls never. In the provinces the old national feeling is stronger, and few fail to attend. Bulls cost 4000 to 5000 reals, in other words £40 to £50.

CHAPTER VI.

CROSSING THE ALPS—ARRIVAL IN ITALY—VENICE—GONDOLAS
AND GONDOLIERS—THE BRIDGE OF SIGHS—MILAN—ROME—
HUMOROUS REMARKS OF AN AMERICAN TOURIST—THE BAY
OF NAPLES — VESUVIUS — HERCULANEUM AND POMPEII —
BRINDISI.

CROSSING the Alps, we call to mind Ruskin's words as he contemplated the stupendous masses of rock, the rushing rivers, the towering mountains built 'like great cathedrals, with gates of granite, pavements of clouds, choirs of stream, altars of snow, and vaults of purple.'

There is nothing better calculated to contrast human insignificance with human resource, than a contemplation of the roads over the Simplon and the St. Gothard Passes. In these delightful parts we often meet 'far from the madding crowd,' in some dear quiet little spot, perched perhaps on some overhanging cliff, or nestling in a secluded valley, people possessing those grand, but so rarely met with, human traits 'charity which spieth no man's faults; and tenderness towards all that suffer.'

'What struck you most in Italy?' a newly returned traveller was asked. 'The sun,' said he. But we will suppose we visit that lovely country early in the Spring, before the hot weather sets in. Is there any trip, I wonder, in the world so delightful as one to Italy! Well, if there is I am not acquainted with it. If I had my choice, I would never want to leave it—the Northern Lakes in the summer, and Naples during the winter. La Bella Italia is becoming, however, a terribly prosaic land. There are tramways in Rome and at Bologna; there are steam launches on the Canalazzo at Venice; and these many years past the cosy little Milanese four-wheeler has been called a 'broum.'

Venice. We at last reach this city, and enter a hearse belonging to the Grand Hotel d' Europe. At any rate the strange-looking conveyance was more like a hearse than anything else, though to speak by the card it's a gondola. And is this the famed gondola, and this the gorgeous gondolier? we ask ourselves. One's first impression of

16

Venice is not to last long, though. In a few minutes we sweep gracefully out into the Grand Canal. Right from the water's edge rise long lines of stately palaces of marble ; while ponderous stone bridges throw their shadows athwart the glittering waves. What a strange old city this Queen of the Adriatic is ! Narrow streets, vast, gloomy marble palaces black with the corroding damp of centuries, all partly submerged ; no dry land visible anywhere, and no side-walks worth mentioning; if you want to go to church, to the theatre, or to the restaurant you must call a gondola.

Venice must be a paradise for cripples, for verily a man has no use for- legs here. In the glare of day, there is little poetry about Venice, but under the charitable moon her stained palaces are white again, their battered sculptures are hidden in shadows, and the old city seems crowned once more with the grandeur that was hers 500 years ago. It is easy, then, in fancy, to people these silent canals with plumed gallants and fair ladies—with Shylocks in gaberdine and sandals venturing loans upon the rich argosies of Venetian commerce ; with Othellos and Desdemonas— with Iagos and Roderigos ; with noble fleets and victorious legions returning from the wars.

In the treacherous sunlight we see Venice decayed, forlorn, poverty-stricken, and commerceless—forgotten and utterly insignificant. But in the moonlight,. her fourteen centuries of greatness fling their glories about her, and once more is she the princeliest among the nations of the earth.

Of course, we go and see the. Bridge of Sighs, and next the Church and the Great Square of St. Mark—the Bronze Horses and the famous Lion of St. Mark, the campanile, and Byron's house, and Balbi's, the geographer.

At Milan, we enter our 'broum' and drive through the charming city. It is a most enjoyable ride, believe me, and one you would not soon forget. Nothing short of the highest poetry, or, the noblest art can paint it truly, or dimly shadow forth the grandeur of Milan Cathedral. Gazing at this beautiful Cathedral, we almost fancy we can hear :

> 'The pealing organ blow
> To the full-voiced choir below.'

as the incense, with its ' odour of sanctity,' rises above. In this sunny land, even the little street urchins hum, or sing snatches from the latest opera. The people in Italy seem to agree with Marmontel's remark : 'Music is the sole talent which gives pleasure of itself ; all the others require witnesses.'

We visit at Rome the tomb of Cœcillii Metella. How changed to what it used to be, is Rome! The Metelli family have been renowned here for centuries. Metella, the daughter of a general of this name, was taken by the Goddess Vesta to Lanuvium, when offered up to her as a sacrifice for her father's disrespect to the goddess.

> 'Imperial Cæsar, who, being dead and turned to clay
> May stop a hole to keep the wind away.'

To wile away the time we visit St. Peter's, and at night the Sala Dante, where the writer has frequently performed.

An American tourist says : ' I was delighted to know that the families of Brutus, Caius Fabricius, and Appius Claudius, were still in existence ; their names are on the door-plates in the principal street, though their founders had been dead several years—at least, so our guide informed us.' ' And whose residence is that ? ' I asked, drawing attention to a stately mansion which was unoccupied, and having a large card displayed in the window, with ' To Let, 700 lire per month.' ' That signor, is the home of the younger Casca ; but he is an envious, miserly man, and can never get a tenant ; he makes the rent so large.' ' Is he the son of the Casca who made the rent in Cæsar's garment ? ' ' He is, signor, and the trait runs in the family.' ' Thank you,' replied I, handing Lucius a lira for being so truthful.

Our guide next conducted us to the Roman Museum, where we viewed the numerous curiosities so well-known in history, but only observable to a few. Lucius Junius pointed out a large glass-case containing a flock of seven stuffed geese, headed by a solemn-looking gander. ' And pray, what does all this mean, Lucius ? ' asked I of the guide. ' These, signor, are what saved the city. ' And what is that garment hanging on yonder peg ? ' ' The toga of the illustrious Cæsar,' he replied. ' What are those auger-bits on the shelf there ? ' ' Those, signor, are the four augurs that interpreted omens.' ' What are those wax figures arrayed in white ? ' asked I, pointing to a row of six or eight lay figures ranged against a wall. ' The vestal virgins, signor.' ' You haven't got any Sabine women in your collection ? ' ' No, signor, they were all carried away several months ago.' ' What are those two wax babies ? ' General Prat spoke up and informed me that they were Romulus and Remus. ' Where is the wolf ? ' I asked of Lucius. ' They are feeding him, signor, in the back yard.'

By common consent of ' Globe trotters,' who are competent

to form an opinion, the three loveliest bays on earth are those of Naples, Rio Janeiro, and New York.

Let us suppose we have arrived at Naples by steamer, and enjoyed at daybreak, as we enter the Bay, a view unequalled in this world. After doing dear old dirty Naples, our first excursion must, most assuredly, be to Pompeii by road ; so, jumping into one of those rickety, one-horsed, native, bone-shaking conveyances, we tell our Jehu to drive us to Pompeii, in preference to taking the train. That ride to Castlemare will never be forgotten, as all the way you skirt the beautiful Bay of Naples.

Pompeii claims much of our attention. When Sir Walter Scott visited the place with Sir William Gell, almost his only remark was the exclamation : 'The City of the Dead !—The City of the Dead !' And to think that nineteen hundred years ago the inhabitants of this place knew more of comfort than we, with all our boasted civilisation, know to day ! Take the baths, for instance. We think we have reached the acme with our now popular Turkish Baths, but the ancients, after a bath of that description, returned to the *tepidarium*, and then the main delight and extravagance of the bath commenced. Their slaves anointed the bathers from vials of gold, of alabaster, or of crystal, studded with profusest gems, and containing the rarest unguents gathered from all quarters of the world. The number of these smegmata used by the wealthy would fill a modern volume, while soft music played in an adjacent chamber, and the bather lay on the soft cushions of the bronze seats, chatting to those around, having been previously powdered and pumice-stoned.

Near the principal street, the Via Domitiana, which used, over 1200 years ago, to be as crowded with passengers and equipages and chariots, exhibiting the gay and animated exuberance of life and motion, as we find in Naples to day, stood the Amphitheatre. This city was destroyed (A.D. 79, on the 24th August, and was first discovered A.D. 750. Various theories as to the exact mode it was destroyed have been invented by the ingenious, but little doubt exists but that it was destroyed by showers of ashes and boiling water, aided by partial convulsions of the earth.

Herculaneum, on the contrary, appears to have received not only the showers of ashes, but also inundations from molten lava. Volcanic lightnings were also among the engines of ruin at Pompeii, as Papyrus, and other of the more inflammable materials are found in a burnt state, and a bronze statue is completely shivered, as if by lightning.

The small but graceful Temple consecrated to Isis stands close here. Sylla is said to have transported to Italy the worship of the Egyptian Isis, whose priests arrogated a knowledge of magic, and of the future. Voltaire, with much plausible ingenuity, endeavours to prove that the gipsies are a remnant of the ancient priests and priestesses of Isis, intermixed with those of the goddess of Syria. The superstition of the 'Evil Eye' still flourishes in these parts, and at Naples the superstition works well for the jewellers, many charms and talismans in the course of the year they sell for the ominous fascination of the *mal-occhio.*

In Pompeii the talismans were equally numerous, but not always of so elegant a shape, nor of so decorous a character. But, generally speaking, a coral ornament was, as it now is, among the favourite averters of the Evil influence.

In the Amphitheatre at Pompeii, the gladiatorial displays took, place, the wild beasts (lions and tigers) were confined in *vivaria* looking out from the outer walls. Imagine this huge place full of people. Suddenly Mount Vesuvius breaks out into eruption. Such is Vesuvius, and these things take place in it every year! But all eruptions which have happened since would be trifling, even if all summed into one, compared to what occurred at the period I refer to, A.D. '79. Day was turned into night, and light into darkness ; an inexpressible quantity of dust and ashes was poured out, deluging land, sea, and air, and burying two entire cities, while the people were sitting in this very theatre. Pompeii was the miniature of the civilisation of that age, a sort of Brighton or Nice. Within the narrow compass of its walls was contained, as it were, a specimen of every gift which luxury offered to power. In its minute but glittering shops, its tiny palaces, its baths, its forum, its theatre, its circus—in the energy, yet corruption, in the refinement, yet the vice, of its people, you beheld a model of the whole empire. It was a toy—a plaything—a show-box, in which the gods seemed pleased to keep the representation of the great monarchy of earth, and which they afterwards hid from time, to give to the wonder of posterity, the moral of the maxim, 'that under the sun there is nothing new.'

The discoveries here have controverted the long-established error of the antiquaries, that glass windows were unknown to the Romans the use of them was not, however, common among the middle and inferior classes in their private dwellings. In the *apody-terium* (that is a place where the bathers prepared themselves for their luxurious ablutions) attached to the different baths these windows have been discovered.

In Pompeii, a rough sketch of Pluto delineates that fearful

deity in the shape we at present ascribe to Satan, and decorates him with the paraphernalia of horns and a tail. But in all probability, it was from the mysterious Pan, the haunter of solitary places, the inspirer of vague and soul-shaking terrors, that we took the vulgar notion of the outward likeness of the fiend, it corresponds exactly to the cloven-footed Satan.

And in the unhallowed and profligate rites of Pan, Christians might well imagine they traced the deceptions of the devil. Of all the statues in this world commend me to that one dug up here —that mutilated, but all wondrous statue—that Parian face before which all the beauty of the Florentine Venus is poor and earthly—that aspect so full of harmony—of youth—of genius—of the soul—which modern critics have supposed the representation of Psyche. It is now in the Museo Borbonico, and is decidedly the most beautiful of all which ancient sculpture has bequeathed to us.

Nearly seventeen centuries had rolled away when the city was disinterred from its silent tomb, all vivid with undimmed hues ; its walls fresh as if painted yesterday, not a hue faded on the rich mosaic of its floors ; in its forum the half-finished columns as left by the workman's hand—in its gardens the sacrificial tripod—in its halls the chest of treasure—in its baths the strigil ; in its theatres the counter of admission ; in its saloons, the furniture and the lamp—in its triclinia, the fragments of the Last Feast—in its cubicula, the perfumes, and the rouge of faded beauty, and everywhere the bones and skeletons of those who once moved the springs of that minute, yet gorgeous, machine of luxury and of life.

In the house of Diomed, in the subterranean vaults twenty skeletons (one a babe) were discovered in one spot by the door, covered by fine ashen dust, that had evidently been wafted slowly through the apertures, until it had filled the whole space.

There were jewels and coins, candelabra for unavailing light, and wine hardened in the amphora for a prolongation of agonised life. The sand consolidated by damps had taken the forms of the skeletons as in a cast ; and you may yet see the impression of a female neck and bosom of young and round proportions. It seems to the inquirer as if the air had been gradually changed into a sulphurous vapour ; the inmates of the vaults had rushed to the door to find it closed and blocked up by the scoria without, and in their attempts to force it, had been suffocated with the atmosphere.

In the garden was found a skeleton with a key by its bony hand,

and near it a bag of coins. This is believed to have been the master of the house, the unfortunate Diomed, who had probably sought to escape by the garden, and had been destroyed either by the vapours, or some fragment of stone. Beside some silver vases lay another skeleton, probably a slave.

The houses of Sallust, and of Pausa, the Temple of Isis with the juggling concealments behind the statues, the lurking place of its holy oracles, are now bared to the gaze of the curious. In one of the chambers of that temple was found a huge skeleton with an axe beside it; two walls had been pierced by the axe— the victim could penetrate no further. This might, from the conformation of the skull so boldly marked in its intellectual, as well as its worse physical developments, be the identical Arbaces, the Egyptian himself for what we know! Arbaces the Wise Magician, the Hermes of the Burning Belt, the last of the Royalty of Egypt! The skeletons of more than one sentry were found at their posts. The Roman sentry, even in those days, remained erect and motionless at his post, whilst the terrified people rushed past. That hour itself had not animated the machine of the ruthless Majesty of Rome into the reasoning and self-acting man. There he stood, amidst the crashing elements; he had not received the permission to desert his station and escape.

Pliny says 'In proportion as the blackness gathered did the lightnings around Vesuvius increase in their vivid and scorching glare. Nor was their horrible beauty confined to the usual hues of fire; no rainbow ever rivalled their varying and prodigal dyes. Now brightly blue as the most azure depth of a southern sky— now of a livid and snake-like green, darting restlessly to and fro as the folds of an enormous serpent—now of a lurid and intolerable crimson gushing forth through the columns of smoke, far and wide, and lighting up the whole city from arch to arch— then suddenly dying into a sickly paleness, like the ghost of their own life!'

Dion Cassius says 'Far and wide, borne by the winds the showers of ashes descended upon the remotest climes, startling even the swarthy African; and whirled along the antique soil of Syria and of Egypt.'

Professor Palmieri of the Vesuvian Observatory has made some wonderful improvements with his electro-magnetic *Seismograph*. This beautiful instrument accurately notes the slightest upheaving of the earth. Sitting in his rooms at the University of Naples, and with his back to the mountain he can tell exactly what is going on nine or ten miles distant.

Naples delights one more than anything in the way of continental sight-seeing I know of. The balmy air as it blows across the lovely bay, the odd odours of roasting coffee and pine nuts, the noise and haggling of the market people around you as you indulge, *al fresco*, in delicious flavoured oysters, with a panorama in front of you unequalled, all the world over, is perfectly enchanting. The sky is like a lapis lazuli, not a cloud dims it. Orange trees hang over the walls of the gardens by you. Palm trees and other tropical plants abound everywhere ; the dresses are of all the colours of the rainbow !

CHAPTER VII.

A TRIP TO AUSTRALIA—MELBOURNE—SYDNEY—HONOLULU— THE CAROLINE ISLANDS.

SUPPOSE we find ourselves at the extreme end of the world— Australia. What do ninety-nine out of every hundred people you meet know about it, except that it's noted for its tinned meat, and is bounded on the N., &c., &c. Bother its tinned meat and what it's bounded by. How would it suit you or me? In the first place it is the most loyal colony I know of to Her Most Gracious Majesty the Queen, and yet its political constitution is as purely democratic as the constitution of the United States, and their social manners are even more democratic than those of the Americans. Politically they already enjoy all the franchises for which the extreme Radicals at home are clamouring. Here there is no Established Church, no law of primogeniture, no law of entail; and education is secular, compulsory and gratuitous—or all but gratuitous. It's the land of Topsyturvydom. The vast mass of the people are out and out Radicals, as Radicalism is understood in England, but, at the same time, as regards the foreign policy of Great Britain, they are as out and out Tories, and the very mention at a public meeting of the name of the late Lord Beaconsfield at once provokes the most enthusiastic cheering.

Topsyturvydom! The Australian Liberals are protectionists; the Conservatives are free-traders, or almost free-traders.

Suppose we find ourselves at the city of Melbourne in the colony of Victoria. It is just as well to be precise about the locality of the place, for did not His Excellency Sir Frederick Napier Broome, Governor of Western Australia, inform us not long ago, that when in Paris, he was addressed as 'M. le Gouverneur de l'Australie,' while at the Colonial Post Office, mail matter is frequently received addressed, say: 'John Smith, Victoria, Adelaide, New South Wales.' The rateable property of Melbourne, I was given to understand, was worth ten millions sterling, with a nett annual value of nearly a million, and the place is not much more than fifty years old.

In the year 1836, the year before Queen Victoria ascended the throne, the present site of Melbourne was known as Beargrass, and there were just thirteen buildings—three of weatherboard, two of slate and eight turf hovels. Only the year before one of the virtual founders of Melbourne, John Prascoe Fawkner, landed in the bush on the banks or the Yara River, bringing with him a party of five men, two horses, a couple of pigs, three Kangaroo dogs, and a cat. The place crept along, so to speak, till 1851, when the discovery of gold transformed it into a mighty city. 'God made the country, and man made the town,' wrote Cowper. It was gold that made Melbourne!

Charles Lamb once said that were he not an independent gentleman, he would choose the vocation of a beggar. After a visit to Australia, I have come to the conclusion that I should very much like to be an Australian squatter, provided, always, that the drought refrained from decimating my flocks and herds, or destroying them right out, and that I had not over-drawn my account at the bank, and mortgaged my stations to the mysterious powers in the grandiose palaces of finance—Ionic, Doric, Corinthian, Composite in their architecture, which confront one everywhere in the Australian cities.

Omnibuses, hansoms, and hackney waggonettes swarm the streets, and tram-cars will soon be all over the place. Splendid places of public worship, a fine Town Hall, Post Office and University are found here, but the Government House, like Buckingham Palace, is not architecturally a 'thing of beauty which should live for ever.' There are several theatres, a grand permanent Exhibition, and a handsome Aquarium, very differently managed to the one at Westminster. At the Melbourne Aquarium you can take your sisters or daughters any evening, and enjoy a little innocent amusement. One of these days possibly local manufacturers may find a chance of competing with English goods ; artesian wells and dams and a proper system of irrigation may give the country an efficient supply of water ; the towns may then no longer be dependent for their supply of green vegetables on the crapulous Chinamen, who, at present, have a monopoly of the market-gardening industry. Australian cooks may then not be expected to be washerwomen as well, and will not then be allowed by their mistresses to spoil good meat, which should not be wasted by shoving it into colonial ovens to be badly baked ; then the time may come when the Australian working-man may be content with moderate wages, no longer oppose immigration and cease to 'scamp' his work. Let us hope this problematical 'good time coming' will not be long before it does come. There is plenty of room for improvement in Greater Britain, believe me! You soon, in this country, get Eucalyptus trees on the brain; go where you may, it is red gums, blue gums, white gums—Eucalypti for ever and ever, too often startling and horrifying the eye in their skeleton nakedness, due to the ruthless axe of the 'ring-barker.' There is one throughly excellent and comfortable hotel here, in Melbourne, viz., 'Menzies,' and a few other far from uncomfortable caravanserais.

There are, of course, asylums, markets, hospitals, coffee-palaces, public and private schools, clubs, parks, gardens, racecourses, and recreation grounds in profusion, in and about the city. The whole city in short, teems with wealth, even as it does with humanity. Melbourne is the prosperous capital of a prosperous British Colony. It is the same in our colonies as at home; in the lower classes the women are not only superior to the men, but as a rule govern them completely. A friend out there who has been a great traveller, assures me, from personal observation, that about one married woman in forty-five is free from a look of worried care. He thinks that, possibly, the fact that most husbands now get their hair cut with clippers may have something to do with it.

I noticed that the lads out here, if not quite so robust-looking as Young England, had all the go in them our lads have at home in the Mother Country, so well described by Mr. Max O'Rell in his amusing book, 'Nos Chers Voisins;' where he writes: 'It is a sturdy, hardy, robust, well-knitted lad, with muscles of steel and mule-like obstinacy, who, sooner than let go the football which he fiercely cuddles, will perform prodigies of valour; who, merely for the chance of making that ball pass between two goals, will bite the dust, will let his flesh be torn, his jaw dislocated, his ribs staved in; and would even be carried off to die upon a bed of anguish, with a smile upon his lips, if he could only hear as his young eyes closed that his side had scored the game. Multiply such an English youth up to the number of the stars of the firmament, and you will get an idea of the martial, if not the military, strength of England.'

Whether it is eating so much animal food, and so little green vegetable food causes the young Australians to run long and have such sallow complexions, I do not know, but the fact remains all the same. Climate might have something to do with it, but I

doubt it. The Australian 'larrikin' is a very undesirable acquaintance, and yet he is always cropping up. 'Soup, meat, and
pudding, 6d.' I once noticed on the window of a cheap restaurant
off Bourke Street, Melbourne. How much solid food, I thought,
could the growing lad, the junior clerk, get in London for that
price! The abundance of food throughout Australia, and the
phenomenally cheap prices of butcher's meat may be one of the
reasons for the existence of that most detestable nuisance known
as 'larrikinism.' 'It's not madness, mum, it's meat,' quoth Mr.
Bumble, the beadle, when the parish apprentice, Oliver Twist,
resented the insults of Noah Claypole. In the workhouse the
poor little fellow had had little to eat beyond bread and 'skilly.'
At Mr. Sowerberry, the undertaker's, he got a scrap of animal
food now and then, and meat, according to Mr. Bumble, had
made the poor little parish brat rebellious. Meat three times a
day, and a complete dinner—what the Americans term 'a
square meal' may have had much to do with the making of the
Australian 'larrikin.'

The arcades of Melbourne are a great feature, and, indeed, some
kind of shelter from the intolerable heat of the sun, occasionally
120° in the shade, is necessary out here. The witty remark of
that Spanish Ambassador to the Court of James I. (Gondomar,
was it not?) who, when one of his secretaries was returning to
Spain, ironically bade him present on his arrival, his compliments
to El Senor Sol: 'For I have not seen that luminary since my
arrival in England,' would have had little cause for his sarcastic
remarks in sunny Melbourne. One might spend many pleasant
hours wandering up and down Bourke and Collins Streets, and
that arcade nearly opposite the Post Office, and the Victoria, I
think it is called, opposite the Theatre Royal. Then there is the
Eastern Arcade. In each is the notice, 'no smoking allowed,'
the *crême-de-la-crême* of the fair sex of Melbourne using these
pleasant avenues, and objecting, I suppose, to the odours of the
vile German cigars and bad tobacco sold out there.

Nineteen hours railway ride through the bush, about 600 miles
run, changing at Wodonga, brings you from Melbourne to
Sydney.

Standing on the steps of the New General Post Office, Sydney,
New South Wales, one must be indeed struck by the fine *coup
d'œil* he gets. What crowds of busy people flock along! Why,
you might almost fancy you were back in 'the little village,' but
for the absence of the smoke and fog. George Street, Pitt Street,
Market Street, Hunter Street, are all busy, handsome thorough-

fares, full of well-stocked shops and warehouses. The New Post Office, Town Hall, Treasury Buildings, Houses of Parliament, the Courts of Law, are all magnificent buildings, difficult to surpass anywhere; whilst one of the most beautiful pleasaunces in the world, a great recreation-ground, overlooks the harbour. The Anglican and Roman Catholic Cathedrals, and a multitude of other places of worship, a host of banks and insurance offices with the splendid Gothic Hall of the Sydney University, lend a great charm to the picture. Urban Sydney is not unlike urban Boston, in Massachusetts, but it does not bear the slightest resemblance to any other city I have seen in the United States. With very few exceptions the place is thoroughly and entirely English in its actual aspect and suggestiveness. Now you may fancy you are in Church Street, Liverpool, or in Dale Street; or in Market Street, Manchester—anon you might, so you think, be in Birmingham, or Leeds. Pitt Street has a savour of our Strand; Hunter Street might be part of our Holborn. The shops are well-dressed in pleasing contradistinction to the dressing of American shop-windows, which is, as a rule, careless, ugly, and tasteless. The chemist's shops especially are magnificently stocked, but drugs are dearer than they should be in a free-trade country. The Australians are, as a race, great smokers; but it's a hard job to find a shop in Sydney where you can get a good cigar, so one has to fall back on the always safe Manilla, as the detestable German cigars they sell are not fit to give to a camel. The youth of the country are to a certain extent partial to cigarette smoking; but that baleful practice in Australia strikes one as falling very short of the almost monstrous—the maniacal—proportions which the habit of cigarette-smoking has attained in England and in the States. Almost everything sold seems to be imported from home. Some things, of course, are very dear, often twenty per cent. or more dearer than in England. Fresh flowers—the loveliest I have ever seen out of Nice or Florence—are dirt cheap.

Verandahs are found on nearly every house, on the first floor, whilst the arcades—or 'squaricades,' if I may so call them, in contradistinction to the Australian arcades proper, which combine the features of the Parisian *passages* and our Burlington and Lowther, afford a cool and shady promenade in hot weather, and a very convenient shelter on wet days. In this marvellous climate where the sun shines brilliantly, I should say at least three hundred days in the year, the verandah and the arcades are absolute necessities. They lend as much picturesque variety to the streets of Sydney as our own Quadrant—Nash's masterpiece, one of the few examples of street architecture of which Londoners could reasonably be proud, and the wanton destruction of which should ever be regretted—imparted picturesqueness to Regent Street. You can get a good idea of this love of verandahs if you call to mind the Marina at St. Leonard's-by-Hastings, and the dear old pantiles at Tunbridge Wells.

If George IV., when Prince of Wales, found Brighton a humble little fishing village, and converted it into an aristocratic and splendid place ; and Lord Brougham, driven from Nice through the cholera, found out Cannes, and made it what it is, I suppose Governor Philip must be credited with having found out, and made the splendid place it has become, of Sydney, New South Wales, the 'Land of the Golden Fleece.' He little thought on that bright summer morning of 10th January, 1758, Sydney would magnify as it has! It is true the modern capital of Russia was, from a mundane point of view, absolutely and literally the creation of Peter the Great. When it was determined to build in the morass, hard by the Lake of Ladoga, a window which, as he paraphrased it, should look out into Europe, he took up his abode in his little log cabin on the bank of the Neva, and decreed the erection of a 'City of Palaces' as arbitrarily as Kubla Khan in Coleridge's magnificent fragment of verse decreed the stately pleasure dome at Xanadu. There were tens of thousands of Peter's slaves to lay wooden foundations in the shape of piles in the marsh ; there were thousands more slaves to build the palaces, the churches, the barracks, the prisons. Autocracy rubbed its hands with glee, and Petropolis was created. Instead of slaves, convicts, 600 males, 250 females, created Sydney, which more than realises Thackeray's enthusiastic description of 'Limerick prodigious,' standing 'with quays and bridges,' and bringing 'muslin from the Indies, with ships up to the windies ' on the Shannon shore. It is the same here at Sydney, reminding one very much indeed of the Boompijs at Rotterdam, where you can sit at your open window and watch the gigantic East Indiamen bound to or from Batavia, taking in or discharging their immense cargoes. You can do the like at the Circular Quay, Sydney. You can jump in a hansom, at Mr. L. Uhde's Grand Hotel, in Wynward Square, close to George Street, and the New General Post Office right down to almost on board the P. and O. steamer which is to take you home.

In Australia, meat is absolutely superabundant, and ridiculously cheap to anyone coming from dear old England. Mutton from 2d. to 4d. a pound, beef 3½d. to 6d. a pound, veal 5½d., fresh pork at 6d. cannot be considered too high; whilst the cauliflowers are almost as fine as those grown at Valencia, in Spain, or at Salt Lake City, in Utah. The fruit is magnificent, the apples in particular. Oranges are grown to a great extent as near to Sydney as Paramatta, only fourteen miles off; whilst there is a teeming wealth of pine-apples and bananas from Queensland and Fiji. Sydney gets its supply of potatoes from New Zealand and I must say, might improve her supply of green stuff a little more than she does at present; in this there is plenty of room for improvement. The vineyards are splendid; delicious grapes are procurable at from 1d. to 3d. a pound, so the manufacture of wine is steadily improving. I may mention Albury in New South Wales where Mr. Fallon has a store of not less than 350,000 gallons; also Inverell, on a flat bordering the Macintyre river nearly 100 miles from Sydney. I would, for my part, far sooner drink the Australian wines, which, after all, are the pure juice of the grape, than potato sherry from the river Elbe.

'What is meant by the Antipodes?' I once asked. No one knew. 'Well listen, my little friends, and I will explain: If I, standing here in London, you know, were to bore a hole right through the earth, and go down, it till I came to the other side, where should I come out?' 'Out of the hole,' was the unanimous answer. Suppose by way of change we look in at the islands of the Hawaiian group. A break in a long sea voyage is always a joyful occurrence, and marks the almost inevitably monstrous calendar of your log with the whitest of stones. To catch sight of a shark even, or of a 'school' of porpoises, is a kind of relief; while the descent of a shoal of flying fish reminds you of Voltaire's bitter apothegm, in which he likens unto fish that fly those men of letters who are so foolish as to seek to shine in 'society.' 'The fish that remain in the sea hate them for soaring up so high; and when they fall, exhausted, on the deck of the ship, the sailors knock them on the head.'

The advent, too, of an albatross is a boon, since it enables you to refresh your memories of Coleridge's 'Ancient Mariner,' but land—even the dimmest, the most transient glimpse of blue—that is the oäsis in the vast desert of ultramarine for which you most passionately yearn. We have it at last within seven days of San Francisco; first in the guise of jutting headlands and promontories, then of low lying undulating chains of hills, glorious in purple and gold in the rays of the morning sun as our good ship 'Australia,' Captain Ghest, steams up alongside the harbour of Honolulu. Jumping into a buggy, away we go, and 'do' the place in about four hours, meeting on our way King Kalakaua and the Hon. J. O. Dominis, Governor of Oahu, Commander-in-Chief of the Forces, who are reviewing the native troops, which consisted, when last I visited Honolulu, of the Prince's Own Artillery Corps, the Leleioku Cavalary Corps, the Mamalahoa Infantry, the King's Own Volunteers and the Honolulu Rifles.

Pretty gardens laid out in all styles, one like a willow-pattern plate, deep valleys and towering mountains with well-cultivated fields, and sugar plantations, looked after by hard-working Japs, just imported, form a delightful drive. A most useful garment, worn by the inhabitants, you cannot help noticing, it is like a bedgown of white, or coloured calico, and nothing else. A most sensible and suitable garment for this climate—as 'mighty convanient' as were Mr. Brian O'Lynn's nether garments of sheepskin, of which he turned the woolly side outwards in summer, and inwards in winter. The Russian *moujiki*, as you well know, acts in precisely the same manner with his sheepskin gaberdene or *touloupe*. Aloha! It is a matter of etiquette to be continually crying 'Aloha' while you are at Honolulu. Not being skilled in the Hawaiian tongue, I cannot quite make out what it signifies; but fancy it is a convertible term for the American 'Bully for you!' for the French, 'On dirait du veau!' for the Italian, 'Viva la bella famiglia!' and for the English, 'All serene.'

Honolulu is serener than ever was the 'Serenissima' Republic of Venice. It is the loveliest spot that my eyes have ever gazed upon—lovelier even than Sorrento, lovelier than Ventnor, lovelier than the view of the Thames from the terrace of the Star and Garter at Richmond, lovelier than Jackson Square, New Orleans by moonlight. What more can I say? It is a terrestrial Paradise but for its mosquitos.

In these go-ahead days, what surprises you meet with! In a beautiful bungalow here, I have still pleasant memories of an elegant collation—Heidseck's Dry Monopole—or was it Pommery and Greno?—in 'spuming' chalices, with agreeable company, and society small talk of London and Paris, of New York, and Washington, and San Francisco. 'The Ladies' Gazette of Fashion,' I remember, was lying on one table, the 'Girls' Own Paper' and 'Young England' on another. I rubbed for a moment the eyes of my mind, and wondered for a moment where I was. Have you not occasionally fallen into a similar condition of temporary uncertainty, wanderer on the face of the earth? 'Society,' the whole world over, has grown to be so much alike. Rub the eyes of your mind—where the dickens are you?

Sometimes you see, in a splendid saloon, a swarthy gentleman in a black surtout buttoned to the throat, and with a scarlet fez worn at the back of his head. You are in 'society' at Pera or Constantinople. Again, your neighbour at dinner is a charming lady, who speaks French with much more purity than many Parisiennes do, and who is talking enthusiastically about Patti, Nilsson, and Van Zandt, Sardou and Sarah Bernhardt, and the wonderful doings of Dr. Holden, the English Magician. But the gentlemen present are mainly in military uniform, and wear large epaulettes of loose bullion. You are dining out in society at St Petersburg. Again you are at dinner. The ices and the coffee are of exquisite quality. You are at Vienna. Somebody is smoking a *papelito* between the courses. You are at Madrid. As you pass from the dining-room to the drawing-room, you espy a shovel-hat or so on the table in the vestibule, and, among the male guests, there may be some old gentlemen in red stockings, and some younger gentlemen in purple hose. You are at Rome.

Interest has lately been taken in the Caroline Islands. Few people ever dreamed there were such isles. I have a pleasant memory of a trip which I once took to those localities. The principal island, Peu, is one of 48 other smaller islets, some only mere coral-reefs. It is, I should say, from fifty to sixty miles round, with a population of about 20,000 souls, all very mixed. The Malay element predominates, even over the native population. I was most favourably impressed with the people; they seemed to me more intelligent and ruly than many other tribes met with in those latitudes. They grow the bread-fruit to a great extent, the land being most fertile. I do not wonder at the non-residence of a Spanish Governor. Bribery exists to an alarming extent in the Civil Service of Spain. I know, for a fact, of a Governor, in one of her Colonies, remitting, year after year, the *whole of his salary* as commission to the patron who obtained for him the appointment. *What he made out of it paid him,* and paid him well. The Portuguese are just as bad—the Mexicans worse. They follow out the dictum: ' 'Make money, my son ; honestly, if you can, but make money !'

CHAPTER VIII.

A TRIP TO INDIA—BOMBAY—INDIAN RAILWAY—BENARES—THE
GANGES — DELHI — THE BUDDHISTS — HYDERABAD — THE
AUTHOR'S PROFESSIONAL SUCCESS AT THAT FAMOUS CITY—
EUROPEAN REQUISITES FOR THE INDIAN CLIMATE—MORNING
AND NIGHT IN INDIA—THE 'LOGANS' OR ROCKING STONES—
THE MOSQUES OF AHMEDABAD—HINDOO CHILDREN—INDIAN
PILGRIMS.

INDIA as a resort for the pleasure-seeker, or the invalid in search
of healthful change, would seem to be coming into fashion. The
steamers which at one time carried only officials, soldiers, men
of business, and occasional sportsmen to the East, now include in
their lists of passengers many individuals, even sometimes whole
families, who are going out 'for the sake of the trip,' or to pay
relatives a short visit in their distant homes. Sportsmen, young
men of means in quest, as they call it, of 'a little shooting,' have
become a regular feature of every saloon's company, and the
Himalayas and the Anamullis familiar hunting-grounds to the
members of London clubs. Sightseers, also—recognisable at the
first glance by the old Anglo-Indian from the abundance and
diversity of their brand-new 'outfit'—are shipped as punctually
as civilians, hurrying back with a couple of old portmanteaus and
a veteran hatbox to rejoin their appointments.

The knowledge of the actual pleasures of the journey itself
has grown into popular recognition: the Overland trip upon the
Continent—the run across the Mediterranean—a glimpse of Egypt,
and the passage down the Canal; then Suez and Aden, short
snatches of a world that had hitherto seemed to belong only to
remote travel, and so over the Indian Ocean to the wondrous
city of Bombay, which fairly beggars Naples in beauty as seen from
the sea. In all this there is enjoyment of a very vivid and unusual
kind. When, however, as is now the case, physicians are advising
patients to make the trip for health's sake another motive for an
Indian visit is added, and one which, with a great number, will
probably outweigh all considerations of mere pleasure. Nor
indeed, in those cases in which change of scene is beneficial can
any transition be imagined more complete or more invigorating
than this, from the routine of London and the all too-gloomy atmosphere of an English winter to the rapid and beautiful alternations

of foreign scenery and the pleasantly equable climate of 'cold weather' in the East, which four months spent in going to India, and in it, offer to the invalid.

Nor are other considerations wanting to make this change in the fashion of travel thoroughly admirable and its continuance in favour desirable. Even the superficial knowledge which the 'cold weather' visitor obtains of the manner of Anglo-Indian life and thought is sufficient to make all his future judgments more rational, more in sympathy with the East than before, while here and there one or other of the pleasure-seekers is sure to chance upon solid facts which, on his return, go to swell the general aggregate of public information about our Empire of Hindostan. There can never, therefore, be too many visitors to India.

European travel is of course highly beneficial. It is an education in contemporary history. But the tour of the Continent does not expand the mental horizons. It gives no broader margins to ideas. The journeys are so frequently broken, the 'places of interest,' or designated as such in the guide-books, follow so rapidly, that the mind and memory become really crowded up, cramped, and perplexed. There is no grand total at the end. The sum stands as so many castles, so many cathedrals, so many bridges, so many hotels stopped at. Recollection fails to call up any spacious, mind-filling scenes; no connected scheme suggests itself; no broad and deep effects are appreciable. The constant changes of language, the differences in details, the small variations in habit, as the traveller rattles from one country to another, break up the journey into little bits which the memory can never piece together again as a whole. Nor was there time enough for any one nation to impress its character and spirit upon the tourist. Now, in the Indian trip the result is the very reverse. One immense and overwhelming nationality is perpetually present. The traveller is always amongst people of a different costume, tongue, and even colour from his own. Their languages, though locally different, have combined in a Lingua-Franca along the thoroughfares of travel which makes them all seem one to the newly-arrived European. The words that he catches from a Mahratta servant on landing serve him among the Sikhs in the far North, or the Bengalees in the remote East. This unity is in itself a prodigious experience. The real meaning of the word 'India' then sinks of its own weight into the most indifferent mind. Next, perhaps, he remembers that the vast peninsula is really filled with two mighty and rival creeds—the Hindoo and the Mohammedan —but until the difference in the buttoning of the vest is pointed out to him he cannot tell the one from the other. What is it that has welded them together into this single and indistinguishable nation? The traveller soon finds it out—the persistent and irresistible prestige of his own race. He finds scattered up and down the peninsula little handfuls of Englishmen, who hold the great fabric of our Empire together by the integrity with which they carry on, in a just and sympathetic spirit, the administration of the country. So the lesson is learned, which no libraries can teach, of that wondrous position of England in India, and for the first time the traveller understands what the power of his people is in the East. Thus he arrives at broad ideas of the vastness, the wealth, the importance of India, and unconsciously joins the ranks of those who resent the flippant indifference to the possession of that dominion which is affected by a certain limited but noisy class. To turn, however, from these valuable and patriotic results of a tour in India, what can we say as to the pleasures of such a trip? From the moment that Bombay is first seen, sweeping round its harbours in a fringe of tropical vegetation, and backed by vast masses of gigantic mountains—a revelation of beauty to the last, when the homeward-bound steamer threads its way out through the crowding commerce of the world gathered in the great city's roadsteads—there is a perpetual succession of surprise and enjoyment.

The railway journey itself from Bombay, ' over the Ghâts,' is a novelty in engineering, a wonder in landscape, while every stoppage along the line gives glimpses of a life and scenery which, to the European, are full of freshness and suggestiveness. Arrived in the north of the peninsula, the traveller finds himself on a great line of railway stretching from the Bay of Bengal in the east to the frontiers of Afghanistan on the west, and along it are ranged the great cities of the old Asiatic Empire, and the places made ever memorable by the mutinies of 1857 and 1858. To wander even for a day among the temples of Benares is worth a year of Paris, and a week of the Ganges counts for more than a month of the Rhine. Can any excursion be imagined or devised more enchanting than that which, making Agra its centre, is spent in visiting the neighbourhood? Futtehpore Sikri, the most sumptuous ' folly ' the world has ever seen, is of itself worth all the voyage to India, for surely nowhere else, in one single day's contemplation, could such impossibilities of grandeur, such dreams of Imperial caprice be forced to the front as facts of history as in this labyrinth of palace and pleasaunce in which an Emperor held his court for a day, and then departed. Delhi, again!

Where in all the world could an Englishman go to receive so rapidly and so delightfully a knowledge of a splendid past, or anyone, let his nationality be what it may, so just, so overpowering a conception of the 'harlequinade' of Empires?

Indian travel cannot help imparting, in spite of the agreeable excitement of its incidents, a really solid measure of information. Even the sportsman who goes out simply to worry the bears in their leafy strongholds beyond the hills, to have tigers driven before him from the tall grass as he sits upon his elephant waiting for the jungle-raja to pass ; to ride the pig down on the Cawnpore levees ; to lie up by the pools and wait for sambhur, to see the far-famed 'honqua' where the wild occupants of the forest are beaten out indiscriminately in confused procession from their lairs and homes, and made to defile past his ambuscade, to bag his fifty brace of quail or as many snipe in a morning, to 'have a crack' at an elephant, a buffalo, a rhinoceros—even the sportsman with one special object before him cannot help being affected by, at any rate, the two great facts that India insists upon stamping upon every mind—its vast importance to us and the dignity of the Englishman's position in the East. For the ordinary travellers going out to see the country and take any enjoyment that may offer, the three months of exquisite English summer weather—without any of its rain—which they will experience almost suffice to make the adventure a perpetual pleasure. When, however, to this are added the innumerable objects of beauty or novelty which everywhere present themselves, both in Nature and in Art, the tour cannot fail to remain on the memory as 'a joy for ever.' The people, their habitations and vehicles, their ways of life, are each and all so utterly different from every idea acquired by Continental travel that a new world is virtually opened up to the imagination, while the charms of the natural history of the country, of beast and bird, tree and flower, are numberless and fascinating in the extreme. The philosopher and the man of science, the statesman, poet, political economist, artist, man of letters—everyone down to the ordinary pleasure-seeker—stands assured of more than enough to interest and amuse him for all his time ; while medical authority has now come forward to add its weight to the value of the trip. So, as I have already said, too many Englishmen cannot go to India—it only 'just to see what it is like,' while it certainly would not tend to the decrease of the value of their public utterances if Members of Parliament were to spend a year or two in the Peninsula before aking their seats in the House.

A Buddhist priest must not eat except of food given him from a charitable hand, nor drink any beverage except water. Possibly you have, like myself, often wondered at seeing such numbers of acolytes of the monasteries pacing quietly in the streets and lanes with the melon-shaped begging-bowl strapped on their shoulder, but on thinking over to oneself the tenets of Buddhism it is impossible to do other than admire and respect it.

A visit to India would be incomplete without a visit to 'Ooty.' You leave the Coimbatur plain seething in the early heat of the Indian summer, and within six or seven hours are plucking the flowers of home in a climate like that of Perthshire in spring; a hoar-frost at daybreak overspreading the grass, and the rising sun shining mildly upon a sea of white clouds laid near and far upon the face of the lower country, through which a black mountain summit here and there lifts itself precisely like an island from the ocean.

Invalids, it is true, might not be able thus to pass from summer to spring or winter, without due precautions, and even Ootacamund does not, it is said, suit all constitutions. To the merely wearied or fever-stricken denizen of the Indian plains, however, it must be like Paradise to climb to the lap of the great green Dolabetta, and drink in new life with every cool breeze, and every change of the fair and peaceful landscape. If the Romans had conquered India they would have founded a spacious and impregnable city upon this grand upland, colonised it with veteran legionaries, and made a dozen easy roadways up from the Malabar and Coromandel seaports to the gates of their Imperial Sanatorium.

Hyderabad struck me as one of the most curious and interesting cities in India. Everyone seemed armed to the teeth, and yet a pleasanter, nicer lot of people I never once met out there. The whole capital gives the idea of being as it were 'on half-cock,' and ready to go off at a touch into turmoil and revolution. You see here perpetually the snow-white turban of the 'true believer' mingling with the red tarboosh of the Mohammedan negro and the green caftan worn by the Syed, or the Hadji, who has made the pilgrimage to Mecca. In truth, it is hardly less the fashion to wear pistols, sabres, daggers, guns, and spears, in Hyderabad, than to carry umbrellas in Piccadilly. The Nizam has a most magnificent palace here. Of course we should visit the famous 'Rock of Golcondah,' a favourite retreat, by-the-by, of His Royal Highness the Nizam. I remember an armourer here showing me a *johurdar*, or watered blade, worth five thousand rupees, whilst the display he had of *abbassis*, a sort of Persian rapier, *asils*, *nimchas, tegahs, kirichis, dhopes,* and *nawas kihanis*—these last and most murderous looking scimitars—made my mouth water. Five hundred miles only from Bombay, and you seem in a different land altogether.

The railway carriages *en route* seem always full of natives, who appear quite contented, and enjoy the wayside refreshment of gratuitous water, cheap bananas, and cocoa-nuts, or the sticky amrita sweetmeats. And, truly, a thirsty traveller might fare worse than to quaff a deep draught from the green bowl of the cocoa-nut when the vendor slices off the crown with a stroke of his knife and discloses a pint or so of cool limpid beverage of Nature's own concoction, fragrant and fresh in its white and sweet goblet.

During my last professional tour from 'China to Peru,' I happened to find myself, one fine day, at Hyderabad. I had given my Magical Performance at the Nizam's City Palace before a large company of Muslim Court officials, dignitaries and ladies from the garrison at Secunderabad, when, a day or two afterwards, I was sent for, with a request that His Highness wished to confer with me. I was ushered into his presence, wondering what was on the *tapis*. He is of less than middle stature, with dark, expressive eyes, and a mild countenance, and was attired in a black coat crossed by the azure riband of the Star of India, a diamond-studded sabre swinging at his waist. His get up, in the words of Tallyrand : '*Je le trouve bien distingué.*' A brilliant staff of officials stood around, each of whom, in approaching the greatest Prince of India, made six several and profoundly low salaams, acknowledged from the Throne by a slight wave of the hand.

Turning affably to me, he remarked : 'I was very impressed with your 'Mind-revealing '—I think you called it ?'—I bowed low to indicate he was right—'when you appeared here yesterday, and I want to see if you can—but our Minister, Salar Jung, will explain matters more fully to you, Doctor Holden,' said His Highness, with a pleasant and gracious smile, as he took his departure. Here is an adventure, I thought, and tried to look grave, to be in harmony with my character. What is it? I wondered, as I inwardly took in the magnificent surroundings as I hoped, presently, to take them in ! Only a short distance from where I was, stands Golcondah, noted for its diamonds and Sindbad's story of the eagles and the joints of mutton in the " Valley of Jewels." Here the celebrated Koh-i-noor was found. The last famous diamond found here was the 'Nizam,' I believe, which, after a peasant had rashly splintered it by a blow on the apex, still fur nished a fragment valued at seven hundred and twenty thousand pounds. I could not help thinking of this as I stood on the platform of marble, under that exquisite pillared portico looking over the vast, well-lighted quadrangle, surrounded by the white palace buildings.

How little we 'who live at home at ease' know of the glories, in the way of palaces and temples, of India. How different from all our preconceived ideas do we find the reality ! Thus I mused as the Nizam slowly walked away leaving me a most peculiar and unprofessional duty to undertake, as I shall now try and explain. I was surrounded by all the notabilities of the Court, all quizzing me, I fully believed, but all as courteous and gracious as only Muslim gentlemen can be. Salar Jung, a very tall young man, of thoughtful and intellectual countenance, and graceful manners, and Syed Ali, Director of Public Instruction to the State, who, besides talking English with fluent accuracy, and the Hindustani of the Deccan, is a proficient in Persian, Arabic, and Murathi, as well as Sanscrit, between them, explained that His Highness had lost a rare and magnificent diamond from the hilt of his scimitar, some famous stone handed down from—well, whether he said *Vehchaisravai*, the Divine Stallion, or something or somebody else, I could not catch—at all events, it was evidently highly prized.

'Could I by any means find the thief, or if not stolen, could I find where it lay *perdu ?*'

Well this was a poser for me ! 'Give me twelve hours in this palace,' said I 'and I will see what can be done.' I was made right royally welcome, enjoyed a banquet in a private room served upon gold, I remember, the cooking being quite European, except for the profusion of pillaws and curries, in which the Moghul chef of the palace excels any rival. I doubt muchly if the genius of Soyer, of Francatelli, and of Baron Brisse, all combined, could have concocted such an appetising, highly-flavoured repast. I had *carte blanche* to do things, I suppose, no other European ever did there. I set my wits to work and inquired here, inquired there, and still could see no way of solving the problem. Poor old Thucydides would have been shocked had he lived in Hyderabad to-day, as everyone seems armed to the teeth ; even in the palace it was the same. Does he not say in his First Book, that no civilised citizens should carry iron? If the Nizam had taken the sage's advice, this would not have occurred, "well I won't carry iron, but 'brass,' instead," I said to myself. An idea had struck me : arms are never carried into the presence of ladies of the court here, so it must have been when outside those sacred precincts the stone was lost.

I sauntered to that entrance and found it guarded by a black-faced Sidi, whilst a Rohilla, with blue caftan and blunderbuss, lounged close by. Eight men formed the guard of that particular part of the palace, and they had not been changed since the stone had been lost, but had all been searched and thoroughly examined when the loss was discovered, as here the Nizam was in the habit of throwing off any superfluous article he might have on his person, depositing the same in an alcove hard by. I minutely examined the _pesh-khats_, and those little villainous knives named _bichwas_ or 'scorpions' to see if their points had been broken by unsetting the missing diamond; also each _sher bucha_ 'tiger's child,' and _saf shikan_ 'line sweeper,' as they call their wretched blunderbuss, to see if it might not be concealed therein. All to no purpose. At last a happy thought inspired me. I got the Ministers and other officials to witness this my last test, trusting to the chapter of accidents to pull me through.

Whilst waiting for their arrival, I could not but help admiring the view of the city from the palace window where I stood. Koolub Shah created this capital in 1589, A.D., having migrated from Golcondah for want of good water, and called it after his favourite concubine, Bhagmati, beautifying the place with a stately edifice called _Chahar Minar_ or the 'four Minarets,' through the archways of which the main traffic of the bazaars still passes; outside the gray and white walls of the city runs the river Musah, in stony channels which are filled with a turbid flood during the rains, but at other seasons trickle feebly with a chain of shallow pools, where elephants bathe, and the town washing is clamorously done. This rocky stream is spanned by three broad bridges, separating the Hindoo suburbs from the town proper, wherein all, or almost all, is Mohammedan in character.

The long, whitewashed streets of the capital with their shop-fronts formed by Saracenic arches; the Mosques, the tall, sculptured Minarets, the sign-hoards bearing Persian, Arabic, or Hindu inscriptions, and the multiplicity of beggars on the Mosque steps and at the gateways, give the general impression of a sort of Indian Damascus or Cairo. The main streets exhibit more varieties of the Indian races, and it may be added, more elephants than those of any other city from Peshawur to Comorin.

At the bottom of the staircase were drawn up a body of well-mounted short and square Arab troopers, with drawn sabres and silver-bound matchlocks, which they advanced as His Highness and his courtiers came towards where I was standing, shaded by the royal colour or flag of Hyderabad which is yellow with a circular disc in its middle (if I remember rightly) a sort of *Kulcha.* 'And now, Dr. Holden, let us see what we *shall* see,' graciously remarked the Nizam. I bowed, and they sate about on cushions of silk and gold, or carved alabaster benches on the very spot I had a day or so previously 'fooled them to the top of their bent.' It is a scientific fact, of which you may not possibly be aware, that fear and anxiety diminish the digestion of anyone, and stop the secretion of the gastric juice; this fact I had often heard of before, and now determined to put it to the test.

And what a scene presented itself. What colour, what effect. How well it would look, I thought, on one of our best metropolitan theatres! In the distance peering through the gates was the black-faced Sidi; the Rohilla, with blue caftan and blunderbuss. the Pathan, the Afghan, dirty and long-haired, the Rajpoot with his shield of oiled and polished hide; Persians, Bokhara men, Turks, Mahrattas, Madrasees, Parsees an dothers. The suspected ones were marched up, and appeared to me to show more servility than one notices even in the effete courts of Europe. They seemed to have a weakness 'to crook the pregnant hinges of the knee' with a vengeance!

I procured eight brass dishes, each containing a few handfuls of dry rice, and had the eight guards placed in front of me. Being a mesmerist, I saw, at once, I had them under my control entirely. But that would have been no use in detecting crime, you say. True, it would not; but I was going to apply the simpler test, but combined with the magnetic force or will-power. Putting on Cato-like sternness I looked into each man's eyes, and never saw such unflinching, dare-devil subjects. The interpreter was then called for, and was told to explain to these eight men that I, 'Dr. Holden, Magician to the Queen-Empress,' was possessed of supernatural power, and could read men's thoughts. Let each man take a handful of rice and chew it, spitting it on to the plate he held in his hand, when told to do so. They did as requested, without a muscle moving. Now, somehow or another, I felt the guilty man was amongst these eight, and possibly I put forth will-power to a greater extent than I should have done, had I not suspected one of them.

'If the guilty man is amongst you, he cannot chew his rice,' I said, looking them well into the face. 'Spit out on your plate what you have in your mouths,' I said. They did so, and there sure enough, amongst those eight plates of chewed rice, was *one dry mouthful.* Placing my face against that man's, I glared at him and accused him of the theft. I was right. He confessed his crime, and showed us where the concealed stone was. As a lady was mixed up in this affair, and as these lines may very possibly reach Hyderabad, it might be considered, possibly, a breach of confidence if I said any more on this strange subject. The President, Mr. Cordery, will understand my motives for so doing, I have no doubt. Amongst the presents made me is one I shall ever revere. It was a magnificent abbassis, a sort of Persian rapier, on which was engraved the Gayatri, or 'Sacred Verse' of the Brahmins.

Of course, my success got bruited about, and made my sojourn in that hospitable country most enjoyable ; so much so, that it was with considerable reluctance I tore myself away from Hyderabad —the Mohammedan Capua. Some believe it was here Cupid played 'Campaspe,' a game of cards for kisses. However that may be, I shall always console myself with the thought that I played my cards pretty well here.

The morning and the night in India compensate well for her somewhat too fiery noons. From the time when the Dum-i-gurg, the 'grey wolf's tail,' first shows in the East until the sun is a lance's length above the horizon, the air and the fields are almost all the year wholly delightful, and when the sun has sunk—leaving the East all golden and the West all rose—the peace and softness of the land become again indescribable ; unless you have been there, you can scarcely conceive the beauties of a moonlight ride through these parts. One can then understand on such a night of silvery radiance—cooling the hot atmosphere and turning the jungle into a fairyland of mysterious beauty—all those endearing phrases which the Hindoos lavish upon those hours of moontime. *Rat Ma Ka pet* is one of their popular proverbs. 'The night is like the bosom of a mother,' and the fondest phrase which the Indian lover can address to his *Dilkoosha* or sweetheart is to call her ' *Chand Ka tookra,*' a 'piece of the moon '

Those 'logans,' or rocking stones, which attract so much notice when they occur singly with us, as in Cornwall or Scotland, are here, at Hyderabad, to be seen in thousands. Amid these prodigious reefs, fifty, seventy, eighty tons balanced on each other and looking as if the touch of a child's hand would send them crashing down into the jungle, are found gold, iron, and precious stones. It struck me a good opening might be made here with proper appliances, and steam or electric power, to start a paying

'Valley of Jewels Liability Company,' which would very soon put Kimberley into the shade.

The old Mohammedan Mosques of Ahmedabad have been written about so often, that nothing is left to say on the subject, they are built, as everyone knows, mainly of white marble, delicately and marvellously carved. Northern Guzerat and Rajpootana abound in a milky marble, often as pure in grain, I noticed, as Parian. Words fail to describe the dainty loveliness of many among these memorials, dusty and decayed as they are at present. Some of them, like Haibat Khan's Mosque, interest by exhibiting the way in which Muslim and Hindoo styles of architecture were combined.

I am afraid that my tastes led me oftener to the pretty Kankaria tank and Nagina Gardens near the city with its enchanting island in the centre, than to the Mosques, to sport with Amaryllis in the shade. You frequently see the impress of a hand in red ochre on the temple gates, or wall of the city out here, whilst the walls of the Burning-ghâts often bear the same token of that passionate love, or the deep despair which, in old days, moved so many Hindoo widows to die beside their husbands on the funeral pyre. It was never very common, however, I believe in India, which, indeed, the eager perpetuation of their memory proves. Some of them may have been due, no doubt, to the miserable prospects of the widows here, for the lot of a Hindoo widow was, and still is, almost worse than any death. How different in our own country I Only the other day I overheard a lady trying to console a young widow, ' Be reasonable, my dear, bear up, don't you know.'

' Don't be alarmed, Clara, I am. resigned at heart, only you know what my nerves are. It takes very little to upset them.'

The Hindoo is quite assured that he has lived many previous lives, and has many more to experience, and, whether Vaishnav or Shivaite, is troubled with none of the dismal doubts of modern materialism. It may be safely believed that the great majority of those little red-hands stamped upon temple walls, city gate, or house front, commemorate martyrdoms of faithful love, well meriting the respect in which they are held by the common people as examples forbidden henceforward, but in bygone times holy, admirable and elevating.

In the grey light of the ' wolf's brush '—that dim gleam which comes before the true dawn, jackals are seen, as you pass through the country, gun in hand, enjoying the sport, stealing home from their nocturnal forage, and the rising sun shines on the backs of a herd of antelopes. What nimble little creatures those Kangaroo-rats, a kind of jerboa, are. In the dust, at the door of the peasants' hut, the small brown children 'mother-naked' crouch in groups, gravely playing *ekee dôkee*—'odd and even.' Inside the hut the 'two women' are grinding at the mill preparing the meal for the day, with the accompaniment of not unpleasing songs. Villagers on their way to work, stop to prostrate themselves before the reddened 'Lingury-stone,' or the marble 'Bull of Shiva,' enshrined under the fig-tree, and deposit there a bright flower or two, a sweetmeat or a nut. The pilgrims with their *bhugwa* or salmon-coloured flags pass over the field-path on their march to the holy places of the district you happen to be in. The noise of the water-wheels, and the creaking of the ox-carts, mingled with the cry of the parrots, and 'cheep' of the sand grouse, linger long on one's memory.

You find nothing but friendliness and courtesy among the count-less millions of this land; from strangers, townsfolk peasants, servants, men, women, and children, a thousand instances of simple virtues—of charity, of domestic affection—of natural courtesy—of inherent modesty, of honest dignity, of devotion, of piety, of glad human life do you encounter in passing, as one encounters bright birds and fair flowers. I write warmly on the subject because I feel it is due to this great nation to paint them as they really are. It is not that I am ignorant of the crime, super-stition, and ignorance yet to be combated among the masses. A healthy man needs only to keep himself temperate and good-humoured, and avoid unboiled water and chills in order to enjoy the hottest days which India knows, and for every trait of brutality, ingratitude, or folly which can be cited against the Indian peoples, those who love and know them could relate many true and striking proofs of their innate goodness.

I wish that there were space to speak here of the Indian wives and mothers, among whom are to be counted humble saints and angels by the lakh—gentle, patient, laborious, faithful, pure, contented, cheerful, and affectionate souls. Let us hope that some day they will be educated, but not over much, so as to know how to enjoy life more, and to save their infants from dying so needlessly ; that Hindoos will some day respect their own shastras which forbid that a girl be married against her choice, or before she is orientally of age ; it will then be a bright day for India !

CHAPTER IX.

ARRIVAL AT CEYLON—GENERAL DESCRIPTION OF THE ISLAND—
OF BANKOK—THE CAPITAL OF SIAM—THE WHITE ELEPHANT—
SUNDAY MORNING'S DIVINE SERVICE AT SEA—THE MAHARAJAH
OF JOHORE.

CEYLON is one prodigious garden, where the forces of Nature almost oppress and tyrannise the mind, so lush and lavish is the vegetation. This is most of all evident in the remarkable journey between Kandy and Colombo by the railway which climbs the central hills. Leaving the coast, you first of all travel through interminable groves of palms, between which lie sodden but fruitful flats of rice ground and jungly swamp, steaming, and teeming with life. It is all one hotbed of boundless propagation. Every corner, where water lodges, or sun-rays fall, is seen choked with struggling stems, furious to live and blossom and bear seed.

Then, as the train mounts amid splendid highland scenery, the hill sides and deep valleys display the same irrepressible fertility. Your carriage rolls at the bottom of one immense precipice of ferns and palms ; and hangs over another clothed for a thousand feet down with this same endless garment of verdure, scarcely allowing the red soil and gray rocks to show through. Left to themselves, every road, every village, every city in Ceylon, would quickly revert to jungle, so rich is the soil and sun-light, so keen the contest of these wild trees and wilful shrubs to live and thrive. The place is a huge tangled tyranny of the floral world, where man is in danger from the very plants which feed and shade him —an irrepressible natural garden, too thick and flourishing even for birds and beasts.

It has always struck me that good Bishop Heber must have been temporarily suffering from derangement of the liver, when *à propos* of lovely Ceylon, he wrote :

> 'Where every prospect pleases,
> And only man is vile !'

'Man' is very much the same in this beautiful island as elsewhere—genial and friendly if you treat him well, suspicious and dishonest if you distrust and over-reach him ; and the children as

45

comely and intelligent as need be seen, but growing up often under the hot sun and stress of poverty into plain-featured men and women. Anyone weak in the chest, or vexed with chronic-bronchitis, would find this spot an earthly paradise, as the average reading of the thermometer for the year, is 76°.

Nothing, to my mind, is more impressive than a Sunday morning's service on board the steamer, as we pass round the world on the open waters, and in the saloon of our magnificent steamer.

Some who never go to church ashore are drawn to bear part in the simplicity and pathos of this maritime act of reverence. The table draped with the Union Jack of Old England, the books of worship decorously laid out by the quarter-master for the captain's use; the captain himself, gallant, solemn, his hair 'sable-silvered,' his gold eye-glass rigged to tackle the psalms and prayers; the longs rows of beautiful, or gentle, or high-bred feminine faces, of brave and dutiful English gentlemen bound on the service of the Queen, or the honourable toils of business abroad, all these assembled on the great deep for worship combine into a noble picture of British gravity and veneration.

Near to an illustrious traveller kneel veteran colonels, with every one an honourable history, and young officers who will make it in China, and when the captain has finished his supplication for the 'safety of all those who sail on this ship,' the harmonium touched by skilful fingers leads off a hymn of praise, and the sound of a hundred blended voices passes with the wind over the blue expanse upon which we are speeding. The little children, kneeling round their mothers, the dark-skinned ayahs in their gay saris, grouped outside the saloon doors, the punkahs waving to and fro, the Indian boys at the window in snow-white garments and scarlet turbans dreamily working them, the beat of the tireless screw, the hiss of the sweeping seas, the rattle of cordage and chains, and the ship's bell striking the watches, furnish elements to the little floating church which deepen the solemn effect when the good captain's voice is heard praying for the peace and welfare of the Queen, and that glorious British Empire, of which we are here a little moving isolated fragment. No wild theorist has yet proposed to democratise a ship. There are famous men in plenty aboard our good ship, with names known all over the civilised world, but the authority of our captain is disputed in nothing, what he says and does is law for all alike; we live under a benevolent but absolute monarchy, our accepted sovereign being the man who, by forty years of experience, knows better than anybody else what is safe for the ship, and has, humanly speaking, the lives of all in his hands. The Caucus would have no chance of influence upon the deep sea, where people come face to face with the Elemental Powers, and with the Eternal Law that the wisest ought to command, and the unwise ought to obey.

> ' India, farewell! I shall not see again
> Thy shining shores, thy peoples of the sun,
> Gentle, soft-mannered, by a kind word won
> To such quick kindness! O'er the Arab main
> Our flying flag streams back; and backwards stream
> My thoughts to those fair, open fields I love—
> City, and village, maidan, jungle, grove,
> The temples, and the rivers! Must it seem
> Too great for one man's heart to say it holds
> So many unknown brothers? that it folds
> Lakhs of loved friends, in parting? Ah! but there
> Lingers my heart, leave-taking: and it roves
> From hut to hut, whispering 'He knows, and loves.'
> Good-bye! Good-night! Sweet may your slumbers be,
> Gunga! and Kasi! and Saraswati!'

The Maharajah of Jahore has some strange subjects, viz., the *Jakoons*. The ordinary notion is that they are a species of monkey, who live in trees, but possess some of the attributes of humanity. This is a mistake. The *Jakoons* are real human beings without tails, have a language of their own, and are susceptible of cultivation. They have a fancy for living in trees, but they are harmless, and not disinclined to intercourse with strangers. Their settlement can only be compared to huge crow-nests stuck about in the clefts of tall trees, made of twigs—a mere platform of sticks—no walls, doors, or windows; no roof but the leaves overhead; no furniture except a few stones holding a heap of ashes with cocoa-nut shells as cooking utensils, and a hollow bamboo, answering the purpose of a water jug. Humanity can hardly be found anywhere in a more mean and primitive condition. The dress worn is of the most scanty description, and you would find that many of the Jakoons are imbued with the spirit of hospitality. The youngsters clamber up the trees for cocoa-nuts like monkeys, for you, not as boys at home, but clasping the tree with the palms of the hands and feet, and so walking up on all fours. Each family seems to keep a monkey as a companion, as well as a help for pulling down cocoa nuts. They eat monkey-flesh, and the boa-constrictor is a favourite article of diet—families will gorge on one of these massive reptiles for weeks together. An aged Frenchman out here has settled down and has hard work to civilise the Jakoons. He has a school of about thirty children, with copper-coloured skins, projecting jaws, and long toes which they can make use of like fingers. It is strange to hear them singing hymns in Malay and French, and going through the Gregorian Chant with surprising time and precision. A small harmonium is played by one of them with surprising time and precision; you can scarcely believe your eyes or ears as you look upon his jaw projecting so far in advance of his eyes.

From Galle to Singapore, passing Penang and going through the Straits of Malacca, is 1,594 miles, and occupies eight days. Visits to the charming botanical and private gardens, the cocoanut groves, the pineapple plantations, and other tropical attractions fully occupy your time here. A railway will soon perforate, at the southern extremity of Asia and Jahore, Mount Ophir, from whence gifts of gold and precious gems were brought to Solomon 2,800 years ago.

You would find Bankok, the modern capital of Siam, the strangest city in the world. It consists of 70,000 floating houses or shops, and has a population of about 350,000 souls, of which number 70,000 are Chinese, 20,000 Burmese, 20,000 Arabs and Indians; the remainder, or about 240,000 being Siamese. The Catholic Missionary Society at Bankok when I was there, consisted of one bishop and about ten priests, besides one or two proselyte Chinese priests, a somewhat *rara avis*, the latter, I take it?

They were well skilled in medicine, and even a few in surgery, and if anything can win over a savage idolator to lend ear to the marvellous facts of faith, it is surely when he meets a man who has to him, apparently miraculously, relieved him from the greatest sufferings, and whose doctrine in one point of view, and that one by the Siamese considered an all-important one, entirely coincides with his own faith and religion. I allude to the celibacy of the priesthood.

The ' Chief Watt,' the residence of that most beautiful animal the white elephant, the most revered of all the Siamese deities, is situated on the east bank of the Menan. We followed our cicerone and were admitted into the presence of this noble animal. I never saw so large an elephant, his skin was as smooth and spotless and white as the driven snow, with the exception of a large scarlet rim round the eyes.

The room itself was an unpresuming one, exceedingly lofty, with windows all round the loftiest part; but the flooring was covered with a mat-work, wrought *of pure chased gold*, each interwoven seam being about half an inch wide, and about the thickness of a half sovereign ! ! !   If this was not *a sin to snakes*, as the Yankees say, I don't know what was !

The idea of a great unwieldy brute, like the elephant, trampling under foot and wearing out more gold in one year than many hardworking people gain in ten.   And then the soiled mess that this costly carpeting was in in many parts would have been sufficient to cause a miser to go off instantly into a fit of insanity ! !

Several priests were busily engaged in different parts of the room polishing up tarnished spots ; others, professionally goldsmiths, were extracting the worn strips, and replacing them with new ones, so heavy and so bright that it made our eyes and mouths water to see such shameful waste.

The Siamese ladies may, without the smallest fear of competition, proclaim themselves to be *the* ugliest race of females upon the face of the globe.   With their hair worn in the same fashion as the men, the same features, same complexion, and the same amount of clothing, the man must be a gay Lothario indeed who would be captivated by their leering glances ; but as though nature had not formed them sufficiently ugly, these most neglected of all the human species resort to dyes wherewith to dye their teeth and lips of a jet black colour.   The darker the teeth the more beautiful is a Siamese belle considered ; and in order that their gums should be of a brilliant red to form a pleasant contrast to the black lips and teeth, they resort to the pleasant pastime of chewing *betel* from morning till night.   This *betel* consists, first, of the green leaf of the betel, which has a very tart flavour, something like the leaf of the pepper plant ; in this leaf is placed a piece of *chunam* (the common lime used for building), then a bit of the betel nut is broken into small pieces, and placed on the chunam, and the leaf being rolled up into something very much like a sailor's quid is then thrust into the lady's cheek, and is munched and crunched and chewed so long as the slightest flavour lasts ; it has the effect of dyeing their gums and the whole of the palate and tongue a blood red colour.

The people here believe in the transmigration of souls—a creed highly beneficial to snakes and other nauseous reptiles, who but for this, as the population spread in the East, would be in the course of time utterly exterminated.   They believe that at the worst after death, they may be metamorphosed into a snail, or a lizard, or some such agreeable tenant of earth or sea.

Upon the whole I found the Siamese a civil, humble and willing people, wrapped in the grossest ignorance and superstition, and lost to all sentiments of moral virtue ; but a reform on

E

this score can never be hoped till they have been made partakers of 'the benefits of knowledge and the blessings of religion.'

Let us now return to Singapore famed for its strange admixture of races and nationalities, Chinese, Malays, Singalese and other tribes. The great George Stephenson once said : 'that if rich and poor, great folk and small in worldly position, were all to undress they would be found pretty much alike.' But the almost naked bronzes of Singapore bore obvious marks of difference of races that might be a prolific theme for *Ruskinesque* dissertation and discrimination.

I was pleased, indeed, to see the 'Temperance Star' reading and refreshment room, with files of 'Band of Hope Reviews,' 'Children's Friend,' 'Animal World.' I thought it brighter than even the Southern Cross.

CHAPTER X.

A VOYAGE TO CHINA—PEKIN—THE OPIUM SMOKER—THE CHINESE AND THE BRITISH CHINESE PROVERBS—LEGEND OF THE ORIGIN OF THE FAN—THE JOSS HOUSE.

Now for a few words about the strange land China, with its 450,000,000 inhabitants, as we steam along its coast and Yellow Sea.

Peking is one of the largest cities in the world—being 25 miles in circumference and containing, in 1867, 1,600,000 inhabitants. The city has been compared to a great fair. This is especially the case with Circular Street, corresponding to the Regent Street, or Quadrant of London. The custom of the tradesmen here is to attract attention from the shop of their neighbour, by hanging out signs · of all descriptions, written in the picturesque Chinese characters, yellow and gold—running down their neighbour's goods and praising their own, till the street is more gay than a fleet dressed with flags for a royal reception.

The effect of opium-smoking is almost instantaneous on the smoker. He sinks gently against the cushion set at his back, and becomes perfectly insensible to what is passing around. It lasts about five minutes. One old inveterate opium-smoker told me, that if he knew his life would be forfeited by the act, he could no more resist the temptation than he could curb a fiery steed with a thread bridle. It carried him into the seventh heaven; he heard and saw things no tongue could utter, and felt as though his soul soared so high above things earthly during those precious moments of oblivion as to have flown beyond the reach of its heavy, burthensome cage.

Now let us suppose ourselves in Pekin. The delightful surroundings, verdant foliage and shady nooks and corners where we sip our own tea à la russe (that is, sans milk, and out of a glass, with a slice of lemon in it), make us rub our eyes and ask ourselves, 'is this really China?' If we remained very long in this, *par excellence*, wonderful country, I fancy we should lose a lot of our old, absurd British views about China and the Chinese! No sensible being can for one moment gainsay the fact that here we have the country from whence originated nearly everything we so highly prize.   For my own part, I doubt if anything worth inventing could not (were it possible) be traced to Chinese origin.[¶]   Every year brings us fresh proof.   We laugh and sneer at this wonderful people.   We think ourselves so very much superior to them.   But are we?   They choose to go on in the same hum-drum way, century after century never making the slightest change.

Why should they not do so?   They are perfectly satisfied with their lot.   It is quite certain some of us are not.

In no country I have yet travelled in have I ever seen such true religious equality and tolerance as in China.   All honour to them for so doing.   I cannot say I like the people, or their ways, but that does not prevent me speaking well of them.   Possibly they thought just as little of me and my occidental hauteur as I did of them.   Oh, for less of our hateful British egotism, and more of true Cosmopolitan brotherhood.   Heaven knows we have faults enough, and to spare, of our own, what with our mismanaged Hospitals, Poor Houses, and School Boards.

Some of the ordinary expressions of the Chinese are pointedly sarcastic enough.   A blustering harmless fellow they call a 'paper tiger.'   When a man values himself over much, they compare him to 'a rat falling into a scale, and weighing itself.'   Overdoing a thing they call 'a hunchback making a bow.'   A spendthrift they compare to 'a rocket' which goes off at once.   Those who expend their charity on remote objects, but neglect their family, are said to 'hang a lantern on a pole, which is seen afar, but gives no light below.'

Gold fish were originally natives from China and Japan, they were carried by the English to St. Helena, and from thence the captain of one of our East Indian ships brought some of them to England in the year 1788.

The treadmill was invented by the Chinese to raise water for the irrigation of the fields.   It was introduced into England about 1818.

The greater part of the land in China is owned in small properties of five acres and under, even to the sixth of an acre, so 'Three acres and a cow' is, after all, not original.

' 'The tongue of woman,' says a Chinese maxim, 'is their sword, and they never suffer it to grow rusty.'   'Nature has given us two ears and but one tongue, in order that we may repeat but one half of what we hear,' is another sound Chinese proverb.

This is the Chinese legend of the origin of the fan.   'One evening, when the beautiful Kau Si, daughter of a powerful

Chinese mandarin, was assisting at the great feast of ' Lanterns,' she was so overcome by the heat that she was obliged to take off her mask. But to expose her face to the eyes of the profane and vulgar was a serious offence against the law ; so, holding the mask as closely as possible to her features, she fluttered it rapidly to give herself air, and the rapidity of the movement still concealed her. The other ladies present, witnessing this hardy but charming innovation, imitated it, and at once ten thousand hands were fluttering ten thousand masks.' Thus the fan was evoked, and took the place of the mask.

Marriage here, is neither a civil nor a religious ceremony, no priest or any person in authority being present ; the only witnesses are the family and friends. In the middle of the drawing-room is a table, upon which have been placed a censer, fruits, and wine. In their idea, this table is exposed to the sight of Heaven. The pair then prostrate themselves before the table to thank the Supreme Being for having created them, the earth for having nourished them, the emperor for protecting, and their parents for educating them. Then the bridegroom presents his bride to the members of his family, and to those of his friends who are present.

The Chinese have a proverb : ' That every man who rules himself is a king.' Royal blood is not scarce in England, it would seem, if every woman who rules her husband is a queen.

In China, if you are wise, you must not inquire too closely into what you eat. ' What the eye does not see, &c., &c.' It is all very well to go over the floating restaurants, where the cookery is exclusively Chinese, and the use of chop-sticks in preference to knives and forks *de rigueur*. What the little round saucers contain—pickled eels' feet *à la daube* or *salmi* of frogs' giblets, birds-nest soup, dried ducks, bêche de mer, snips or snails or puppy dogs' tails—I never could quite make out. The maidens who wait on you are clad in loose *casaquins* and wide trousers of rich materials sumptuously brocaded. None of them are ' golden lilies,' or small-footed. Their complexions are ivory-white, their eyes almond-shaped and sable as sloes, their hair very black and lustrous, and very well dressed. They wear plenty of jewellery, and their eyebrows and lips are manifestly painted. They would really be pretty but for the sickly, dejected, downtrodden, almost imbecile simper playing about their ruddled lips—the simper of the slave continually deprecating the always imminent bamboo. The singing out here is the usual Chinese whine, rising now and again to a screech, an ululation no doubt delightful to

Oriental ears, but to the Occidental tympanum distressingly dissonant, as bad indeed as the " Music of the future."

We have a look, of course, into the Joss house, which is always kept scrupulously clean and carefully oil-clothed. It is an octagonal apartment, with a high altar covered with painted mats, and behind it a kind of reredos of wood, elaborately carved, gilt in some places and in others daubed with garish hues. An inscrutable race! John Chinaman always reminds me of a cat, from Montaigne's point of view ' you may laugh at Grimalkin ; but don't be too sure that he is not laughing at you.' John Chinaman, I fancy, knows a great deal more about you, than you do about him. They are great gamblers, and the pawnbroker a great institution. A Chinaman, when he is gambling, will stake not only his money to the last coin, but the worth of his wearing apparel and his minutest personal belongings—so it follows ' mine uncle ' is a very convenient accessory to the gaming-table. Is our avuncular kinsman wholly unknown in the luxurious haunts of Monte Carlo ? When Madame la Princesse Katerichasoff has been losing heavily by backing Zero, has she not been known over and over again, *en plein tripot*, to strip from her fair arms her dazzling diamond bracelets, to pluck from her rosy ear-lobes their gleaming pendants, and by the hands of a watchful servitor, send the glittering gewgaws to the pawnbroker? The world, after all, is not so big a village as we sometimes take it to be. Humanity in far-distant lands does not vary half so much as we think, or pretend we think that it varies. There is a closer bond of union between distant parts than we often wot of.

The signs over the restaurants and hotels are peculiar, such as ' the Heavenly Jewel,' or the ' Chamber of Fragrant Almonds,' while a druggist calls his shop the ' Hall of Everlasting Life.' There are no windows to the shops-—the front takes out, showing the goods inside. Wheelbarrows are the only wheeled vehicles seen in the streets. The passenger sits on one side balanced by his luggage on the other.

Butcher's shops are numerous, in them are exposed for sale, beef, pork, dried fish, cats, puppies, sea slugs, edible birds'-nests, and frogs' legs. But my readers can easily conceive how varied and full of colour the scene must be. My greatest successes were made in China. Magical performances seeming to be very much to the taste of the Chinese. In no part of the world have I been more kindly treated, and nowhere else have I acquired such excellent ideas in occult wonders as out here. Many of my most effective feats were acquired in China.

CHAPTER XI.

SHANGHAI is by far the most important station for foreign trade on the coast of China. It exports more than one half of the produce sent out of the country. It is the Great Gate of the Chinese Empire.

In going up the river towards the town a forest of masts meet the eye. Nowhere else in the East can be found so great a collection of sea and river going craft. Off the coast of China you are sometimes caught by that fearful gale of wind known as the 'Typhoon' but called by the Chinese '*Tufan*' or 'Sea Devil.' China, to me, seems the most impregnal of all Eastern nations. They are opposed to railways and telegraphs. The cable from Shanghai to Hong Kong the fishermen fish up and cut, because they say the fish will not cross the line, and because the shade of a wire on land crossed the grave of the dead they cut the wires, and the Mandarins will in neither case protect them. As to beds, the inhabitants sleep on a kind of hard bench, every female having a notch in the wood, into which she fits her head on lying down ; no windows, no doors.

A letter in the *New York Times* having asked for information as to fish culture in China, an answer has been given by Mr. E. H. Colton-Salter, ex-United States Consul at Hankow, 700 miles up the Yang-tse Kiang. This gentleman says :—

'On this great river, 3,000 miles long, are found thousands of nurseries devoted to the artificial production of fish. The river is only open for trade with the Treaty Powers at Ching Tsing, Kin Kian, and Honkow, but I have explored the river as far as Yochow and the Yung-Tsing Lake, the great lake of the Empire. The Chinese are pre-eminently a fish-eating people, and when you consider that the population is estimated by some geographers at 500,000,000 souls, imagine the vast demand for fish which can only be supplied by artificial means. The "shad" is called by the Chinese " sam-li ; " it is of superior flavour and great size. I can only repeat the information given me on the great river, that they are produced by artificial means and conveyed in congs, large vessels made of course earthenware, to all parts of the empire. The dense population of China has stimulated human ingenuity to the highest degree so as to provide means of subsistence. Take the subject of artificial incubation, for instance. How little we know of it in this country, although we assume that we know everything ! The traveller in China may see in every village flocks of tiny chickens, ducks, and geese—say, 500 at a time—led by a mere boy with a little wand of the familiar bamboo, and all hatched by the artificial process. As a natural sequence of this system, they are very cheap, and you can purchase from five to ten good fowls for 1,000 copper cash—say 1 dol. gold Eggs are equally cheap, because the people possess secrets to increase the fecundity of the birds, and you can buy, even in the cities, five eggs for the equivalent of our cent. Our people are profoundly ignorant about the resources of this wonderful country, only twenty days' sail from San Francisco by a swift steamer.'

When the sky turns leaden and yellow, and banks of black and ragged cloud gather in a direction away from the wind—when the sea rises and rolls in heavy, restless and confused billows—then the China junks get out their sweeps and make for shore, because the ' Storm Devil ' is out upon the waters. At Shanghai you find a number of Flower Boats or floating restaurants where dinners are served.

Here the wealthy Chinese entertain their friends. The boats are gaily decorated, the elegantly furnished cabins have numerous lanterns hanging from the roof.

There are as many kind of boats here as there are vehicles in Fleet Street. Ferry boats ply as briskly and are as heavily laden as omnibuses. Heavy cargo boats lumber along and get in every one's way as our brewers' drays do. Light Tauka boats with one or two passengers cut in and out like hansoms.

Nearly everything you see done by mechanics in our large cities you will find being imitated in China, only with simpler tools and in a slower manner.

Gamblers are constantly seen here, for the Chinaman will gamble as long as he has cash or a garment to pawn. They have sometimes been known to sell themselves. When persons quarrel in China, they call each other the most abusive names, then separate without coming to blows.

CHAPTER XII.

A TRIP TO JAPAN —YOKOHAMA—TOKIO—YEDDO—JAPANESE
WINDOW GARDENING—THE LANGUAGE OF FLOWERS—HOW TO
KEEP YOURSELF COOL IN HOT CLIMATES—THE AINOS OF JAPAN—
MANNERS AND CUSTOMS OF THE JAPANESE.

WE leave Hong Kong and start for Japan—reaching Yokohama, 1,620 miles distant from that port, eight days after—I had heard a great deal about the beauty of this part of the tour, but the sail over the inland sea of Japan surpassed all dreams of the beauty of that island and mountain—studded lake, of 500 miles of panoramic scenery, with its charming bays of *Hiogo*, and *Naga-saki*, and the river port of *Osaka*, at all of which European and American vessels have free access. I have seen almost every lake in England, Scotland, Ireland, Switzerland, and Italy, but this surpasses each of them, and combines the best features of them all in one.

That Yokohama is ruled more by the alien than the native will be readily admitted.

It's a most hospitable place and boasts one of the finest clubs in the world—whilst several excellent hotels are to be found. The houses are well built, the streets wide, and the English language is heard everywhere.

To see the Japanese at his best, one must either select a country village, where he lives in primitive simplicity, or go to the capital, Tokio, or Yedo, as it used to be called, so at Yokohama, which we find about half European ; we jump in the train, showing our railway tickets which are printed in English and Japanese to the civil ticket collector, and find the railway carriages very English-looking affairs although 12,000 miles away from the old country. The ride is through a flat country planted everywhere with rice. Half an hour's ride brings to our view Fugiama, the great volcano of the island, about 12,000 feet high, if I remember rightly, and generally covered with snow at the top. As it is the fashion out here to make the ascent, of course up we go, and the view one gets from its summit, is worth all the trouble taken.

There is a pretty custom in Japan with regard to window-gardening, which is not, I take it, generally known. In houses wherein reside one or more daughters of a marriageable age, an empty flower-pot of an ornamental character is encircled by a ring and suspended from the window or verandah by three light chains. The Juliets of Japan are, of course, attractive, and their Romeos as anxious as those of other lands. But, instead of serenades by moonlight, and other delicate ways of making an impression, it is etiquette for the Japanese lover to approach the dwelling of his lady bearing some choice plant in his hand, which he boldly, but let us hope, reverently, proceeds to plant in the empty vase. This takes place at a time when he is fully assured that both mother and daughter are at home, neither of whom, of course, is at all conscious that the young man is taking such a liberty with the flower-pot outside their window. It is believed that a young lover so engaged has never been seen by his lady or by her mamma in this act of sacrilege.

This act of placing a pretty plant in the empty flower-pot is equivalent to a formal proposal to the young lady who dwells within, and this Eastern fashion is a most delicate and harmless way of proposing to a lady. The youthful gardener, having settled his plant to his mind, retires, and the lady is free to act as she pleases. If he is the right man, she takes every care of his gift, waters it and tends it carefully with her own hands, that all the world may see the donor is accepted as a suitor. But, if he is not a favourite, or if the stern parents object, the poor plant is torn from the vase, and the next morning lies limp and withered on the verandah, or on the path below. Japan, though very interesting to travel through, is getting too many absurd Occidental ideas in her head to please me.

A capital way to keep cool in hot climates is to spread a piece of Chinese straw matting the size of your bed under the sheet upon which you lie at night, and you will be surprised to find how much it will enhance your comfort. Or, better still, if you can do it get a very big hammock, and sleep in that. If the atmosphere at night seems heavy with suffocating, oppressive heat, you will find much relief from sprinkling water on the floor and hanging up an outspread sheet, thoroughly wet, where, whatever little draught there may be will fall upon it. If you are still too hot to sleep take a cool bath, dry your skin lightly, and if you do not then cool off, it will most probably be because you have a fever or a bad conscience. It seems very odd in Malabar, India, to see the way the natives have civilised the monkeys, making them work the punkas. You see thousands of them at this useful work, and they seem to like it. They are a fine species indigenous in this quarter—the 'neilgherry langur.'

Osaka is second only to Yeddo in population and commerce; its river-sides being crowded with junks laden with bales of produce and commerce, and the streets, shops, and habitations of the citizens 'as clean as a new pin.' Here the new Mint is established and the people, you may be sure, are very proud of their beautiful new gold and silver coinage, made by steam power and ingenious mechanism.

Yeddo is a city of gardens, and palaces, and, with its thirty hills, is unequalled in the world. It stretches out beyond the limits of sight, like a vast park—built on sea—river runs through it. The 'Siro,' or Taïkoun's palace, rises in the centre like a huge citadel, from wide-spreading glacis of turf which descend to circular lakes and canals. Thirty bridges of granite unite it to the city of the Princes or *Soto-siro*, which is quite unlike other Japanese towns. From *Soto* to *Midzi*, the commercial city, the way lies along a hillside, and between great granite walls which enclose immense parks. Immediately above these walls are hedges six feet wide and forty feet high, cut and trained to marvellous perfection ; they are formed of camellias, azaleas and rose laurels, and whole flocks of sacred birds, white plumaged, are always fluttering among them like the hanging gardens of Babylon. It is a mark of politeness to put food in the mouth of the guest. Another custom is for the guest to carry a quantity of food from the dinner table to eat' at home. At a dinner given by Lord Elgin, a Japanese Governor put in the folds of his shirt any food that took his fancy, and one of his suite attempted to carry some strawberry jam in his bosom. We visit the gardens of the Taïkoun, with its wondrous falconries and summer-houses; the famous temple of Asaxa 33,333 divinities. Crossing the *Lokungo* river, we find the great tea-house of *Meïaski*, which is an epitome of the utter strangeness of things in Japan.

A few years ago when I was at Yeddo, it was quite unsafe to walk through many of the streets; this last time, I was drawn by two coolies in a *Gin-rick-sha* right through the city, the natives laughing good humouredly, and cheering, and crowding round us when we stopped at a shop or exhibition. Through the three miles of streets not a solitary unfriendly disposition was manifested in that great city of nearly a million inhabitants. I was astonished to see such a large number of book and picture shops, and was told that the Japanese are a great reading people, and fond especially of story. It is easy to see that they are very sagacious, and ready to adopt whatever is likely to contribute to their interest.

Japanese ladies' hair is *grown* on their heads, and here ladies have quite as much liberty as Europeans. Their complexion is fair, their hair is arranged in massive rolls like the chignons of European belles; they wear robes of rich materials with long flowing sleeves, and round the waist a sash of bright colours is tied in the form of a 'pannier.' They have been worn here from time immemorial. Previous to marriage a Japanese belle increases her charms by painting her cheeks and lips—but after that event she shows the affection she bears her husband by pulling out her eyebrows and blacking her teeth. This the Japanese think adds to the beauty of the lady.

Mr. De Long, lately United States Minister in Japan, made the following statement in his lecture at Sacramento:—

'The Japanese estimate their population at about 40,000,000. This I think an over-estimate by from 10,000,000 to 15,000,000, although their reckoning is supported by their census returns. There is found inhabiting the island of Jesso and the Kurile Islands a race of men called by the Japanese "Ainos," or "hairy men." This appellation they well sustain, as they have full flowing black beards, reaching, in many cases, below the middle of the breast. We are told that they are aborigines of Japan, originally occupying all of the islands embraced in that group; and Japanese history records the fact that Jimoo Tenno, the first Japanese Emperor, with some followers, came from heaven in a boat, landed at or near Nagasaki, on the Island of Sikoke, from whom sprang the present Japanese nation; that gradually they beat back and destroyed the Aino race, as we have done the Indian, until the nation attained its present greatness, and the aborigines sank to their present weak condition. This is all the Japanese know of their origin and their race.'

'Nothing interests their leading men more than a study of their probable origin, as they treat with levity the legend recorded in their country. The Embassy which accompanied me to Washington brought with them a large collection of stone beads, arrow heads, and other evidences of the "Stone Age." These they brought for the purpose of comparing them with similar relics found in our own and other countries. The Embassy studied with great regard such Indians as we met, and such relics as could be found at Salt Lake City and other places. Iwakura assured me that the appearance of our Indians, their dress, costume, and weapons were identical with such ornamentation as their geologists had discovered upon rude images marking the "Stone Age" in Japan, and he further remarked to me that he would be almost prepared to believe they were akin but for the circumstance that our Indians could not be civilised.'

The Ainos form, in my mind, a curious subject of reflection. They seem to bear no relation in customs, language, or appearance to either the Japanese, Chinese, Manchoos, or other Oriental nations. They are extremely kind, mild-mannered, skilful as hunters and fishermen, intelligent, and brave. Crime is almost unknown among them, yet they are so completely savage or barbarous that they have no idea of their origin, no mode of reckoning time, no knowledge of the value of money, nor even proper names. They call their children, 'One,' 'Two,' 'Three,' &c. Their mode of saluting a superior is to sit down upon the earth cross-legged, bow the head, and, placing their hands together with the palms upward, raise them three times towards their faces, as if in the act of casting dust or water upon themselves, after which they complacently stroke their long black beards with both hands three times. This mode of salutation, I believe, is analogous to that of the ancient Hebrews, while the beard and physiognomy of the people, in my mind, strongly resemble that interesting and wonderful nation.

Ancient mining works of a very extensive character are found upon the island of Jesso, where these people live, and are mentioned by Professor Pompelly, who resided there for a period, while in long service in his work entitled, 'A Tour Around the World.' I trust you will pardon me for indulging for a moment in what may seem to you to be a vagary. We know that Solomon sent forth ships to a place called Ophir after gold. The rude character of sailing craft of that period forbids the supposition that they could have voyaged to either Australia or California. Sailing, as we are informed, from Arabia eastward, and, like all small craft, naturally keeping near the shore, they would, after crossing the northern portion of the Indian Ocean, reach the Gulf Stream of the Pacific, which, without effort upon their part, would bear them to the Japanese Islands. With the death of Solomon, or the fall and captivity of the nation, it is presumable that this commerce with Ophir suddenly ceased. In such a case it is fairly presumable that workmen sent abroad may have been left there by this accident, or that they voluntarily remained there, rather than return and share in the enslavement of their people.   Only by this theory·can I account for this strange and interesting race of men, for their customs, which I have mentioned, or for the existence of those ancient mining works, which is unaccounted for by Japanese history or Aino legendry.

When death appears inevitable in a family the patient's clothes are removed, and their places supplied by others.

These are put on *topsy-turvy*, the sleeves at the feet, and the lower part upwards.   When dead a powder called *dosia* is introduced into his ears, mouth and nostrils, to render the limbs flexible.   The floors of rooms in Japan are covered with soft mats made of rice or wheat straw neatly plaited 6ft. + 3ft. and 4ins. thick.   At night they are used for beds, with the addition of a quilt, and a block of wood for a pillow.

The land is one of great beauty and rich fertility, also of extraordinary interest, natural, historical, political, and social.   The inhabitants and the Government are rapidly transforming into enlightened, peaceful, and cordial citizens.   In the department of the Imperial Government Proper, 214 foreigners are employed, on salaries ranging from 480 to 16,000 dollars.   In the interior there are a number of foreigners, teachers, surgeons, engineers, &c.   The superiority of Japanese acrobats and jugglers is sufficiently well-known in Europe, but their performances in the Sacred City reach a point of such marvellous perfection, that, no doubt, the masters of those arts are too well paid ever to wish to leave Japan, so that the extraordinary things we have seen done by them in England are only, in reality, second-rate performances.

In Japan children are rarely threatened or struck by their parents—the love, obedience, and reverence manifested by them is unbounded—while the confidence placed by parents in their children is without limit.

The Japanese are far in advance of us in matters of private cleanliness and sanitary arrangements, baths being found in every respectable house.

There are public baths in every street, known by a black flag suspended over the doorway.

In the large towns there are streams of clear water running on each side of the street.

The streets in most towns here are open, well paved, and well swept, and the houses of all classes have their floors covered with neatly-worked matting.

The people are pictures of gentleness and kindness ; docile as lambs, and eager (many of them) to be led in the right way.

The Mikado, too, unlike the exclusive and secluded emperors of many ages ago, mingles with the people, and holds converse with the representatives of foreign states; and the numerous embassies and delegations to Europe are all designed to collect information and cull the best examples of 'law and order.' At the present time there is a general expectation of an early decree of religious toleration.

The national religion of Japan is Sintooism, or the worship of deified heroes, the head of which is the *Mikado* or Spiritual Emperor. Next to this is Buddhism, the faith of over 300 millions of the human race, teaching, them morality, cleanliness, and the care of the poor. Then there are thirty-three religious sects off-shoots of these.

Numbers of young Japanese are now learning the European languages.

There are two large foundries in the country with foreign machinery, and several extensive dockyards.

Newspapers are published, there are four or five dailies published at Yokohama alone.

While the old temples of Buddhism are going to decay, new School-houses for both sexes are rising up in every direction, and teachers are engaged by Government from England and America, at good salaries, who are expected to teach English and other European languages.

The Japanese now have omnibuses, steamers, gas, telegraphs, an efficient lighthouse department, sewing machines, and even a railroad—they will be trying a School Board next!

The Army and Navy have been remodelled upon our system down to the drum, fife, and cat-o'-nine-tails.

A scheme of general education has also been established throughout the Empire and a Japanese law tribunal has been established at one or two of the principal ports.

At Yokohama you are 12,000 miles from old England 8,500 sea, 3,500 land. Suppose you were here and wanted to come home by the route we have just taken, you would have to pay £104 8s. 6d. for a first and £61 19s. 6d. for a second class ticket on the P. and O. Co.'s steamer. If you returned by Malta and Gibraltar, it would be cheaper, viz. £95 and £55.

The United States mail steamers leave Yokohama every fourteen days for San Francisco.

CHAPTER XIII.

CROSSING THE PACIFIC—SAN FRANCISCO—THE CHINESE IN CALIFORNIA—GIANT TREES OF CALIFORNIA—OGDEN—SPLENDID SCENERY IN AMERICA.

CROSSING the Pacific is terribly monotonous if you go from Japan to San Francisco direct. One vast undulating rolling sea of molten glass. You feel ashamed to ask the Captain orally, too often, as to when he thinks you will arrive, remembering that master-mariners have much to put up with both on sea and land from passengers ; and I have known captains who had quick tempers and who could give, upon occasions, short answers. How stinging was the rebuke administered by the late Commodore Judkins, of the Cunard service, to the lady passenger who, when the ship was off the banks of Newfoundland, asked him 'if it were always foggy there?' 'Do you think I live here, mum?' quoth stern Commodore Judkins.

A group of Catholic Sisters of Charity in their wide-sleeved robes and white wimples and pinners beneath their snowy veils, and with their sweet, smiling, rosy faces as they sit on deck, working at some embroidery or whatnot, teach us poor fretting, discontented, rationalistic humbugs a lesson, I think. How contented and happy they look ! I fear, cynic that I am, I have but a poor opinion of my fellow men, but Diogenes himself might well be proud that such good people do exist as these Sisters. Yes, their pure, rosy faces are still the same even beneath this torrid sun. All the world over you meet their kindly faces. Rome ! Rome ! You know what you are about, in sending forth such angel Missionaries to convert the heathen !

The crew you will find on board are all Chinamen with the exception of a few leading seamen and engineers. There is a terrible outcry and strong agitation among the Sydney Trade-Unionists connected with shipping against the employment of coloured hands on board the ships of the Pacific Steam Navigation Company— the *Australia*, the *Zealandia*, and the *City of Sydney*—The Seamen's Union, the firemen, the stokers, the cooks, the stewards of the capital of New South Wales, were all literally up in arms against the shipping of Mongol hands on board British ships. Even the cook on board, we find, is Taas, a Celestial, who seems, however, to stick to English cookery.

To my mind all ocean steamer cookery is too substantial not to say gross, heavy and insipid. The only lesson he had learnt from the kitchen of California was his buckwheat cakes for breakfast quite *à l'Américaine*, albeit we had to put up with clarified molasses, in lieu of maple syrup, to lubricate our cakes withal. That loss of a day on the Pacific in the 180° of longitude has always puzzled me and, possibly, some of you, my readers, as well. I remember going to rest one Friday night and on waking up in the morning was dumbfounded to find it was Sunday morning, and the crew preparing for Divine service. It is more curious still, and a study for Sabbatarians, that on one of the Pacific islands Saturday is observed as the Christian Sabbath, and on another island, on the opposite side of the line, Monday is kept as the Lord's Day, Sunday being the dropped day, according to Dr. Prime of New York in his 'Voyage Round the World'; on reaching the 180ß of longitude we are at the antipodes of Greenwich, and London time is twelve hours in advance. We then take a leap of twenty-four hours, leaving Greenwich twelve hours in the rear, but crossing the Meridian line we put back our time an hour for every 15 degrees, and by the time we reach London the clocks and time will have righted themselves.

Lounging under the shady trees of Golden Gate Park in your spider-waggon, and then on to famous Cliff House, and the Seal Rock, with the broad Pacific before you, with the knowledge that you have a week's rest before you and 'belonging,' for the time to Mr. Sharon, the manager of the Palace Hotel, San Francisco, and his obliging, courteous chief clerk Mr. George H. Smith—is really very agreeable. It is worth while—well worth while—to have come so many thousand miles to behold this enchanting scene, and looking eastward you think of the delightful railway journey you have in front of you—the ascent of the Pacific slope—threading the gorges of the Sierras Nevadas: running the gauntlet of the Devil's Slide, Webber's Canon, and the snow-sheds, traversing Wearyfoot Common, otherwise the Rocky Mountains—Sacramento to Ogden—Ogden to Omaha, till at last you find repose at the Grand Pacific Hotel at Chicago. Union and Pacific, the Chicago and North-Western, and the Erie Railways, and so by a Cunard steamship to Liverpool.

There is something about 'Frisco I like very much, it is not

F

only the people, but the surroundings; fancy leaving snowed up Eastern cities in furs, and a day or so afterwards in delightful El Dorado, buying in the market fresh strawberries, green peas, oranges and japonicas, which all flourish in the open.

Of course some hospitable friend makes us try that peculiar Californian punch, which I am informed contains twelve ingredients, comprising, its concoctors proudly boast, not one single drop of water. You know what the Romans say of the Fountain of Trevi. The stranger, they declare, who has once drunk of the Trevi waters is bound to return again and again to the Eternal City. And, indeed, as I am penning these lines, I am thinking of what a very nice thing it will be if I am spared to appear one of these fine days in Rome again. In 'Frisco, though, there are not any fountains, but I can remember, yet, the glass of iced water you quaff at your breakfast at the Palace Hotel, Market Street, as you devour a couple of oranges to put you in trim for the fried oysters, the tomcod, the tender loin steaks, the scrambled eggs, the stuffed tomatoes, the fish balls, the buckwheat cakes, and the strawberries and cream which are to follow. Pio Nono once told Kaiser Wilhelm that all Christians belonged, somehow or another, to the Pope. The Imperial Hohenzollern was unable to recognise the cogency of the assertion; still I am fatalist enough to think that when a traveller has once drunk his glass of iced water and sucked his oranges in the breakfast-room of the Palace Hotel, he is unconsciously subjected to an obligation to cross the Rockies and the Sierras Nevadas again and again, to 'do the block' in Kearney Street, and be fascinated by the beauty of the ladies engaged in afternon shopping in that fashionable thoroughfare, to be amazed at the architectural magnificence of the Californian millionaires' red-wood palaces on 'Nob Hill.' San Francisco is one of the pleasantest cities in the whole world. Being at 'Frisco we naturally enough visit China Town.

John Chinaman's picturesqueness is apt to become, after a time, monotonous, and then to cloy, to satiate, and at length to revolt. Take him at his best, and with the most favourable surroundings, the celestial, somehow, leaves a slightly unpleasant táste in your mouth. The Roman epigrammatist who didn't like Zabidus, and the Oxford undergraduate who didn't like Dr. Fell, might be unanimous in the expression of their dislike for the Heathen Chinee, yet as incapable of giving a definite reason for their aversion. If all the celestials you met resembled the merchants and manufacturers of China Town generally, there would be no need to recall the unreasoning ill-nature of the epigrams on Zabidus and Dr. Fell. Unfortunately the mass of the inhabitants are the nastiest of nasty creatures, I am sure some of the faces, I have seen in the lowest quarters, I shall never get out of my eyes—faces awfully abominable in their distortion and depravation from the normal aspect of humanity—faces which in their grotesqueness and their horror made pale and jejune the wildest efforts of the graphic imagination of Jacques Callot, and Breughel d'Enfer, and the Spaniard Francisco Goya.

You might not possibly be aware of the fact, but most of the Indians of Alaska believe in cremation, and hardly a day passes when one cannot witness the peculiar ceremony gone through during the burning and after it is completed. No dead Indian is taken out through the door, but is either taken out through the roof or through the side of the house. The body is then placed on a pile of logs and the fire started, while the people stand round and sing, beating time with carved poles while the body burns. When all is consumed, the ashes are placed in a box, and, together with many articles belonging to the deceased, are placed in one of the Dead-houses, or houses built near the town for the purpose of holding the ashes of each particular family.

The luxury of this Pacific country is amazing. The restaurants and cafés of each petty digging town put forth bills-of-fare which the *Trois Frères* could not equal for ingenuity; wine lists such as *Delmonico's* cannot beat. The dishes smell of the Californian soil; baked rock-cod à la Buena Vista, boiled Californian quail with Russian River bacon, Sacramento snipes on toast, Oregon ham with champagne sauce, and a dozen other toothsome things. A few Atlantic States dishes, however, you find down—hominy, cod chowder—hardly equal to that of Salem—sassafras candy, and squash tart, but never a mention of pork and molasses, dear to the Massachusetts boy. All these good things the diggers, when 'dirt is plenty,' moisten with Clicquot, or *Heidsick* cabinet; when returns are small, with their excellent Sonoma wine.

Americans certainly need not go to Europe to find scenery. The world can show few scenes more winning than *Israel's River Valley* in the White Mountains of New Hampshire, or *North Conway* in the Southern slopes of the same range. Nothing can be more full of grandeur than the passage of the James at Balcony Falls, where the river rushes through a crack in the Appalachian chain. As for river scenery, the Hudson is grander than the Rhine, the *Susquehanna* is lovelier than the *Meuse*, the Schuylkill prettier than the Seine; the Mohawk more enchanting than the

Dart. Of the rivers of North Europe, the Neckar alone is not beaten in the States.

In Pennsylvania, you may sometimes fancy yourself in Sussex ; while in only New England you seem to be in some part of Europe that you have never happened to light on before ; in California, you are, at all events, at last in a new world. The names, The Golden State and El Dorado are doubly applicable to California ; her light and landscape, as well as her soil are golden. On the Pacific side, Nature wears a robe of deep rich yellow, even the distant hills are wrapped in golden haze. All is rounded, soft, and warm. A Coloradon going West was asked in Nevada if in his country they could beat the ' Comstock lode ?' ' Dear, no !' he said. ' The boys with us are plaguy discouraged jess at present.' The Nevadans were down upon the word. ' Discouraged, air they ?' 'Why yes! They've jess found they've got ter dig through three feet of solid silver 'fore ever they come ter gold.'

The giant trees of California are situated in the Mammoth Tree Valley, Calaveros Co. and in the Mariposa Valley, about 150 miles east and south of San Francisco. In the former you find the 'Big Tree Stump.' It is perfectly smooth, sound, and level. Upon it on the 4th July, '64, thirty-two persons were engaged in dancing four sets of cotillions at one time. At 5½ ft. from the ground the stump measures 28ft. across. This tree employed five men 22 days in felling it. It was 302ft. high and 96ft. in circumference at the base. The largest tree in the entire group is called the 'Father of the Forest' it lies on the ground, half buried in the soil, 435ft. high, i.e. 31ft. higher than the top of St. Paul's Cathedral, and 110ft. in circumference. Our wonder at the magnitude of these trees, becomes amazement, when we look at the *Cones* produced by them and find that they are not larger than a hen's egg, and the seeds a mere speck.

It would take a dozen to weigh down an apple seed. Some of these giant trees are over 3,000 years old. A concentric circle is formed on the bark of each tree every year, and more than 3,000 circles can be counted on the trunk of the fallen tree. 881 miles from San Francisco you find Ogden. We will suppose we leave the train here and after a détour of thirty-seven miles reach Salt Lake City.

It is possible the few words I am now about to say about the Mormons, will occasion some surprise. They will differ materially from accounts written by several visitors to these parts. I cannot confirm all their statements without making an unpardonable sacrifice of truth. Doubtless they were honest in their eulogy; but, then, they must either have deliberately shut their eyes, or else have been incompetent and superficial observers.

It may be, that, going forth laden with foregone conclusions, they returned home rejoicing that they were in the right.

You will find the Mormons very backward and ignorant, when compared with other dwellers on the American Continent. Neither Jew nor Christian can safely and easily establish himself in Utah. As for the energy displayed by the Mormons of which we hear so much—look at the Norwegian settlement in Wisconsin—more than seventy-five per cent. in advance in point of wealth, intelligence, culture, and everything which goes under the name of civilisation; and they have no grog shops nor houses of prostitution amongst them.

At the northern end of the principal street you find the Tithing-office, the Endowment House, the residence of President Young, and the Tabernacle, holding, in my opinion, not more than 5,000 sitters, though some say 8,000. It is an oblong or egg-shaped structure, devoid of ornament and wholly destitute of beauty in proportion or outline. In front of the elders' pew there are barrels containing water which often being blessed is handed about in tin cans to all. A sip and bit of bread—Sacrament.

CHAPTER XIV.

DESCRIPTION OF NEW YORK—THE BROADWAY—THE FALLS OF NIAGARA—THE TERRAPIN TOWER—A VISIT TO THE FALLS—THE LAKES.

WHEN I first saw New York it did not appear to me a foreign city in the same sense as Paris, or Frankfort, or Milan. A closer and more leisurely examination produced a different impression. To walk along Broadway recalls a walk along Regent Street, but it also recalls a walk along the Rue de la Paix. What seems to be English is rivalled, if not outdone, by what is unmistakably French, while many things have neither a French nor an English impress. The architectural effects are extraordinary in their variety. The want of simplicity and repose is as marked as the absence of a distinctively national style. Everyone has apparently followed the bent of his fancy, and the straining after originality has led to a confusion of ideas and a clashing of ideas. Half the languages of Europe are spoken by the motley gathering.

In my opinion scant justice has yet been done to New York on the whole. It has its drawbacks, as has every city on the face of the globe, but it possesses excellences which more than outweigh them. The man of business finds it as good a centre for his operations as London. The pleasure-seeker can amuse himself as well as in Paris, while men of letters and students of art affirm that the prospects of New York becoming an honoured home of literature and art, grow brighter every day. The scenery of the Hudson has been highly lauded, but not overpraised. It is quite as romantic as that of the Rhine.

A gentleman, who had been here three days, but who had been paying attention to a prominent New York belle, wanted to propropose, but was afraid he would be thought too hasty. He delicately broached the subject as follows: 'If I were to ask you to allow me to speak of marriage, after having made your acquaintance only three days ago, what would you say to it?' 'Well, I should say, never put off till to-morrow that which you should have done the day before yesterday.'

With money in your pocket everything that the most polished Sybarite could desire is procurable.

'Why celebrate George Washington's birthday more than mine?' asked a schoolmaster here one day of one of his pupils. 'Because he never told a lie,' was the reply.

Out here they thoroughly believe the earth turns on its axis every twenty-four hours, subject to the constitution of the United States.

The leap from spring to summer is the only spring they have in these parts.

Niagàra is an old Indian word meaning the *Thunder of Waters.* The roar of the cataract can be heard ten miles off, over one hundred million tons of water rush over this precipice every hour, still the great lakes above are never dry, they do not vary six inches in height each year. On the brink of the precipice are a few scattered rocks, on one of which is built the *Terrapin Tower.* From this point you obtain the most magnificent view of the Falls. The Tower is forty-five feet high—the bridge connecting it with Goat Island is made of wood, and is always wet with spray, thus rendering it slippery and dangerous. Close to Clifton House there is a circular staircase which conducts you to a ledge of rock running, *under the Fall*—(the Canadian side).

If you have courage enough, you pay a half dollar—a guide dresses you in a flannel suit, and drags you from rock to rock till you are under the Fall. You can touch Niagara as it rushes down, while deafened with the roar and drenched to the skin with the spray. You are not at all sorry to get back again to your comfortable hotel. Between Goat Island and the American mainland is Luna Island—the best point for seeing on a moonlight night the beautiful Lunar bow.

Those who say that America has no scenery forget the Hudson, while they can never have explored *Lake George, Lake Champlain,* and the *Mohawk.* That Poole's exquisite scene from the *Decameron, Philomel's Song,* could have been realised on earth, I never dreamt until I saw the singers at a New Yorker's Villa, on the Hudson, grouped in the deep shades of a glen, from which there was an outlook upon the basaltic palisades and lake-like *Tappan Zee.*

It was in some such spot that *De Tocqueville* wrote the brightest of his brilliant letters—that dated 'Sing Sing,'—for he speaks of himself as lying on a hill that overhung the Hudson, watching the white sails gleaming in the hot sun ; and trying in vain to fancy what became of the river where it disappeared in the blue Highlands.

CHAPTER XV.

A VOYAGE TO MADEIRA—DESCRIPTION OE FUNCHAL—OUR FELLOW
VOYAGERS—A CRUISE IN SEARCH OF HEALTH—REMINISCENCES
OF HOME—OUR BRITISH SAILORS.

To a man who requires (or thinks he requires) a little rest
sea air, and a change of scene, a trip by one of Donald Currie's
mail-steamers to Cape Town should prove to be the very identical
thing he needed. What an easy thing to just run down to the
City a day or so beforehand, take a return ticket and secure your
berth ; and the day the 'Something or other *Castle*' leaves the
West India Docks, London, jump into a hansom, light up a full
flavoured Havanna cigar, which will reduce the not over savoury
smells of the far east (of London) to a minimum, and after a
rather long ride drive up almost alongside the magnificent
steamer. One look at her, as she lays steam up and everything
ready for departure, is enough. You feel you are as safe aboard
her as if in the Grosvenor Hotel itself. The interior arrangements are as near perfection as possible, nothing seems wanting,
and a look in at the bath-room makes the vista of the Tropics
ioose half its horrors. Why, with such accommodations, a supply
of good weeds, and the well-known high quality of the Company's
Wine List, one might comfortably do the Styx itself in her. After
leaving Gravesend, and a day or so later, Dartmouth, that bad
quarter of an hour leave-taking is got over. To me, it is ever a
most painful sight. As you have about twenty days or more with
nothing to bore you, no letters to answer, no news to speak of
from the other world, you feel—well—that simply depends on
your constitution. For my part, I know of nothing so delightful
as (say, once every few years) twenty days at sea with nothing
to bother you, and pleasant company. London fogs, and smoke,
and chilly weather, give place to delightful Dartmouth, which in
its turn makes way tor Madeira, where you get ashore for a few
hours. I like the inhabitants here, there is no sham about them.
They do not pose themselves as saints, like the Dutch settlers in
the Cape, in fact, there is more of the sinner, I fear, about them.

72

Madeira seems to mark the boundary line between the capricious weather north of it and the delightful climates and smooth seas south to as far as the Cape of Good Hope. I marked the change when, the island being a faint bluish smudge on the horizon, I climbed to the bridge of the steamer and gazed around. The long fabric of the great vessel swept below me through the smooth dark blue waters. Our speed was a fair fourteen knots, there was nothing to stop us, and the engines were storming in a regulated thunder of sound in the metal caverns beneath, whirling with resistless velocity the giant propeller with its diameter of nineteen feet and its twenty-seven foot pitch. I gazed along the length of three hundred and seventy-seven feet, and upon a breadth of over forty-seven feet. The shapely configuration of the thrashing and thrusting structure was thrown out in brilliantly clear black lines by the white waters seething past on either hand like the foaming race at the foot of a mountain cataract. Brass and glass flashed out to the steady pouring sunshine. Looking right aft I marked the elegant curve of the elliptical stern showing sharp upon the tremulous snow-like surface that went rushing from under the counter into the tender distant blueness and faintness.

There was a satin sheen upon the sea. Only the faintest fold of swell came to put a motion as of soft breathing into the powerful steamer. The sun was westering fast, layers of pearl-like clouds caught a golden tinge from the slowly crimsoning luminary upon their delicate brows. In the distance that seemed measureless in the amazing transparency of the sweet and sunlit atmosphere you saw the moonlike gleaming of a sail, otherwise the circle of the sea went round unbroken to the heavens, a glorious sapphire cincture east and south and north, but gathering fast in the west a reddish splendour from the approach of the sun to its liquid verge, and from the ruddy glorifying of the sky down which the orb was floating. The change from the Biscayan latitudes was strongly marked now, and felt by me more keenly even than when Madeira lay steady and rich before me half in weeping shadow and half in sunshine, with the white houses to give an inter-tropical aspect to it, and its nude, dark-skinned boys, laughing, diving, and shouting out their language of the sun alongside.

I remember when the evening came down dark, and after I had stood watching the dull, cloudy light of phosphorus in the roaring surge that coiled over and broke into milk from the vessel's bow, seating myself abaft the ladies' saloon for the shelter of it from the wind which the steamer's progress through the water was making to blow at the velocity of very nearly half a gale. An engine-room hatchway was directly in front of me, protected by gratings, and, peering down, I could see through another grating into the black depths, a distance of forty feet beneath. There were scarlet lights at the bottom ; the glow of one or more of the eighteen furnaces. You could see phantom figures moving, catching, now and again, as they passed from darkness into darkness, a gleam from the fires that seemed to give them an outline of flame. The effect was extraordinary. Often voices broke into song down in those mysterious, resonant depths. The shovelling of coal was incessant. By listening a little you found words distinctly articulated by the engines. You fitted the rhythmic, metallic pulsations with syllables which became a sentence that was fast repeated over and over and over again. It seemed to me as though there were some mighty giant working below there in the fire-touched darkness you saw through the gratings ; he breathed harshly and heavily, often with a fierce hissing through his clenched teeth, as though the burden of his tremendous labour grew at moments too heavy for him, and he expended his impatience in a wild and bitter sigh. There were a hundred sounds to suggest the presence below of some powerful human spirit, rather than the mechanical soulless action of beams of metal and lengths of massive steel revolved by steam. It was the heavy panting that made you think of the hidden giant. Seated on deck with the stars shining in glory, the refreshing noises of foaming waters alongside, and the wind sweeping past either hand of the structure that sheltered me, raising tempestuous melodies as it flew, I listened to the sounds, human and mechanical, which rose through that engine-room grating, as I would to expressions of a life utterly distinct from and wholly separated from our own. The gushes of air coming up through the hatch were unendurably hot. A whole forest of windsails swinging with distended arms in the gloom, carried the cool wind into the region of fire beneath ; but the heat, as suggested by the fervid puffings rising from the engine-room, made one wonder how men could be found capable of discharging the laborious duties of firemen and trimmers, in an atmosphere of which the merest whiff snatched from the deck oppressed and enervated the whole system. The stokers and firemen have the hardest times of it on board-ship in these days, I think. Jack inhabits a fine forecastle compared to what he used to sling his hammock in in the old times of slush lamps, blackened beams, dripping carlings, and rats as big as cats. His food, if it be not better, is surely not worse than it was, anyhow. There is nothing particular to be done aloft, at least in such three-masted schooners as the *Tartar*. There is no deep-sea lead to heave, and the duties of the sailor are restricted to cleaning, scrubbing, and swabbing. Besides all this, he is in the fresh air when his watch comes on. But when I thought of the lot of the firemen, and of those whose day-and-night work lies in the engine-room ; when I contrasted the mild delightful breezes I was breathing with that stagnant feverish atmosphere where the fire-god was doing his work, and when I listened to the incessant sounds of shovelling, and the perpetual metallic roaring of the fabric of cylinders, piston rods, crank shafts, connecting rods, and the like revolving a propeller weighing eleven tons, I confess it was with amazement that I listened to the cheery and hearty singing of the poor fellows at their toil. For it seemed to me that if I had to work in an engine-room, I should have but small heart to pipe out even the most lugubrious ditty I am acquainted with.

After a hurried look over the town of Funchal, a purchase at the Bazaar of a few curiosities, you make for the boat on the beach to reach your steamer. The return fare is generally 50 per cent. more than what you paid to land, and the wretches won't put off from shore until they are paid in advance. You may abuse their religious opinions like the very late member for Carlisle himself, you may make use of stronger language than ever Franchise demonstrator made before the Carlton Club—you may even, as I have done myself, hit the fellows with force enough to send them sprawling on the bottom of the boat, the crew may play the fire-hose over them, but lay not the flattering unction to your soul that that will stop their thieving, cheating proclivities. If the steamer takes in coal at Madeira by day, you can amuse yourself by throwing coins into the sea and watching the natives dive off their boats into the sea after them. It is a very good job, perhaps, that I do not understand the Portuguese language, or my ears might have been shocked the last time I visited that place. Using penny-pieces electro-plated in preference to half-crowns for my Magical Entertainments, I happened to have a pocket full of them, and amused myself by holding one up at a time and giving some half-a-dozen or so divers a good view of the coin. I threw it into the sea. The fighting and scuffling they had over those wretched coins ! They took me for a millionaire, I suppose, until one sharper than the others found out they were only the humble pennies. Then the bad language !

The experienced surgeon carried on board the 'Castle

steamers as a rule finds he gets a little busier a few days after leaving Madeira.   Looking over some old papers, I have just come across the Bill of Fare for the fourteenth day out.   Here it is; it may prove interesting to some.

SOUPS.
Mock Turtle.

— —

FISH AND ENTRÉES.
Jugged Hare and Red Currant Jelly.
Braised Sheep's Head.   Fricassée of Fowl.

— —

JOINTS.
Roast Saddle of Mutton (English).
Roast Sirloin Beef.   Yorkshire Pudding.
Boiled Neck Mutton and Turnips.   Corned Beef and Carrots.

— —

POULTRY.
Roast Goose, Apple Sauce.
Boiled Fowls.   Parsley Sauce.
Curry of Rice.

— —

SWEETS.
Macédoines of Fruit.
Tipsy Cakes.   Plum Pudding.
Boiled Vanilla Custards.

— —

DESSERT.
Assorted.

Better regulated mail steamers, I will defy anyone to name. Everything works like clockwork, and such a thing as a grumble is rarely heard, at all events, in the saloon part of the ship, but even the second-class passengers on this line fare better than the first-class passengers do on many lines I have travelled by; a more bountifully supplied second-class table I never saw.   The steerage passengers also are well looked after.

Of Madeira so much has been written that little or nothing remains to be said.   The green and beautiful island is a noble refreshment to the sight after the tedious and tossing days of a stormy sea passage.   The lofty mass of land breaks like a slow revelation of beauty upon the gaze, and it first darkens and then brightens out into clear sunny and many-coloured proportions from the faint blue shadow it submits to the eye when it is first seen.   I was haunted, as we approached, with the memory of the picturesque old legend of the Englishman running away, three or four hundred years ago, with the beautiful lady of his love,

who died soon after their arrival, and whose early death reads
like the historic anticipation of the melancholy uses to which this
fertile and gilded spot of land would be put by future travellers
in search of health. From the waters abreast of Funchal the
island offers a spectacle of soft and tender loveliness ; the towering
peaks have nothing forbidding in their elevation ; the vapour in
soft white masses wreathes itself like garlands of snow about the
heads of the mountain tops. The atmosphere has the brilliancy
of burnished glass, but it imparts, for all that, a singular tenderness of prismatic tint to what you view through it, and every
colour strikes the sight with a sort of mellowness in its purity.
The white houses, dwarfed by distance, shine like ivory toys—
the foam winks in fitful flashes at the foot of the rocks. A
shower of rain was falling over one part of the island when we
brought up, and many rainbows spanned the numerous ravines,
gorges, and scars, with here and there the dense foliage breaking
through the iridescent arches ; whilst further on, where the
shadow of the squall lay deep, the land faded into a dim blue,
looming with a clear head or two of hill above it ; and the sea
line swept round it sharp, azure, and sparkling to its foot. If
you remain on board ship off Madeira, there are plenty of
clamorous swimming boys to take good care that repose shall
form no element of your survey. Dingy-skinned lads, black-
skinned-lads, yellow-haired lads with coffee-coloured bodies raise
a thousand distracting yells over the ship's side in their solicita-
tions to you to throw money for them to dive after. The
adjacent islands hung dark and blue in the distance, with the
sunshine feebly illuminating the more accentuated features. The
bright azure water spreading smooth into boundless distance
formed a perfect setting for these gems of land. A yacht with
awning spread lay near us, and our passage of four days from
Southampton grew dream-like when I contrasted that white
covering and the violet shadow it cast upon the decks of the
yacht with the bitter winds and drenching fogs we had left
behind us in the English Channel, and the cold air, the high
swell, and the broken seas of Finisterre and St. Vincent.

We got under weigh in the afternoon, with our company of
passengers somewhat thinned in number. It was now raining
heavily over parts of Madeira, and the atmosphere was rendered
somewhat uncomfortable by the tepid humidity of it. It seemed
extraordinary that so many people should, in defiance of the
strong misgivings which have been expressed as to the health-
yielding qualities of this climate, determine to land there, instead

of proceeding to the magnificent skies and the wide and varied climatic fields which are offered by the colonies of South Africa. Madeira is unquestionably a beautiful island, but it seems to me one of the saddest spots in the world. Its annals are full of death, and hundreds are lured to it only to be bitterly cheated in their dearest hopes. Besides, the passage to the island is the most uncomfortable part of the voyage to the Cape of Good Hope. You have the swells of the Bay of Biscay, and plentiful risks of the rude tempestuous weather of the North Atlantic. But Madeira once passed, you straightway enter upon sunny seas and steam under blue and golden skies; and till Table Bay is entered it is reckoned a novel experience if one meets with more than a light head sea in the tail of the S.E. Trades. I stood leaning over the rail watching the features of the lovely land growing faint at the extremity of our gleaming wake; and whilst thinking over some of the white-faced and trembling people whom we had brought with us and whom I had noticed feebly descending the gangway ladder to enter the shore boats, it came into my head to ask the 'doctor,' as the medical officer is commonly called, some questions touching the benefit to be derived by an invalid from a journey to the Cape. He was a gentleman of experience, had made the voyage many times, had had many kinds of patients under his charge, and was well qualified therefore to give an opinion.

After speaking of some of the people who had left us at Madeira, I inquired what maladies he considered a voyage to the Cape good for? He answered, 'I should say that every chronic disease, no matter of what character, is sure of alleviation, if not of being completely cured, by a fine weather trip like this. The change of scene, the mild, pure, refreshing breezes, the rest, the absolute freedom from all worry and anxiety, are strong adjuncts to the appropriate drugs or treatment in each case. Three sorts of patients are chiefly benefited; I mean the consumptive, the rheumatic, and those who are suffering from what is termed nervous exhaustion, the most distressing perhaps of all human complaints, because of the physical suffering involving mental distress. In the case of consumption, the sweet, exhilarating air and the warm weather almost invariably work wonders; but always providing that the voyage be undertaken in time. Unhappily, as we medical men know, it is too commonly the practice of patients to postpone their departure until the disease has got a strong hold of them; and the result is that we are constantly seeing patients helped on board at Southampton in the last stage of consumption, only to die of exhaustion on entering the tropics through inability to withstand the heat and the consequent profuse perspirations. If,' he continued, 'patients of this sort had determined to trust themselves to our tender mercies at the beginning of their illness, the probability is that the round voyage, with perhaps a stay of a month or two at the Cape, would have perfectly recovered them.' 'And rheumatism?' said I. 'Well,' he replied, ' for chronic muscular rheumatism—I will not speak of arthritis— the warm and equable climate we have in passing through the tropics possesses marvellous curative powers. I can offer myself as an instance. I was almost paralysed by muscular rheumatism; yet, after my first voyage the malady let me, and I have never had an hour's suffering since from it. As to nervous exhaustion, I can only say, that those, whose minds have been almost unhinged by business troubles, by grief, or by mental shock of any kind, find in the peaceful life of a steamer, with the change of scene and the round of innocent amusements you get on board ship, the only effectual kind of treatment it is possible to prescribe. Again, to people recovering from almost any of the acute diseases, a ship offers a nearly perfect convalescent home.' 'Can you,' said I, 'tell me of any cures which have come under your notice?' 'It is difficult to give instances,' he answered; 'I will tell you why. You have your patient under observation for eighteen or twenty days only, because people, as a rule, seldom return in the same ship they sailed in; you lose sight of them, and their further progress can only be a matter of conjecture. But of the comparatively small number of persons who make the round trip I could tell you of several recoveries. One remarkable case was that of a middle-aged gentleman, whose nervous system had been cruelly prostrated by domestic trouble. When he came on board he was the merest wreck of a man, and when he landed in England he was, both mentally and physically, as sound as ever he had been in the healthiest period of his life. Another case was that of a youth suffering from incipient phthisis, which was certified by one of the leading London consultants. The warmth and sea breezes so thoroughly restored him that, on visiting his medical adviser on his return, not the least trace of the malady was discoverable.'

'You think,' I said, 'a residence at the Cape for consumptive people preferable to a residence at Madeira?' 'Assuredly. I have visited the coast towns of the colony only, and cannot therefore speak from personal experience of the climatic conditions of the places up country; but the testimonies that have reached me place beyond all dispute the certainty of cures in the Cape Colonies, and of corresponding failures, not only at Madeira, but at the Mediterranean and other popular South European resorts. Bloemfontein, in the Orange Free State, has a high local reputation for its climatic cures of consumption. I say local, because that part of the world has yet to be discovered by or be made known to our Northern sufferers. Some parts of the Transvaal, too, and of the Northern portion of Natal, at the foot of the Drakensberg Mountains, have also a climate that seems specially designed for this class of patients. One is constantly meeting at the Cape, or whilst travelling to and fro coastwise, with colonists in excellent health, who assure one that when they first went out to South Africa they arrived dying men. Such power does a dry and genial climate possess in arresting the destructive tubercular processes! But to put the thing fairly; those who linger at home and postpone their departure to a time when help is hopeless, run down hill at a fearful pace in the heat of the Cape summer. We have, as you know, a lady on board who is dreadfully ill with consumption; I very much fear that the heat we must expect on our arrival at South Africa will prove more than her small remaining stock of strength can withstand. Should she, however, happily manage to pull through it, there is every reason to believe that, during the ensuing winter, she will so improve as to be practically out of danger by the time the next summer comes round.'

'I notice that there is a good deal of drinking on board; what is your experience in this direction?' 'Well, I must confess that a considerable amount of "nipping" goes on as a rule! It is not often that you see a passenger drunk; in truth, intoxication is of rare occurrence, and a vice which the rules of the ship render difficult of practice; but people get into the habit of having cocktails before and after breakfast, drinks at eleven, sherry and bitters before lunch, and so on, not to mention many incidental adjournments to the bar, when games of bull, or chess, or poker, and the like, are won or lost.' 'This "nipping" as you term it, can hardly serve the end of persons in search of health?' 'Hardly, indeed! but I am quite convinced that passengers do themselves more injury by over-eating than by over-drinking. Nine out of ten persons devour out and away more food on board ship than they do on shore. Of course they should eat very much less, when you consider the temperature, and the little exercise they take. It is anything but an agreeable sight at breakfast, say, on a hot morning in the tropics, to see people plodding steadily through the " Bill of Fare," literally surfeiting themselves, beginning, perhaps, with a plate of porridge, and then working away at fish, a mutton chop, a grilled bone, Irish stew, sausages, bacon and eggs, ham and tongue, and winding-up with a top layer of bread-and-butter and marmalade. I assure you I once at my table watched a lady make just such a breakfast as I have given you the details of.

'The whole ' Bill of Fare,' as it stands morning after morning, accompanied by powerful flushings of tea or coffee, is by no means an unusual breakfast at sea. As a result of all this eating and drinking, a passenger finds himself rather unwell; he doses himself, or comes to me complaining of headache and of feeling heavy and dull. Of course he attributes it all " to the dreadful heat." If passengers would control their appetites and limit themselves to one meal of meat a day, taking care to eat plenty of fruit and fresh vegetables, they would have very few disorders indeed to ascribe to the heat, which, in fact, is never very great, as you may easily ascertain by watching the thermometer.' There is much good sense, I think, in all this, and persons proposing to make a voyage, whether for health, pleasure, or business, may thank me for the suggestions indicated in this brief chat with the doctor. I hope, in due course, to deal with the victualing of ocean steamers, and from the ' Bills of Fare' for breakfast, lunch, and dinner, which I shall probably give as illustrative of the quality of living on board ship, readers will judge that, when passengers are charged with over-eating, the accusation implies a very large volume of food for the indulgence of their voracity. As a matter of curiosity, I asked the steward what he reckoned as the average expenditure per male passenger for drinks. He answered that he would take each passenger as spending from three to four pounds a week, but in many cases the figure rose to as high as nine or ten pounds a week. This is at the rate of from two hundred to five hundred a year for liquor ; and when you consider that spirits and wines are no dearer on board than they are on shore—indeed, in some ships they are cheaper— you may judge that a man who spends, say five pounds a week on drink, must contrive to stow away a pretty large liquid cargo in the course of the seven days.

A passenger steamer is, indeed, a kind of hotel, and obviously among the most important personages on board her must be the head steward and the cook, the two powers who rule the tables of the saloon, and who supply us with the most welcome of all breaks in the monotony of sea existence. The steward, in short, must needs be a feature of weight and moment in the internal economy of the ship. The popularity of the vessel must depend a very great deal upon him. Ill-chosen and badly-cooked provisions, a meagre table, and indifferent wines will be remembered to the prejudice of a vessel when the lively gratitude inspired by the commander's able management in foul weather and amid dangerous seas has long ago faded out. I could never gaze at the head steward of the steamer without an emotion of respect not unmingled with awe. Care lay dark in every seam in his face. How should it have been otherwise ? He had a number of stewards under him who needed close watching. He had two cooks—a butcher, and a baker to confer with, remonstrate with, and quarrel with. I remember a man once complaining to me that his father allowed him but one hundred a year, which was all he had to live upon. 'For, consider,' said he, 'that there are in one year alone not only three hundred and sixty-five breakfasts, but three hundred and sixty-five luncheons and three hundred and sixty-five dinners!' But think of an official having every day whilst he is at sea to provide three sets of breakfast for the three classes of passengers, two dinners and a luncheon, a dinner, and two teas and two suppers! 'It is not,' exclaimed the steward to me, in a voice broken by emotion, ' as if there was a Meat Market over the side where, if I was at a loss to know what change of dish to offer, I could purchase what I wanted: this lies every head steward's difficulty A certain amount of provisions is put on board, and out of what there is a man has to provide as good a dinner as you would get at an excellent *table a'hôte* ashore. How it is done beats my knowledge, but it *is* done.

The conclusion must necessarily be that head stewards are natural geniuses, born to move in culinary and gastronomic spheres, where plenty reigns, where tinned stuff is unknown, and where there are no shipboard limitations to obstruct a choice and expansive taste. I will ask the public to bear with me for a moment, whilst I give examples of the character of a few of the meals furnished to first, second, and third class passengers on board my three-masted steamer. Here are three saloon breakfast illustrations: 1. Bloaters, mutton chops, grilled ham, deviled turkey, Irish stew, savoury omelettes, curry and rice, porridge and potatoes. 2. Fried fish, mutton chops, minced veal, liver and bacon, sausages, deviled bones, curry and rice, boiled eggs, porridge, and potatoes. 3. Haddock, grilled rump steak, eggs and bacon, chicken and rice, grilled bones, Irish stew, and so on. For samples of a second-class breakfast : 1. Fried fish, mutton chops, boiled eggs, porridge, and potatoes.   2. Haddock, grilled steak, eggs and bacon, porridge, and potatoes. This, in my time. would have been thought an exceptionally fine repast to serve in a cuddy where they charged you seventy and ninety guineas for a cabin. For the third class the head steward manages to make out a plentiful meal of Irish stew, salt fish, steak, hashed meats, and porridge without limit. As an example of a saloon luncheon, the 'Bill of Fare' offered soup, two entrées, potatoes, cold meats of every description, and, when I questioned the steward, he told me that in hot weather he gives brawn, pressed tongue, raised pies, cold poultry, fish, four kinds of pastry, fruit, and salads. How is it done? I have before me a list of the dry and wet stores on board the vessel, and, on looking over it, I still find myself saying, 'How is it done?'

One sees many things to look at and to find amusement in on board an ocean passenger boat. The show of human nature not, indeed, great; perfectly natural people are not very common either on sea or on shore, and voyages are scarcely long enough now-a-days to suffer the mind to lapse into ingenuousness. Yet an attentive observer will often observe human nature breaking out here and there, chiefly in unexpected places. One thing I noticed ; the pride fathers and husbands had in the children and wives they left behind them. After a week or two a man would come up and break off in his chat to put his hand in his pocket and produce a little packet of photographs—his wife and his children, and particularly the baby—and though there might be nothing remarkable to admire in the little fat object, the sight of whose portrait put a kind of yearning into the father's eyes as he glanced at it a moment before returning it to his pocket, yet the tenderness of the thing touched and pleased one. It would take a long time to bring a man into this state of communicativeness on shore ; but the feeling of distance and of isolation is strong at sea, and thoughts of home and the dear ones there will thaw the iciest reserve, and instil a spirit of kindliness and goodwill fore and aft. It was impossible to look over the side, to feel the glorious breeze full upon the cheek and whistling through the teeth, to understand that the roasting African coast was, com-paratively speaking, but a few leagues distant, without thinking of those British sailors whose stern duty it is to watch over the interests of our country in the torrid climes from between Saldanha Bay and Sierra Leone. On board an ocean steamer, always making a breeze of wind by her rapid progress, or stem-ming the blue and invigorating breath of the South-East Trades, with awnings protecting her decks fore and aft, with ports wide open, with many tons of ice in her hold, and with a bar at which all day long you'may get cool drinks passing under fifty names, it is not very easy to realise the fate of Royal naval officers and men anchored within an easy run of the spot through which your steamer is sweeping, or creeping in gunboats or small corvettes from one fiery village coast to another.

At Cape Town I met a lieutenant of a well-known vessel that had been stationed for many months upon the barbarous African coast. His little ship had just arrived at Simon's Bay, and this officer, a fine, hearty, genial fellow, had come to the old Cape Settlement for a day or two to enjoy himself and forget, if he could, life on shipboard on the West African Station. He was burnt up to the complexion of a coloured man, and told me some desperate stories of the sick list and of fever, of thirty grains of quinine for a dose, of horrible morbid thoughts causing a man as he lies in his coffin of a cabin, reeking with cockroaches, to cast his languid gaze about in search of any implement to end his life. I remember when we met that it was a beautiful moonlight night; the air was deliciously cool; a light breeze coming in soft gusts down Table Mountain shook many sweet odours from trees of the drooping morn-lily and from the red petals of the oleander, silvered by the moon-gleams. The lieutenant stood awhile in a kind of rapture, with his hands clasped. The posture and the emotion were absolutely unaffected. He breathed deep, and exclaimed, 'I have not set my foot off the ship for seven months. You may conceive what this scene means to me.' He behaved like a man in a dream. Before parting we entered a little drawing-room, where there was a piano. He turned to me with a smile, and said, 'Time was when I could play this thing. I wonder if West Africa has left any music in me!' He sat down and played over a tune or two, and you saw how the very sound of the melodies affected him, and how they carried him many thousands of miles away home to where his wife and his little children were. To watch him getting up and looking at the piano was like seeing a shipwrecked stranded man welcoming some sign of life and of help washing up to him. It gave me a better idea of the true signification of banishment to the West African Coast than I could have gathered from a whole volume of description. 'He also serves who only stands and waits,' says Milton, in one of the sublimest of his sonnets, and it is not necessary that there should be war to test the courage, the dutifulness, and wonderful capacity of self-sacrifice of the Queen's sailor.

CHAPTER XVI.

THE APPROACH TO TABLE BAY—SOUTH AFRICAN SCENERY—THE
LION'S HEAD—TABLE MOUNTAIN—ARRIVAL OF AN AMERICAN
WHALE SHIP—THE PHANTOM SHIP OF VANDERDECKEN—
STRANGE TRADITIONS—SPECIAL FEATURES OF CAPE TOWN.

AN element of grandeur enters into the beauty of the scene of
Table Bay as you survey it from the spot where the ocean steamers
drop anchor before entering the docks. The general notion
amongst Europeans of South African scenery is that of leagues of
roasting white sands, with an inland flatness of parched and
stunted vegetation. This delusion is largely owing to the accounts
sailors have given of their shipwreck on the African coast.
In all the old stories it is always mile upon mile of sand, with
nothing in view but the distant figures of a horde of Arabs or
nude barbarians, restlessly awaiting an opportunity to pounce
down upon poor Jack, strip him of his boots and jacket, and carry
him off, secured to the tail of a camel, into captivity to some village
of small huts, filled with sable ladies and picaninnies, commonly
about five hundred miles inland, and, therefore, a very long and
thirsty walk for the castaway mariner. The real truth is that the
coast of Africa, certainly in its southern part, abounds in many
beautiful bays, enriched with romantic scenery, and ennobled by
towering mountains, near or distant. Table Bay is an example.
You get something of the impression of wonder that is produced
upon you by Sydney Harbour when you enter this bay for the
first time. The mountains lifting their eternal heads, crowned
with snow-white vapour, give a majesty to the perspective. The
water of the bay is of an exquisitely soft blue.

At the base of that grand and picturesque height named the
Lion's Head you see the houses standing like ivory toys, whilst
the white surf gleams in masses upon the beach, beautified with
the greenery of gardens just beyond. The mountain sides seem
draped in velvets of green and brown. It is the purity and
transparency of the atmosphere that imparts this surprising softness of tone. You specially note the charming effect in the view

of the Hottentot Holland Mountains which, even in their dim distance, gather a sort of richness in their azure tint and fascinate the eye with a cloud-like tenderness, bland as the shining fulness of swelling summer vapour slowly sailing above the horizon to the wind, but with a sky-line too cleanly cut and too deliberately fantastic in its irregularity tô be mistaken for anything but the high sierra of a range of lofty mountains. The many colours of that morning supplied me with just such a picture of Cape Town as one would most like to see. From the flat summit of Table Mountain, where the white vapour was beginning to gather against the unspeakable blue of the sky beyond, the gaze descended into the dark violet shadows of solemn ravines, took in the twilight in deep scars, the metallic lustre of groups of silvery trees, the vivid green of tracts of vine bushes, with now and again a large cloud-shadow sweeping a sort of faint purple light over the sun-lit patches of red soil, of granite-like prominences, and of abrupt falls of rock bronzed in their massive flats as though the hand of old Time had coated them with iron —I say—the gaze descending into those heights of nearly four thousand feet came to a most lovely grouping of houses, low-roofed, with windows shining, with much shrubbery between, and verandahs veiling the white fronts with a delicate violet gloom. In the foreground were the docks with the heavy spars of a man-of-war or two giving a density to the complex tracery of the lighter masts and rigging of merchant vessels and steamers. A red powder-flag, fluttering at the masthead of a small vessel anchored close in, sufficed to give a sharp distinctness to the houses on a line with it on the hillside. It was a contrast, calculated to lend to distance the precision you obtain by looking through a lens ; and all other notes of colours, I observed, produced the same effect, such as a red funnel, the American stars and stripes, the English ensign floating at a peak. And still a wonderful complexity of tints took the eye as it swept round the margin of the bay past Woodstock, with its foreground of pleasure-boats and quaintly imagined bathing-machines and the ruddy patches of the soil on the mountains—of the windmill bold against the airy azure of the far inland heights. The water always came round in a brilliant blue to the throbbings of its own surf upon the shore of dazzling white sand, of shining houses, of little spaces of soft green, and the mighty flanking of the cathedral mountains. But the magic that works so much of beauty here can neither be expressed nor suggested. I speak of the enchantment of the radiant atmosphere. Nothing is lost in this marvellous transparency, and you think of the towns and plains at a dreamlike distance away inland that would be visible to you from the commanding altitude of Table Mountain if those stately peaks lying fifty miles distant, stretching as far as Tulbagh, did not barricade the regions beyond them with their mystical altitudes.

In the days preceding the Suez Canal, and when sailing ships were making the voyage to Australia and India, Table Bay was a much more familiar sight to Englishmen than it now is. Vessels full of passengers were repeatedly calling here for one reason or another, and the impressions people received they carried away and talked about at home and elsewhere. It is seldom nowadays that you see the big passenger sailing ship in the bay. Reports come from L'Agulhas of many kinds of craft passing that stormy point ; but the times are gone when the cold blue waters of this splendid haven reflected the checkered sides and the burnished masts of tall ships which had dropped anchor here as a place of call and a break in the tediousness of four or five months of passage to Pacific coasts, or to the hot regions to the north of the Indian Ocean. Hence, often as the scene has been described, a man may yet with a resonable amount of conscience venture to offer a sketch of Table Bay, and of its town and neighbourhood as they now are. I must confess that all the while that I remained in Cape Town I was never weary of admiring the scenery of its noble tract of waters, of the bright mountain-shadowed bays, and the granite giants which looked down upon the town. The dock officials very kindly placed a small steamer at my disposal for a trip, and in company with several gentlemen I made one of the most delightful little voyages that can be imagined. To as far as Camp's Bay we opened a hundred novel beauties. The mountains for ever accompanied us. Go where we would their dominating presence was a mighty shadow in the blue heavens. To me, Table Mountain looked like the ruins of some immense cathedral raised by hands in days when there were Titans in the land. From the centre of the bay it resembles the remains of a vast wall, and round the slope of the Lion's Head you seem to find the theory of giants having constructed this amazing edifice confirmed by vast blocks of rock and granite which might well pass for the headstones and churchyard memorials of the burial grounds of a vanished colossal race. It is here, especially, that you observe a hundred startling phantasies in the shapes and postures of these stones, prone or upright ; enormous owls, cowled monks of huge stature, prodigious women in drapery carved, as one would suppose, to perfection. You would say, indeed, that the remains of giants reposed upon this rocky massive slope, that their sportive fancies were perpetuated in these wild and grotesque shapes, just as traces of their serious and splendid genius remained in the spacious front of a mountain, cathedral-like in its immensity, and to this day reverberating the old giant organ notes of praise in the low melodious thunder of every blast sweeping down the sheer abrupt from the white cloud resting upon its brow. It is the cloud, the 'table-cloth,' as it is called, that gives to Table Mountain and to the sentinel eminences that stand on either hand of it, much of the wonder and not a little even of the magnificence you find in it.

Whilst taking that cruise about the bay which I have just now mentioned, I came across a ship that I would not very willingly have missed. She was an American whaler, and had been out for twenty-two months bagging whales in about latitude 42° South. She had 800 barrels of oil aboard, and was certainly one of the queerest and rustiest old hulls I ever had the fortune to encounter. I was told that whalers are rare birds in Table Bay now-a-days, though in former times they were plentiful enough. I kept the steamer alongside of her for some time that I might inspect her. Her metal sheathing was green as grass, and you saw the barnacles upon it through the transparency a little way below to where the sheathing came. The large blocks employed in 'cutting in' had scraped her sides clean all about her gangway. She appeared to have worked half the oakum out of her, and her seams were hollow. Her name was the *Sea Queen*, Joseph Thomson, master, and she hailed, as might easily have been conjectured, from New Bedford. Boats exhibiting every symptom of hard wear stood bottom up on chocks, or hung from massive wooden davits over the side. Dirt and grime lay thick on the scuttles. The name of Herman Melville rose to my tongue as I looked at her, with her short top-gallant masts and crowfoot rings over top-gallant rigging for the men to keep a look-out from. No one who had read 'Omoo,' or 'The Whaler,' or 'Typee,' and saw this ship, but must have thought of the brilliant Yankee sea-yarner. The *Sea Queen* was just such another old hooker as brought Melville away as a beach-comber from the Marquesas. As I stood looking at the row of heads over the rail I thought to myself: 'Surely the right name for this craft must be the *Little Jule*, and if Mr. Jermin, the chief mate, is aboard I will ask him to show me that wonderful sextant with which at noon, when slightly the worse for rum, he would go hunting for the sun all

over his grass-covered decks!' There is a pleasure in the unexpected confrontment of the perfect realisation of some visionary
favourite in a work of fiction. I have met Bumble, also Noah
Claypole, and I have shaken hands with Parson Adams. Here
now was the *Little Jule* lying in Table Bay under the name of the
Sea Queen. She carried thirty of a crew; they all came to the
rail to look at us, and I heartily wish some artist had been with
us to jot down with his pencil the delightful variety of countenance
and of costume exhibited by that array of whalers. There were
white men and black men; men whose faces were all hair, and
who looked like sailors striving to peer through a mat. There
were Dutch faces and Yankee faces; faces that might have been
carved out of a balk of timber, and faces of the hue of the ship's
bread, which I suspect might have been found crawling about on the
legs of innumerable weevils in the little barky's lazarette. There
were four harpooners, and they came over the side and exhibited
the small brass muskets or guns with which nowadays they kill
whales by firing explosives into them, though of course the old-
fashioned harpoon is carried in plenty and repeatedly used. Each
tub of oil, they told me, contained 310 gallons, and as they had
800 such tubs filled up in their hold, and as, moreover, they had
only been twenty-two months cruising out of the forty months'
voyage their owners had limited them to, there was a good chance
of every man's 'lay' ending in a big pocketful of dollars. A man
might live a hundred years and yet never come across so quaint,
old, seedy, battered, and grimy a whaler as this *Sea Queen,* fresh
as she was from nearly two years' washing about in search of prey
south of the Cape of Good Hope.

The sight was one to stir the fancy, and I certainly found no
great extravagance of imagination in the sudden arising in me of
thoughts of the ' *Flying Dutchman,*' out of that wallowing old
whaler from which our little steamer was now speeding. If
Table Bay and all about the Cape of Good Hope be not the
right neighbourhood wherein to dream and think of the *Phantom
Ship,* I know not what other parallels to choose. It was off
Agulhas, in the teeth of one of the wild north-westers you get in
these seas, that Skipper Vanderdecken swore his dreadful and
lamentable oath not to give up trying to weather the stormy
headland even though he should have to wait till the Day of
Judgment came. Did the Dutchman, before his fierce defiance
of Heaven, ever bring up in Table Bay? No doubt he did. He
was from Batavia, and there is yet living an ancient Hollander,
who, when a boy, remembered his grandfather telling how once

Vanderdecken, when outward bound to Batavia, had called at Table Bay for fruit and tobacco, *on dit*. It was during his return voyage from Batavia, after his visit to Table Bay, that the skipper provoked the wrath of Heaven by his imprecations. The ancient Hollander's grandfather lived long after Vanderdecken had been sighted by ships struggling to windward, and this it was that impressed upon the recollection of the Dutch grandsire the picture of the ship he had seen straining at her hemp cable a little to the westwards of where the breakwater now is. She is described as having a very curious low-built bow, with a mass of timbers curving at the head to the immensely thick cut-water. Her bowsprit is steeved to an angle of 45 deg.; at the end of it is a round top, and standing perpendicularly up out of this top is a small mast with another top at the head of it big enough to admit of its occupation by two or three men. A very heavy square yard hangs by lifts under the bowsprit, and on the little perpendicular mast she carries what may be called a spritsail yard, the foot of whose sail spreads on the yard beneath. She has lower topsail and topgallant yards, with large round tops at the head of her lower masts, and smaller tops, but of a like character, at her topmast's heads, instead of cross-trees. She has a very lofty stern, with a kind of castle at the end of the poop where the taffrail should be; and it is here where Vanderdecken takes his stand, trumpet in hand, when a vessel heaves in sight, and he desires to speak her. Her mizzen-mast rakes aft, and carries a triangular sail set on a gaff, with another jib-headed sail that sets flying outside like a bonnet or a water-sail. The break of the poop comes to before the mainmast, so that that spar pierces the poop deck whilst the athwart-ship rail is set up, so to speak, on either hand the main-mast. The high bulwarks end abruptly just abaft the fore-rigging. She is pierced for eight guns, but it is not certainly known whether she still carries the quaint old pieces that grinned in her hey-day through her ports. The ancient Dutchman affirmed that his grandfather used to say she was painted a pale yellow. Time, probably, has left to the struggling fabric but little of its old garnishings. There can be no doubt, however, that the above description is that of Vanderdecken's ship that sailed from Batavia for Holland in or about the year 1641 on a voyage which, through the wickedness of her profane master, will never come to an end as long as old ocean continues to roll, if one is verdant enough to believe the yarn !

I made many inquiries whilst at Cape Town as to whether there were any traditions in the neighbourhood of Vanderdecken having been sighted, but nobody seemed to know much about him, and if it had not been for the old Dutchman I should not have been able to describe her. I have ascertained, however, that there is no foundation for the statement that Vanderdecken was fired upon by the Dutch whilst seeking to enter Table Bay during the winter season, when no vessel was allowed to come in. It is quite inconsistent with the old tradition to pretend that in consequence of being fired upon the skipper put to sea and was lost. It would be a harsh judgment indeed that should compel the phantom of a ship that had foundered to go on sailing about for ever. It is well known that the sole reason Vanderdecken has for hailing a ship, is, that he may send a boat with letters for the home that he and his crew have not revisited for two centuries and a half. The superstition is that if a captain heaves his ship to receive one of these messages from the Dutchman, he and his vessel are doomed. In this point lies the real pathos of the thing. Poor Vanderdecken and his bald-headed blear-eyed, and tottering sailors are for ever yearning to communicate with those homes which have long ago ceased to exist ; but the mariner, knowing the penalty of accepting the mission, flies at the approach of the *Phantom Ship*, which, after a short chase, desolately shifts her helm and braces once again sharp up against the visionary gale, that prohibits her from doubling the Cape.

Many years, I believe, have now elapsed since Vanderdecken was last sighted. The latest instance I can find is that of the man-of-war *Leven*, commanded by Captain W. F. W. Owen. It was on April 6th, 1823, when this vessel, being off Danger Point, bound to Simon's Bay, saw the *Barracouta*, another ship of war, two miles or thereabouts to leeward. This was considered extraordinary, as it was known on board the *Leven* that the other vessel's sailing orders must have despatched her leagues away from the place in which she was now seen. Captain Owen bore down to speak, but the other stood away, though she was observed some time afterwards to lower a boat. Next day the *Leven* anchored in Simon's Bay. The *Barracouta* arrived a week, later. On inspecting her log, it was seen that she was 300 miles away from the spot where it was believed she had been seen. Twice the *Leven* sighted the *Phantom Ship*. On the second occasion, the Dutchman lowered a boat, but Captain Owen, perfectly aware of the penalty that would attend his undertaking the delivery of a letter for Vanderdecken, packed on canvas, and took to his heels as fast as his ship would carry him. The authority for the following is ' R. Montgomery Martin,' who published the statement in 1835. It will fitly close my reference to perhaps the most picturesque and romantic of all the traditions of the sea: 'We had been in dirty weather, as the sailors say, for several days, and to beguile the afternoon, I commenced, after dinner, narratives to the French officers and passengers (who were strangers to the Eastern seas), current about the *Flying Dutchman*. The wind, which had been refreshing during the evening, now blew a stiff gale, and we proceeded on deck to see the crew make our bark all snug for the night. The clouds, dark and heavy, coursed with peculiar rapidity across the bright moon, whose lustre is so peculiar in the southern hemisphere, and we could see a distance of from eight to ten miles on the horizon. Suddenly, the second officer, a fine Marseilles sailor, who had been among the foremost in the cabin in laughing at and ridiculing the story of the *Flying Dutchman*, ascended the weather-rigging, exclaiming, " *Voilà le volant Hollandais.*" The captain sent for his night-glass, and soon observed : " It is very strange, but there is a ship bearing down upon us with *all sail* set, while we dare scarcely show a pocket-handkerchief to the breeze." In a few minutes the stranger was visible to all on deck, her rig plainly discernible, and people on her poop ; she seemed to near us with the rapidity of lightning, and apparently wished to pass under our quarter, for the purpose of speaking. The captain, a resolute Bordeaux mariner, said it was quite incomprehensible, and sent for the trumpet to hail or answer, when, in an instant, and while we were all on the *qui-vive*, the stranger totally disappeared, and was seen no more.'

One characteristic of Cape Town lies in the number of its Hansom cabs, and another feature that speedily excites the attention is the extraordinary posture of laziness into which the drivers contrive, while their horses are standing still, to fling themselves. You notice the effect of the climate in a little thing of this kind, just as its drowsy influence is illustrated in the indolence of the dogs, which lie about sleeping one on top of the other all day long, though to be sure when the night comes, they atone for their reserve during the day by a widespread barking that is often hideous and distracting. Another feature is the cock-crowing. I recollect one morning being awakened at about dawn. I went to the open window, and saw the green light in the east gradually brightening into a most delicate beautiful blue throught the lacework of greenery that festooned the verandah. I had not stood a moment or two when I was surprised by an extraordinary kind of groaning noise, that apparently rose from the whole surface of the land on which Cape Town stands. It sounded to me like a mourning chorus of fanatics—thousands of Malays, perhaps, smiting themselves and adoring Allah. It was not until a cock in a neighbouring yard rang out its hoarse crow that I could determine the nature of the multitudinous groanings. But this adjacent cock having given me the key-note, I at once discovered that the sounds which had puzzled me were produced by hundreds and perhaps thousands of cocks crowing, for the most part, all at once. Again, I may regard the horns of the fish salesmen as another 'special feature' to employ the language of trade. The town is filled with carts, which are used for hawking fish about, and the men who sell this fish announce their approach by blowing a kind of trumpet. Throughout the day the air is re· sonant with these detestable notes. The reader may conceive for himself the sort of pleasure he would derive from street boys passing his house every five minutes from six in the morning till six at night blowing incessantly, every mother's son of them, a trumpet that may be heard a mile off. This sort of noise the people of Cape Town endure, apparently, for no other reason than that their servants may know that some very tough and tasteless fish is coming their way in a black man's cart. There are thousands of crickets, too, when the blaring of these coloured costermongers has ceased, to start a new sort of music for the night. Their utterance is like the sharp abrupt ringing of electric bells. Heard afar their chimes are not without a kind of melodiousness. The silvery monotonous singing seems always in correspondence with the bright African moonshine, the brilliancy of the twinkling stars, the deep respiration of the soft hot breeze amidst boughs drooping with weight of foliage, or amidst flowers faint in hue but glistening gem-like to the shining with the dew-drops they offer to the moon.

Cape Town is charged with a cosmopolitanism of complexion ; every shade is represented, from the ebony black of the negro-born leagues away upland behind those distant blue mountains there, to the white and sickly hue of the English girl languishing in a climate where the British rose may be sought for in vain. Of all the coloured folks the Malays are the oddest. These people are artisans ; they drive cabs, they sell fish, they wash linen, and so forth. They are all well to do, are aristrocratic from their own standpoint, and are such a power in the place that the one policy practised towards them, I believe, whether from the Governor's table or the magisterial bench, is that of conciliation. When I was in Cape Town some difficulty arose about a new burial-ground that had been assigned to these Malays, who are

Mohammedans. They objected to the site, and affirmed their intention of continuing to bury their dead in the old ground. A dangerous insurrection was theatened; the volunteers dressed and armed themselves, and the troops were called out. Every street corner had its little crowd of excited Malay men and women, dressed in bright colours, who gesticulated furiously and chattered with passionate rapidity about their grievance. Elderly European ladies wandered about calling upon friends or visiting hotels, alarming everybody with conjectures as to what the result must be. We were all to be murdered in our beds; we were all to be poisoned in our cups; we were all to be secretly stabbed with weapons coated with some deadly mixture as we passed through the streets; our houses were to be fired, and we were all to be starved by reason of the Malays (who seem to have the chief victualing of the place in their hands amongst their other privileges and dignities) refusing to sell food and drink to us. Instead of looking for snakes under the bed we searched for Malays coiled up in the darkness there; and if Malay laundry-men approached us with their little bills we kept the table be-tween them and us whilst we inquired into the motive of their visit. Eventually the Malays, on being harangued, consented to the interment of their dead in the new ground, the general terror evaporated, and we ate, drank, and went to bed once more without misgivings. Yet one saw in this incident the sort of footing the Malays have in Cape Town. You would suppose that they were an infinitely more powerful factor than the Dutch, though you hear a very great deal indeed about the latter element, afnd next to nothing at all about the former unless there be a religious riot.

I have no worse criticism to pass than this—nothing worse to say of Capetown than that its drainage is extraordinarily and dis-gracefully imperfect, and that its hotel accommodation should be accepted as a scandal by the people. For the rest all is beauty, all is grandeur. The famous drive round the mountain side called the Kloof Road with its sheer descents of many hundred feet for the gaze to search, the bays mountain-flanked, their green hollows studded with white houses, with the giant comber of the South At-lantic breaking in acres of dazzling foam upon the rugged beach, leave such impressions upon the mind as years of travel amidst famous scenes could not efface. The strong South-eastern sweep-ing down the mountain finds children of its own in the obedient trees leaning along its course. At long intervals a kind of volcanic splendour is observed on the heights of the heaven-seeking eminences by the burning of whole acres of the pine tree; the night is illuminated by the incandescence, the stars are obscured by the masses of smoke settling in a dense fog about the Blaawberg Mountains, and you respire an atmosphere charged with a resinous aroma, and thick with light-grey ash.   All about Wynberg, High Constantia, and Claremont is pure fairy-land; houses of graceful form shine amidst vegetation of tropical luxuriance; the white-faced old Dutch farmhouse stands, as it has stood for years, with draped windows, silent amidst the stillness of high trees, to which the shadow of the looming mountain beyond imparts a deeper repose yet.   A cheerful Cape cart trots by with its happy family party snug under the cool cover.   The lively Africander whistles and shows his teeth to you with a saluting grin, as he lolls upon the burden of his cart behind the slow-moving oxen and the patient mule.   And into all things the marvellous blue of the heavens by day, the marvellous brilliance of the stars by night, put the spirit of gracefulness, of tenderness, and of romance.   It is, indeed, a favoured land, for the climate, for the growth of the soil, for natural beauties of a thousand kinds.

Cape Town is not a sweet place, *bien au contraire.*   It's about as dusty as Llandudno.   Why, even the trees fronting your hotel look ashamed and bow their heads in meek humiliation.   The blacks of the lower orders are about as lazy and independent a lot of people you can well meet with.   The Malays, if you get to know them, you cannot but help liking; the Africanders also, but Heaven save me from some of the Dutch I came across out there, especially at Worcester !

CHAPTER XVII.

WITCHCRAFT IN SOUTH AFRICA—AN IMPOSTOR—STRANGE PREDIC-
TIONS—THE AMAXOSA—HOW THEY WERE DUPED—CETEWAYO'S
WITCH-DOCTORS—HOW CETEWAYO'S HIDING-PLACE WAS DIS-
COVERED—KIMBERLEY—THE DIAMOND FIELDS OF SOUTH AFRICA.

THE adventures I went through in South Africa would fill a three-
volume book, I fear. The Fates forbid that I may ever inflict
the same on the reviewers! I gave my Magical performances
out here more with a view of exposing modern superstition than
anything else.

In South Africa Witchcraft holds a dreadful sway. I need hardly
remind my readers that every rising of the natives during this
century may be fairly ascribed to their witch-doctors. In 1857
when the Cape was almost stripped of troops because of the
Indian mutiny, occurred one of the most extraordinary instances of
self-immolation I ever heard of. The Amaxosa, unwarned by all
they had suffered from similar delusions in the past, suffered themselves to be persuaded by a madman or impostor, of the name of
Mhlakaza, into an act of almost incredible folly, which well-nigh
resulted in the entire extinction of their nation. He foretold that
on a certain day all the dead warriors and great men of old, were
to rise from their graves, and all the living to be endowed with
strength and beauty. Immense herds of the finest cattle were to
come forth out of a cave, and wide fields of corn to spring up, and
the white man to wither like a leaf.

And the one condition of this great Kaffir millennium was faith
—faith that was to prove itself by the utter sacrifice of everything
that they possessed, except the arms of the warriors. The cattle
were to be killed, the grain destroyed, and their fields suffered to
remain unsown. The one exception of the arms seems to show
that there was method in the madness of this Mhlakaza if madness
it was. He was supported by the predictions of a girl, who also
pretended to have communications with the Spirit World; and also
by the chief Magoma who assured the people that he too had

received communications from the Unseen World, and that all that the Prophet said would surely come to pass.

Incredible as it may appear, the Amaxosa not only believed but were willing to prove their faith by their works. Corn and cattle were destroyed. In vain did the Government try to dispel the illusion by sending agents among them. The very interference of Government seemed to confirm them in their extraordinary belief, till at last the whole nation was on the verge of starvation. Nearly 50,000 perished—one third of the entire nation ! ! ! The colonists did what could be done, to provide food for the famished thousands who invaded their homes, not as conquerors but as beggars ; but many ghastly tales I heard of on the spot of the dire extremities to which many were driven. The Amaxosa never fully recovered from this act of national suicide.

In the early part of 1850 it was known that great excitement prevailed in Kaffirland, through the prophecies of another rank impostor named Umlangein. For some time past he had been inciting the Kaffirs to rebellion as secretly as possible, assuring them of supernatural aid in driving the white man into the sea. The late disastrous war in Zululand was likewise brought about by the same causes, Cetewayo's Witch-Doctors having assured him that the Spirits had appeared to them and prophesied that he, the King, would be successful. I shall not forget, for some time, the remark Cetewayo made to me in October, 1879. ' I wish I had had you for my Witch-doctor.' There was not much in the remark itself, but there was in the meaning of it. It was as much as to say, ' I see how I have been humbugged and brought to my present position by believing too implicitly in my native Witch-doctors. It is to be hoped his fate will be a warning to other savage rulers. To see a brave man, as he undoubtedly was—a king with, at one time at least, 50,000 fighting men at his beck and call, ready to lay down their lives for him—a miserable prisoner cramped up in the old Dutch Castle at Cape Town, at the time I visited him ; and all because he put his trust in witchcraft was only a stronger, inducement to me (if I needed it) to persevere and expose this detestable form of humbug. It's a great mistake to suppose Cetewayo was abandoned by his people. He was not ; and, with all their faults, it speaks well for them, that though several of them were flogged to try and get them to divulge the ex-king's hiding-place, it had no effect upon them, and it was only by strategy the desired information was obtained. Three of the prisoners who were flogged, were blindfolded, and each taken to a separate spot when two gun shots were fired, and each of course supposed that the other two were killed.   And so the secret was obtained from one or more of them, by this not very dignified proceeding.

The diamonds fields of South Africa, like the gold-bearing streams and ravines of California, have brought to some fabulous wealth, while to others they have been 'will o' the wisps,' leading to ruin, despair, and death.   As the pan washing and cradling of the adventurous prospector of '49 has given way, on the Pacific slope, to the operations of organised and scientific mining industry, so the individual operations of the individual diamond diggers of Griqualand, South Africa, in 1871, with their rude bucket and windlass, followed by the inclined wire, have been replaced by skilled labour.   Tunnels have been blasted through solid rock, shafts have been sunk hundreds of feet into the earth, and yet the precious bits of carbon are found in quantities to supply the greed of avaricious man and furnish a living to thousands, and wealth to a lucky few.

What is now known as Kimberley was called De Beer's New Rush, and had already been yielding up its carbon crystals until a city of tents and corrugated iron houses, with one huge music hall and between 300 and 400 drinking places had clustered around the enormous excavation, whence the earth had been removed by single bucketfuls.   This marvellous result of the labours of the human ants who swarmed in its depths and on its borders was the spot which became known the world round as the Kolesberg Kopje, before it became the Kimberley mine.

Some idea of the size of the Kopje, and the number of people working on it daily will be gathered from the statement that, at the time now spoken of, 800 claims, each being thirty feet square, and an average of about thirty men —say twenty-six black and four white—worked in each claim, giving a total of 24,000 working there.   The first licenses to work claims at the Kopje were issued on the 20th of July, 1871, and in little more than a year the claims were carried down so deep, many over eighty feet, that none of the roadways were left standing complete, though immense portions of them having the appearance of huge broken walls remained.

Standing on an embankment, many feet high, one looks down on an immense basin-shaped excavation, covered in with a perfect cobweb of ropes.   Wherever one's eyes rest, whether it be on the sides of this excavation or the great chasms below, or down in its lowest depths, there are human beings energetically at work.   The Kopje has been aptly described as a vast human ant-hill. I do not know a more effective simile. Human beings are everywhere moving about with an activity and in numbers, like ants. They pass over the narrow roadways, glide down the face of the excavations, or are at work at a depth which dwarfs their statures into that of mere miniature men. Here men are feverishly risking their necks day after day in the pursuit of wealth. They pass over places where a false step—the slipping of a foot, or the incorrectness of the eye in measuring a distance —will cause their death. They climb up ascents that to the inexpert seem unascendable. They slip down ropes that are only fastened to frail tree branches driven into the loose earth. They stand on ledges that are, perhaps, forty feet from the roadway above, and forty feet above the bottom of the claim below. They wheel barrows along narrow pathways that would startle even some expert mountaineers. They work beneath tottering masses, and every now and then these fall, maiming and killing.

A friend and I visited the Kopje by moonlight, and the picture we witnessed could only be done justice to by the pencil of an artist, and not by the pen of a liner. The lime-like soil thrown up around the Kopje might well have been taken for the sand of a Desert; and the masses of earth standing upon the hollow below, the remnants of the roadways, and the fantastic workings of the various claims as broken pillars and crumbling walls of the monuments left of the gorgeous palaces of the ancients. The galvanised iron ropes were now as a veil of silver falling over the softly-illumined mine, into which the rays of the moonlight streamed, making dark shadows that contrasted strangely and brought out more conspicuously the columns and walls on which the moonbeams played.

On the 25th of November, 1885, the Kimberley Railway from Cape Town to the city of Kimberley, once 'De Beer's New Rush,' was opened with imposing ceremonies participated in by many of the leading officials of South Africa. The excursionists from Cape Town found themselves in a large city with paved streets, elegant buildings and all of the evidences of modern metropolitan prosperity. Thousands and tens of thousands of people, embracing the entire population of the district, which includes several smaller mines, were gathered to welcome the arrival of the train bearing the distinguished guests, some of them riding far beyond the limits of the city and acting as an escort of honour into the municipal boundaries. An immense procession comprising all of the city officers, the mining and business magnates, the various lodges and singing societies of the city, and four companies of local military testified to the marvellous and solid growth of the city.

The Great Mine of to-day is one of the grand enterprises of the age, and the arrival of the excursion party was made the occasion of opening communication between the inner and outer shafts at a distance of 550 feet below the surface, the two shafts being 750 feet apart. The holes had been drilled and charged with explosives in the last curtain of rock in the tunnel—the key of the instruments to cause the explosion was touched by a young lady, the obstruction crumbled, and she was the first to walk through the opening in the bowels of the earth far below the spot where, so short a time ago, the bucket, the windlass and the wire rope had been the only means of bringing to light the sparkling treasures hidden by nature in her ample bosom.

It does not matter what part of the world you may be in, you are morally certain to find a Scotchman there. Whether it be that the Scotch emigrants are, for the most part, men of better education than those of other nations, of whose citizens only the poorest and most ignorant are known to emigrate, or whether the Scotchman owes his uniform success in every climate to his perseverance or his shrewdness, the fact remains that wherever abroad you come across a Scotchman, you invariably find him prosperous and respected. The Scotchman crosses the seas in calculating contentment ; the Irishman, too frequently, in sorrow and despair.

In the hot regions of Central Africa, sheep imported from colder regions lose their wool in the course of a year, and thin hair takes its place. The lion, I noticed, which in Northern Africa has a long thick mane, in Central Africa has none.

The Tunisian gentleman is gifted with a never-failing instinct of good taste ; however violent the juxtaposition in their dress the tints, somehow, never seem to clash ; exactly the right tone is chosen and put by the side of something whose shade harmonises with it to a nicety. I do not believe the colours have been yet invented that would not go together if properly adjusted as to tone. People talk with horror of blue and green, and at the same time the Tunisians are very fond of the amalgamation. They seem to have a *penchant*, however, for extreme delicacy of tint, wearing a rose-coloured robe with a jacket of lovely tea-green, or canary-yellow nether garments, with a pale blue bernouse. The women retain the white linen veil and yashmak while walking in the streets.

CHAPTER XVIII.

THE 'DARK CONTINENT'—STANLEY AND LIVINGSTONE—LORD
WOLSELEY—GORDON—KHARTOUM—A SAIL DOWN THE NILE—
REMINISCENCES OF PAST AGES—UJIJI—THE SIMOON—THE
SPHINX—THE PYRAMIDS.

THE 'Dark Continent!' The very mention of it calls up to our
minds thoughts of dear old Livingstone, and of General Gordon,
the discovery of the former by that marvellous, intrepid explorer
Stanley, and the lamentable failure to save the latter through the
half-hearted grandmotherly policy of—well—somebody. Only
by travelling through this country as I have done, can you
conceive the difficulties which have to be encountered. General
Wolseley's magnificently planned march across the Desert ranks
high in the annals of military glory, although he was unsuccessful
in re-leaving Khartoum. The fault was not his. Those fatal
words, 'Too late,' will haunt those whom the cap fits till their
dying day!

The date forests are very picturesque in Egypt, the early
seat of political civilisation, where the first epoch was the dynasty
of the Pharaohs, or 'great kings,' and commenced, we are taught
to believe, with Mizraim, the son of Ham, second son of Noah,
2188 B.C. The population of the present vice-royalty is about
8,000,000.

We sail down the Nile, occasionally landing to visit the old
temples of the past.

Take, for instance, Denderah. How marvellously distinct are
the hieroglyphics on the columns of this Temple! Athotes, son
of Menes, it is believed, was the author of them, and wrote the
history of the Egyptians, 2122, B.C. Here physic was first practised by the priests. Pythagoras, on these very steps, endeavoured
to explain the philosophy of disease, and the action of medicine,
529, B.C., whilst Hippocrates, the father of medicine, flourished
out here about 422, B.C. Hieroglyphics, or sacred engravings,
have, during the present century, been much elucidated by such

men as Young, Champollion, Rosellini, and others. The population of Egypt Proper is 5,583,000, out of whom 5,000,000 are Egyptians Proper; 95,000 Bedaween, 290,000 Copts, 12,000 Jews and Armenians, 40,000 Negroes and Abyssinians, 16,500 French, 7,000 Germans, 6,000 British. We naturally pay a visit to the Temple of Abone, and likewise the Temple of Maharrakka, Nubia near New Dongola, hard by the third cataract.

Is it not astonishing what a wonderful state of preservation these interesting places are in? In the bright dry climate of these parts, 'time passes with no heavy tread, and leaves light footprints in its track.' Marble and granite are almost perennial in their duration, which is very noticeable as we proceed on our journey from Lake Nyanza, the great feeder of the Nile, to Gondokoro, following the White Nile due north till it meets the Blue Nile at Khartoum.

MEETING OF STANLEY AND LIVINGSTONE.

Let us suppose ourselves in the very centre of Africa. What a marvellous feat of endurance and pluck was there depicted. After a tedious journey of 236 days the gallant American explorer, Stanley, met that glorious pioneer of truth, Dr. David Livingstone, at Ujiji, on the eastern shores of that vast Lake Tanganyika. 'Dr. Livingstone, I believe, sir?' he said, as he raised his cap, just as if he was addressing a friend on 'change. How happy must dear old Livingstone have felt to think he was not forgotten by those at home; only those who have lived away from their fellowmen in an alien country for any period of time can conceive how truly thankful he felt to again speak to a white man, and get news from the outer world. Stanley found him in a very exhausted condition and it was some days before they started together to explore the northern end of the Lake.

You, of course, remember Dr. Livingstone had left England, for the third time on the 16th August, 1865, for Zanzibar, an island off the east coast of Africa, and from 1865 to 1872, various rumours were current that he had lost his life, &c., &c. At last, finding that nothing was to be expected from us 'who live at home, at ease,' here, Mr. Stanley was sent out by the Proprietors of the *New York Herald*, and our *Daily Telegraph*, to try and clear up the mystery and 'find and relieve Livingstone,' at a cost of £8,000 or more. His party consisted of 190 persons, and left Zanzibar in January, 1871. A mutiny broke out, as might be expected, and his company was greatly reduced by the time he met Livingstone.

Slave traders, after devastating a tract of country, say the size of Ireland, have been known to only bring away alive 2,300 female slaves, and 2,000 tusks of ivory, whilst possibly 2,500 people were shot, and 1,300 died on the wayside through scant provisions and the intensity of their hopeless wretchedness.

I noticed that banana beer is drunk by the natives of Equatorial Africa as a preventive of fever.

David Livingstone was born at Blantyre, near Glasgow, March 19th, 1813.

Stanley, after spending four months with him, bade him adieu on March 14th, 1872, at Unyanjembe, and from that day no white man saw Dr. Livingstone alive.

Stanley, Selim, his intrepreter, and party reached Zanzibar, May 7th, 1872.

The Arab's tent is made of camel's hair cloths, their dress is a cotton shirt, over which the more wealthy wear a *kombar*, or long gown of silk or cotton stuff, and the poorer classes a woollen mantle.

They live almost entirely on dates and a coarse kind of bread ; they use coffee in large quantities and smoking is universal, knives and forks are never used, they eat with their fingers.

The knowledge of physic among the Arabs is limited, and the sort of doctoring they do practise is such as to terrify away all complaints. Cauterising the part affected is a certain cure. A red-hot iron clapped on the forehead cures the *headache*, at least few persons are known to complain twice.

Dates are here as large as a finger, and of an orange hue ; their flesh is solid, vinous in taste, sweet, and somewhat viscous ; they contain a nutritive principle helpful to horses. The fruit is softened by boiling in water, and goats' milk is added. The Arabs in their pilgrimages across the desert make a species of bread from them, and use the pulp, extracted by pressure in earthenware colanders, for butter and sugar. Great Britain's trade with West Africa amounts to more than £4,000,000 per annum including both imports and exports.

The climate of Egypt, during the greater part of the year, is remarkably salubrious.

The general height of the thermometer in the depth of winter in Lower Egypt, in the afternoon and in the shade is from 50° to 60° ; in the hottest season it is from 90° to 100° ; and about 10° higher in the southern parts of Upper Egypt.

But though the summer heat is so great, it is seldom very oppressive, being generally accompanied by a refreshing northerly breeze, and the air being extremely dry one great source of discomfort arising from the dryness is the excessive quantity of dust.

The Simoon, as it is called in Arabia, or the Sirocco in Africa, comes in sudden gusts, levelling your tents with the ground, and almost blowing the clothes off your backs. The whole atmosphere appears to be on fire. The heat is very oppressive. Buckhardt has seen thermometer stand at 121° in the shade. The camels kneel down and bury their nostrils in the sand, keeping them there till the squall is over. One passed over as we reached that most wonderful monument of Egypt—the 'Sphinx.' It is cut out of the red sandstone rock, only the head and neck are above the level of the Desert.

What a wonderful land Egypt is if we only think a moment. The land over which Joseph ruled, and in which he glorified the God of Israel! Where Israel groaned under cruel task-masters —Where Jehovah called forth his distinguished servants, Moses and Aaron, to their arduous work, and stretched forth His hand in marvellous and miraculous ministration, on behalf of a people whom He had chosen for Himself, and bound to Him by a lasting covenant.

To this land the tender Babe of Bethlehem was transported by night, in obedience to a divine command, beyond the reach of the tyrant Herod.

The Sphinx has a human head and a lion's body, denoting, according to some—wisdom and strength, the attributes of the ancient Egyptian monarchs—chin to top of forehead twenty-eight feet, at one time painted red. There is yet another opinion which is by far too prevalent, it seems to bear the stamp of contradiction on its front.

It is, that this figure was a representation of *Vice*, which, while it presents a fascinating aspect of beauty, is the treacherous and merciless destroyer. This may form a very pretty allegory, and look very well if made the subject of some two or three cantos, but it seems very doubtful how far it has any application to or with the Sphinx. It is, perhaps, best to take the matter as it stands, and leave it simply as it stands to make its own moral and to point its own tale.

A Bedawee Arab will haggle and drive the hardest bargain, in order to get the very last piastre ; and for that purpose will descend to any meanness ; but when once the contract is made with him, he honestly fulfils it to the minutest particular, and considers that he has enlisted himself—life and heart in your service.   The customary salutation of the Bedawee consists in striking gently the palm of each other's extended hand, and then pressing one's own hand first upon the lips, and next upon the forehead.   They generally go barefoot, or wear sandals of fish skin made at Tor.

It is now, I believe, generally agreed that the Bedaween are all the progeny of *Ishmael.*   I have never met with a deformed Bedawee.   They walk as nature intended.   They have never been drilled into awkwardness by dancing or posture masters. Every muscle, tendon, and sinew, performs its proper office. These men have a *wild-bird-o'-th'-wilderness* look about them.

Dean Stanley says, 'that if the Sphinx was the giant representative of Egyptian royalty, then it fitly guards the greatest of all royal sepulchres, and with its half human, half-animal form, is the best welcome we can have to the history and religion of Egypt.'

This country is now before all eyes beginning a second and more wonderful history, if possible, than that of her old glories. Instead of actually marking the places of sepulture it really seems most probable that the *Pyramids* are merely *Cenotaphs*, commemorating and committing to tradition the memory of those persons whose names they bear.

It may not be out of place to compare the height of the Great Pyramid with other buildings :

The Great Pyramid is	479	feet high.
Antwerp Cathedral	472	,,
Strasburgh Cathedral	466	,,
S. Etienne, Vienna	460	,,
S. Peter's, Rome	434	,,
Porcelain Tower, Nankin	414	,,
Salisbury Cathedral	410	,,
St. Paul's, London	404	,,

The three Great Pyramids contain, it is computed, 4,693,000 cubic metres of masonry, and if a wall was made of the same 9 feet high by 1 foot thick ; it would extend 1,400 leagues—say from Alexandria right across Africa to the Guinea coast.

CHAPTER XIX.

PALESTINE—THE HOLY SEPULCHRE—THE TALMUD—THE MISHNAH —DEAN STANLEY'S BOOK ON THE HOLY LAND—THE CEDARS OF LEBANON — BETHLEHEM — DISTINGUISHED MODERN JEWISH MUSICIANS.

I AM sure, from the tenor of the books I have read, that many who have visited the Holy Land in years gone by were Presbyterians, and came seeking evidences in support of their particular creed ; they found a Presbyterian Palestine, and they had already made up their minds to find no other, though possibly they did not know it, being blinded by their zeal. Others were Baptists, seeking Baptist evidences and a Baptist Palestine. Others were Catholics, Methodists, Episcopalians, seeking evidences endorsing their several creeds, and a Catholic, a Methodist, an Episcopalian Palestine. Honest as these men's intentions may have been, they were full of partialities and prejudices, they entered the country with their verdicts already prepared, and they could no more write dispassionately and impartially about it than they could about their own wives and daughters.

The Holy Sepulchre must, without dispute, be considered as the most important of those sacred places which, in all ages of the Christian dispensation, have commanded the attention of the ⁕Christian world. From the day when Christ consigned His weeping Mother to the care of the beloved apostle, and gave Himself up as a Sin Offering for the whole human family, the exact locality where the greatest crime of man was consummated, must always appeal to his heart as that spot of earth where the deepest curse was converted into the highest blessing.

The Church of the Holy Sepulchre embraces under its roof all the places marked by every peculiar event connected with Christ's death. The Stone of Unction, the Pillar of Flagellation, the spot where His garments were parted, and every other locality connected with the awful wonders of that eventful day. One altar here is dedicated to the Roman soldier, who exclaimed :

106

' Surely this was the son of God ' Here they used to keep the copperplate Pilate had put upon the Cross, 'This is the King of the Jews.' St. Helena, the mother of Constantine found it there. She found many interesting objects. It is in Rome now. The description is very distinct. ' The Talmud,' says a modern Jew, ' is a complete system of all our learning, and a comprehensive rule of all the practical part of our laws and religion.'

The Talmud of Jerusalem was really compiled at Tiberias about the close of the fourth century, the second, viz., the Talmud of Babylon, was drawn up at Syra in Babylonia a few years later, though not completed till the end of the fifth century. In it there are many resemblances to the New Testament. That grand dictum : ' Do unto others as thou wouldst be done by,' was spoken by Hillel, who died ten years after the birth of Christ, ' not as anything new, but as an old and well-known dictum that comprised the whole law.' The law said, ' Thou shalt love thy neighbour as thyself' (Lev. xix. 18.), and an Apocryphal book said, ' Do to no man that which thou hatest,' and Hillel's words were, ' Thou shalt not do to thy neighbour that which is hateful to thyself, for this is the whole law.'

To the Jew the *Mishnah* is the ' Oral Law,' which Moses taught ; and was handed down by word of mouth from age to age until it was written. The *Gemara* is reverenced as embodying the opinions and wisdom of the Fathers.

I am aware that I am upon Holy ground, but I hope I may, without irreverence, be permitted to describe this part of the world, and the manners and customs of the natives as I found them, without giving offence or wounding the slightest susceptibilities of anyone.

That I choose not to take my belief from the mouths of ' babes and sucklings,' is no earthly reason why others should be deterred from so doing.

If any of you are sceptical regarding the Arabic legends, and are prepared to be guided by sound sense, extensive information, and acute reasoning, read the Dean of Westminster's charming book upon the ' Holy Land,' and your local faith will be settled upon a sure foundation.

Fergusson, Robinson and others, consider the true site of the Holy Sepulchre to be the Mosque of Omar—the ' Home of the Rock.' The question is still undecided, I believe, and is likely to be ! What an odd thing it seems that Keble, who had never set foot in the Holy Land, was able to write the magnificent description of that land he has been able to do, and to be even complimented by the late Dean Stanley on his correct description.

Josephus tells us the famous Temple of Solomon here in Jerusalem was seven years in building, yet during the whole term it rained not in the day-time that the workmen might not be obstructed in their labour; and from the sacred history it appears that there was neither the sound of the hammer, nor axe, nor any tool of iron heard in the house while it was building. This famous fabric was supported by 1,453 columns, and 2,906 pilasters all hewn from the finest Parian marble. There were employed in building it three Grand Masters, 3,300 masters or overseers of the work, 80,000 fellow-crafts and 70,000 entered apprentices, or bearers of burdens. All these were classed and arranged in such a manner by the wisdom of King Solomon, that neither envy, discord, nor confusion was suffered to interrupt that universal peace and tranquillity which pervaded the world at that important period

The Cedars of Lebanon (the ancient ones) are twelve in number—seven of them clustered together, and the other five at various parts of the grove. I did not measure the girth of any.

'And are these the trees—the very trees,' you ask—' of which Solomon spake; and which have supplied the inspired penman with imagery to symbolise spiritual dignity, and the glory which is of righteousness?' Why should they not be? I know not. Certainly they bear traces of the lapse of ages upon ages. I have seen noble cedars in Europe—the growth of centuries—but compared with those of Lebanon they are but saplings. They appear as old as Lebanon itself—as if they had never been seedlings. If they are not the very trees, surely they have sprung from the seeds of the most ancient ones. The seven which are clustered together go up like gigantic pillars; and their interlaced arms above—each in itself a vast tree—form a verdant dome through which the vertical sun, never penetrates. I delighted in cherishing the persuasion of their full antiquity, as I mused on Israel's history, and thought of the glory of Lebanon.

The Arabs call the Mirage '*Serab*,' which agrees with the Hebrew שָׁרָב and in both languages it means a glowing sandy plain; which in hot countries, at a distance, has the appearance of water.

Sir John Chardin and others speak of it as the effect of the repercussion of the sun's rays from the sand of the Desert.

It generally has the flickering appearance of a landscape

seen through the columns of heat and vapour proceeding from a brick-kiln or furnace.

Out here there is but a short—scarcely any—interval of twilight between sunset and darkness.

> 'The sun's rim dips; the stars rush out;
>   At one stride comes the dark.'
>   *Coleridge's 'Ancient Mariner.'*

The late General Gordon, as you may possibly have heard, like myself, delighted in being at times, alone, and was an expert camel rider. He was always far ahead of his party, frequently riding miles in advance of anyone else. This desire for solitude was one of the general's strongest characteristics.

The Holy Land is considered to have been settled by the Canaanites, 1965, B.C. The land was divided among the Israelites by Joshua, 1445, B.C.

Travelling out here now is very easy, thanks to such enterprising pioneers as Messrs. Cook and Sons, Gaze, and a few others, but the country, though deeply interesting, is desolate and unlovely. And why, as someone asks, should it be otherwise? Can the curse of the Deity beautify a land?

The best way to thoroughly see the country is to start from Damascus and travel south. At this important city the celebrated attar of roses is manufactured in large quantities. It takes eighty pounds of roses (nearly 200,000 roses) to make an ounce and a half of attar, which is worth, on the spot, about £4 sterling an ounce.

The women are homely, and anything but beautiful. 'They wash clothes at the public tanks half the day but they are probably someone else's,' remarks Mark Twain, 'or may be,' he adds, 'they keep one set to wear, and another to wash, because they ever put on those that ever have been washed. When they see anyone with a clean shirt on it arouses their scorn.'

Damascus was a city even in the time of Abraham, 1913, B.C. It is the most important city in Syria, and the third largest city belonging to Turkey, which country seems to be getting 'small by degrees and beautifully less.' Seen from a distance it is really a charming picture, especially if you visit it, as I did at the time the roses are in full bloom. It takes 800 full-blown roses to make a tablespoonful of perfume; whilst one shilling's-worth of cooked onions will scent a whole neighbourhood.

The Turks are as little complimentary to their own nation as Voltaire to his, for they say, 'the Turks hunt hares in carriages drawn by oxen,' and of the Persians, whom they regard as heretical Mohammedans, they say, 'that in the other world they will be transformed into asses to carry Jews into a locality not to be named to ears polite.' Of a great liar they say : 'Send him to Persia to teach Persians to lie'; and the Russians they describe as 'Bears in kid gloves.' Damascus was taken by David, 1040, B.C.

It is intensely hot here at Damascus. You have here the house where a most wicked, sinful man died—he died impenitent. Three days after his death he sent a message up asking his widow to send him down a few blankets.

Taken with the proverbial particle of granulated chloride of sodium, it might be possible to swallow all you hear in these parts.

Bethlehem contains a large convent enclosing, as is said, the very birth-place of Christ ; a church erected by the Empress Helena in the form of a cross, about the year 325 ; a chapel, called the Chapel of the Nativity, where they show you the manger in which Christ was laid ; and a third, of the Holy Innocents.

Adrian, at the time of his persecution of the Christians erected a Temple of Jupiter on Mount Calvary, and a Temple of Adonis on the manger here.

Bethany takes its name from a boat-house. 'It was a cave, and a stone lay upon it.' Its population cannot possibly amount to more than 500, and they are mostly Latins.

The Tomb of the Virgin Mary is just outside the Garden of Gethsemane, on the Mount of Olives. The eight trees are decidedly old, in one it is possible to crowd in three or four persons, the trunk being hollow.

The Virgin Mary being one of the three holy women appointed by the Prophet Mahomet to be held in reverence by the true believers, the spot which is assumed to be her burial place is shared by them with the Greek and other Christian bodies.

It is partly an excavation, and partly an elevation, enclosing within its limits a cave known as the place of sepulture. Before reaching the Tomb within, you notice an arched recess on either hand, in them the remains of St. Anne, the mother of the Virgin, and of Joseph her husband are said to rest, while further on is the Mausoleum covered with marble, simple in form, and altogether unmarked by any peculiarity.

Here the Turks have their praying place, and here the members of the Greek Church offer up masses, while the chapel itself boasts of a large amount of decoration.

Jews, Christians, and Mohammedans, look for the Great Assize of the Judgement Day to be held just underneath the East Wall of Jerusalem, in the valley of Jehoshaphat.

How little has the country or the people changed! The inhabitants will ever remain the same. 'The leopard cannot change his spots, nor the Ethiopian his skin. These people's one grand aim is to fleece the stranger; it's one of the unpleasant reminiscences of eastern travel. We can only echo Themistocles' wish, 'Give me the art of oblivion,' as we, in after years, think of the way we were swindled.

Jerusalem was razed to the ground, and not one stone allowed to remain on another by the Emperor Adrian in A.D. 130, and who built Ælia Capitolina on its site.

The history of the Jews is a wonderful story. Where are the Egyptians? Taxed by foreign masters! Where the Assyrians, onceso mighty and powerful? Edom and Philistia—great in their ay—what know we of them now?

The Greeks are not the Greeks who, when they met in hostile fight, exhibited in all its force the 'tug of war.' And Rome is well, almost a ruin—Rome twice mistress of the world, once in pagan and imperial splendour, and once again in Catholic Christianity. Nations have risen and decayed, races have mingled with races, and all the rivers run into the sea—but the Jews are the exception the Jews are as much alone now in this nineteenth century as when they wandered in the wilderness. They are still a peculiar people, a waiting people—a people who have stood aloof from the Gentiles and who do so still. Their history since the dispersion is most remarkable and reminds us of their river Jordan, which, it is said, goes through the bituminous lake of the Dead Sea, without in the least degree mingling with its waters. Surely a people thus singularly preserved are designed for some great purpose— something yet to be developed—something yet to be wrought out.

Great had been the privileges of the Jews, and for abused privileges great was the penalty. There is much that is impressive, striking, and instructive in the history of the Jews.

The weird old legend of the Wandering Jew seems but a type of the nation.

> 'And eighteen centuries now have sped
> On the dark wrecks of Rome and Greece;
> They have seen the ashes scattered
> Of thousand shifting dynasties;
> Seen good, unfruitful good, and ill
> Prolific while the tempest rolled,
> Seen two new worlds the circle fill
> Which one world occupied of old;
>   Ever, ever,
> Earth revolves—they rest them never.'

Jews have been by intolerant laws compelled to turn their attention to the accumulation of money.

In every age they have been celebrated for their wealth, '*rich as a Jew,*' has become a proverb. Their supposed wealth has brought upon them cruelty and persecution ; their real wealth is a known fact.

But modern Jews can do something more than make money. The melting music of the ' Midsummer Night's Dream,'—the melancholy strains of ' Elijah,' the solemn music of ' Saul' owe their origin to Felix Mendelssohn, a Jew. Who has not been enchanted with the beautiful fictions of lyric poetry, and charmed with the graceful melodies of Heine ? Jewish genius has enriched our collections of art. Was not Rossini a Jew ? Was not Meyerbeer a Jew ?

The Rev. George Fisk, LL.B., says : ' I shall not weary you with a description of the Holy Sepulchre. I felt myself surrounded in it, by the various kinds of Popish apparatus with which I had become familiar, even to disgust, in France and Italy, and hastened through the mere exhibition that awaited me, perfectly convinced that if any of the scenes of our Blessed Lord's humiliation and suffering were actually beneath that roof, they were as utterly obscured and disfigured by outward decoration, as His finished and perfect work of redemption effected there is obscured and disfigured by the corruptions of an apostate Church.' These beautiful traits of Christian feeling and goodwill one towards another are most charming.

CHAPTER XX.

THE ARABS AND THEIR HORSES—ARABIAN AND TURKISH CUSTOMS
—THE BEARD—STRANGE ADVENTURES OF THE AUTHOR—OUT
AND ABOUT—THE AUTHOR'S BOHEMIAN NOTES.

THE Arabs are famous for their splendid horses. After being foaled, the colt is attended to as though it were a young child It is not mounted until it is two years old, and then the saddle is rarely off its back. It becomes the intimate companion of his master, sharing all his comforts, and, also, all his privations. They thus become docile, gentle and intelligent in a high degree. It is a common practice to give them flesh, both raw and cooked before, commencing a fatiguing journey.

The Arab is very hospitable; he entertains his guest with the best provisions he has at his disposal, and he is careful not to lodge and feed the rich above the poor. Arabs never turn a deaf ear to the complaint of the way-farer, but you must remember that there are Arabs and Arabs.

Among the Arabs and Turks the beard is reckoned the greatest ornament of a man, and is not trimmed or shaved except in cases of extreme grief. Many an Arab would rather risk the loss of his head than part with his beard.

The total absence of it or a spare and stinted sprinkling of hair upon the chin, is thought by the Orientals to be as great a deformity to the features, as the want of a nose would appear to us; while, on the contrary, a long and bushy beard, flowing down in luxuriant profusion to the breast, is considered not only a graceful ornament to the person, but as contributing in no small degree to respectability and dignity of character. When a man's veracity is doubted in the East, 'Look at his beard,' they will say, 'the very sight of it will satisfy you of the truth and probity of the owner.' 'Shame on your beard' is a most severe expression of reproof. To treat the beard with irreverence, has, in the East, been for ages considered the grossest insult. 'May God preserve your beard.' 'It is worth more than one's beard;' and other expressions of regard,

I

show the intense veneration entertained for this appendage. The slaves are shaved as a mark of servitude.

One morning, sauntering into the open space used as a market-place at Fez, with fancy bernouse thrown carelessly over me, I had a look around on the *qui vive* for 'something to turn up,' as poor Micawber used to say. In travelling through Morocco, I always dressed in the Oriental style, and when necessary passed myself off as a native. My readers may easily imagine, without too great a stretch of the imagination, the bright picturesque scene presented. Wild swarthy men from the Atlas slopes bargaining for one thing or another, yelling and shouting and cheapening what they wanted—no such thing as 'prix fixe' seeming to be in vogue at Fez. I used to think Naples the queerest spot under the sun to strike a bargain in, but it is 'nowhere' compared to Fez. Slaves were led through the crowd, in batches of three, or four together, and contented enough they looked poor souls. You see, the unfortunate wretches had had no School Board education crammed into them, neither had they—poor benighted ones—ever had the advantage of attending Exeter Hall; the consequences were that they, knowing no better, were quite satisfied with their lot, and seemed to take things as they came. Piles of juicy fruit, many of them unknown to dear old Covent Garden, lay about, watched over by bright-eyed Moorish women, who seem to work like beasts of burden. There is very little poetry about them, and they are all as ignorant as well can be. The bazaars around were full of people chatting and yelling, who were pushed aside as the Sultan's body-guard strode along in all their glory! And what magnificent looking men they are! They walk along, glancing first on this side, and then on the other, nodding to their friends, with all the grace of Salvini himself. These Moors are bronzed, it is true, but it is not the sooty hue with which our tragedians depict the Swan of Avon's *Othello*. At one stall were hanging a number of partridges, quails, some queer-looking unknown birds, and hares, presided over by a brigandish-looking-penny-plain-twopence-coloured-looking moun-taineer, with fierce moustache and armed *cap-à-pie*. 'What will you take, not what are you asking, Ali, for this wretched, half-starved heaven-forsaken hare?' I asked him in Arabic. 'Salaam, aleikoom' (so and so,) was the reply, 'and it's worth double. I shot it myself,' he added with a proud chuckle, 'the day before yesterday, miles from here.' 'Reach it down,' I said, 'and tell me no more of your lies, Ali. Shot it the day before yesterday? It's pretty high then.' 'Yes,' he answered, 'I shot it up a tree!'

'Why, it is alive, you dog,' I said. Taking it up by the ears I showed it to the crowd around me, and sure enough alive and kicking it was. I then let it jump off the board, and off it bolted down the street, pursued by a number of onlookers and all the mongrel dogs in the city. Ali's face was a study! Shall I ever forget his look—I think not. He thought I was *Yama* himself. Like wild-fire the tale spread, how the Magician had put life into a dead hare, which in due time was run to earth just inside the garden of the Palace, and the tale was told to the Sultan himself who was passing out at the time on his way to the Mosque.

That afternoon, I remember, I was sent for to the Palace, and it was arranged I should give a display of my powers the following day before the Court. For the evening, I had already announced my intention of giving a public performance in the then empty bazaar of Aboulhassen Ebn Becar, which my readers may remember if they have ever visited Fez is, or was, situated close to the Mosque. I need hardly remark, that before publicly anointing myself that night with what the audience took to be Meemi-ke-tale, I had the satisfaction of seeing the place crowded to almost suffocation, scarcely allowing me room to grow the mangosteen in. So full, indeed, was the place, that numbers failed to obtain admission. Over twenty performances did I give there, and all through the simple device I practised.

On my way to Fez from Fighig, after crossing the Atlas range of mountains, my dog caught a hare, which I carefully attended to, and on the morning I have just mentioned this hare was carefully concealed in a pocket, very get-at-able, just underneath my bernouse. As I took the dead hare from Ali's hands, I substituted the living one, and pocketed the dead hare in a far shorter space of time than it takes to tell. The fanatic, ignorant people about, thought I was possessed of supernatural power. This belief was also shared in by far higher people in Morocco, but I do not feel at liberty to mention names, as very likely these lines may be read by many out there who might not feel flattered at reading that they swallowed as gospel truth, and 'divine afflatus,' something the very reverse. I can only add that the chivalrous, hospitable character of the higher classes will never be forgotten by me, and I look forward with much pleasure to another tour through Morocco before long. It is true the dangers of travel there are many, and hardships in plenty have to be met, but the country is so romantic and wild, that it well repays one for any inconvenience experienced. One word of advice, however, I may give to intending tourists, that is, never travel in these parts without an armed escort, or you may repent the day you forgot the old French proverb, 'There is no such thing as small economies.'

In my wanderings through North Africa from Morocco to Egypt (about the most exciting and interesting journey I know of) I found two large mackintosh sheets most useful. They had an opening in the centre, which buttoned and unbuttoned, and they formed a sort of tent by night, and in the wet season an overcoat or cloak. My camel used to form a nice soft warm mattress at night, as we both rested together. What a delightful feeling was that dip in the nearest running stream, whilst a brace of partridges just shot were cooking in my camp kettle, made savoury with fresh-gathered mushrooms and wild carrots, herbs, and sometimes truffles! As a rule I used to prepare these things overnight, never forgetting to bait a few hooks for fish. Land-turtles were so plentiful that one was never at a loss for a good meal, whilst oranges, dates, and numerous kinds of delicious fruit could be had in sackfuls.

When the nights were lighted by Selenë's rays, then was the time I used to like to push along, covering a great distance at a stretch, and resting during the heat of the day under a clump of date trees. During my rides across the Desert, I used often to be thankful for a species of bread made from dates, and for butter and sugar was content with the pulp which was extracted by pressure in an earthenware colander. At those periods of my existence, visions would rise up of the excellent square meals I had in days gone by grumbled at, and I really do believe, just then, I should have been even contented with Loveridge's Strand *cuisine*, and have thought his waiters the very pink of perfection, smartness, and politeness!

If no date palms were at hand, I used to content myself with any shady trees, if I could find them, or even a sage bush to make shift with. At first my camel rather kicked against this un-Oriental style of travelling, but in time soon got used to it. Oh! the heat, and the flies! I don't believe you can conceive what it is like unless you experience it. But it was only for a short time I felt it. Regular living, the leaving off spirits and some secret preparation like a sort of pomatum I obtained from a Moslem fakir, with which I anointed my head, kept off all kinds of flies most effectually, whilst camphor plentifully sprinkled over my clothes was very welcome. The people, when I did come across them (far removed from any city, I mean), were a fine race of people to look at. They were bold and determined fellows, and as they came clustering round you, all speaking together, if you happened to be faint-hearted, God help you. Before now, single-handed, I have come out scot free from a crowd of as murderous-looking wretches as you would never wish to meet, by simply playing on their ignorant superstitious feelings, and passing myself off as gifted with supernatural powers. An eclipse of the moon once even saved my life. I knew by my almanack the exact minute it would take place that night, and having been made prisoner by a tribe of thieves on the borders of the Sahara Desert, who assured me they lived almost entirely on milk (here a rather curious ethnological query will persist in presenting itself: 'When did some of them settle in England?') I told them if they took my life Diana, Queen of the Night, would most surely avenge me; and to prove to them what interest I had with Luna I promised in so many minutes to cause a total veil to cover the moon. It luckily came off to time, or I muchly doubt if ever I should have penned these lines. The miserable, poverty-striken, dirty Arabs will swallow anything. Of course, many of the sheiks are right good fellows.

The Sultan of Morocco has one thousand wives. Solomon had only seven hundred. But Solomon was a wise man; he knew when he had enough!

I have met many noble examples of their good nature and generosity, but then I travelled under exceptional conditions. I had a pass-word or sign worth fabulous wealth, which took me through many parts of the 'Dark Continent,' where I know for certain no European dare travel alone, and even with a large escort it would be full of danger; and yet Sed Hamlah, two slaves, and myself traversed thousands of miles without harm or a scratch, more than a slight sword-cut I received with the tribe I have just mentioned, for which they dearly paid afterwards at Castillejos. I had only to raise my finger to obtain anything I wanted; my magic power awed them into obedience to my will; so my readers can easily conceive I had a right good time of it—sometimes.

On arriving at Cairo, a rather amusing incident occurred, which may not be out of place here. In the delightfully cool general room of the Royal Hotel, which is situated on the Boulevard Esbekich, Cairo, and is about as comfortable a hotel you can well find out there, we were chatting together, enjoying the fragrant weed, when I thought I would play a joke during the evening on W——, and mentioned to one or two present that I would do a trick with his scarf-pin. An hour or so later the chance presented itself. "You might show us a trick before you go to perform at the theatre, Dr. Holden,' said one. 'Do, *mon ami*,' said another. 'Gentlemen,' I said, 'I never perform a magical experiment except on the stage, but as you are so very pressing, and if it will relieve *un mauvais quart d'heure*, as I see the ladies have all left, I will just show you a feat I saw performed once out here. Will anyone kindly lend me a scarf-pin?' I asked. W——, after a little hesitation, said he would. 'Do not let me touch it, nor even see it,' I replied, 'but take this envelope, place your scarf-pin inside, and seal it up with wax, a stick of which I beg to hand you.' By this time all eyes were on me, but by a dexterous move I managed to get hold of the envelope, and instantly changed it for another one, sealed up like the other, and containing a dummy scarf-pin. Having 'rung the changes,' as it were, I now felt secure, and prepared to sit upon poor W——. The airs I gave myself (Englishlike) none can tell. Before now, gentle reader, have you not often felt inclined to hurl the soup-tureen or the spittoon at the head of some egotistical, self-conceited, fellow-countryman abroad, as he makes himself a lineal descendant of Balaam's Ass before a company of sensible foreigners? Well, had you been present that evening at Cairo, you would not have even drawn the line at the sofa itself, I fear, as far as it concerns me. I gave myself more airs than all Gatti's waiters put together. I not only sat on poor W——, but pulverised the fellow. He bore it, I must confess, like a lamb. 'Observe, gentlemen, what a marvellous feat I am about to demonstrate. Waiter, bring me in three lemons, please.' He did so, and I managed to get W——'s pin out of the envelope in my back pocket, palm it, and soon insert it in one of the lemons I had carelessly taken up.

'I shall now command the scarf-pin to leave my hand,' I said, as I took up the sealed envelope by the tips of my fingers; and pass into either of those lemons.' One was selected—of course the one with the pin in it. That I placed in the centre of the table, in a borrowed hat, and vanished by a sleight of hand the dummy pin and sealed envelope.

'I'll bet you a level "pony" my pin is not inside that lemon in the hat,' said W——. 'And champagne round as well for the good of the house?' I added. 'Done,' said W—— and done I was.

I cut open, bombastically, the lemon, and there was a pin right enough, but it was *my* pin, not W——'s. Some kind friend, it seems, had told W—— of the 'sell' I had prepared for him, and he had gone to my room and exchanged pins, they being very much alike, but inside his was his name and where it was presented to him. So I had to pay up.

I think practical jokes are very silly things.

I propose now to conclude our 'globe-trotting,' and to devote a little time to superstition, and magic. My readers will have noticed ere reaching these lines, that I have touched very slightly on the subject, for the reason I mentioned at the commencement. This enables you, gentle reader, to read so far, and if the subject in hand is not to your taste to now, throw the book down and part company—Friends, I hope!

CHAPTER XXI

SUMMONED TO BALMORAL—AN ENTERTAINMENT GIVEN BEFORE
THE QUEEN—A MUSICAL DISTRIBUTION—THE SILK CLOTH—
THE BOUQUET—THE ROYAL PROGRAMME OF THE AUTHOR'S—
PERFORMANCE BEFORE HER MAJESTY—GENERAL REMARKS ON
SCOTLAND.

THOROUGHLY agreeing with Goethe's hero, when he says, ''Twas
for wandering in it that the world was made so wide,' it caused
me but slight surprise one morning in May, 1879, when Mr.
Mitchell, of the Royal Library, informed me that he wanted me
to go to the north of Scotland, to give a conjuring entertainment,
of an hour's duration. 'It's at Balmoral Castle, and Her Majesty
will be there. Just a little private family party, you know,' said
Mr. Mitchell. 'Oh, yes, I understand,' I said, trying to look
as unconcerned as I could. 'Everything shall go *comme il faut.*'
I have often heard about being 'knocked over with a feather,'
but must say I was never nearer the consummation of that peculiar *contretemps.* Never in all my Scottish Castle buildings in Ayr,
had I ever dreamed of such a tour, and performing before the
Queen herself. Double-distilled Conservative that I have always
been, the honour seemed all the greater. The performance was
to take place on the following Saturday, May 24th, 1879, Her
Majesty's sixtieth birthday, and as several of the younger members
of the Royal Family were to be present, it was necessary for a
magical distribution to be made.

As my readers may not understand what that means, I may as
well mention that it is my custom to borrow a silk scarf or a shawl
and, standing in the middle of my audience, produce from the
said shawl a quantity of little presents for the juvenile portion of
the auditory, who, of course, think muchly of any little article of
vertu *produced by magic.* Having procured from Liberty, of
Regent Street, sufficient oriental curiosities for the occasion and
made my preparations. I left London by Midland from St. Pancras,
on Thursday night at 9.15, for Aberdeen.

I know of nothing so pleasant, in the way of travelling, as a
night ride with an agreeable companion (or else nobody at all) in a

fast train on the Midland railway. Was it not Dr. Johnson whose idea of the greatest happiness was to travel in a fast post-chaise, with an intelligent and pretty woman for a companion? I think it was, if I mistake not. What a treat it is to bid adieu, or rather *au revoir*, to noisy, unsociable London! Having visited every city of importance in this wicked world, I speak advisedly when I say take away Regent Street and part of Oxford Street, and London would be anything but my *beau ideal* of what a city should be. Soon after daybreak next morning, Edinburgh was reached, and, having half an hour to wait, I availed myself of the opportunity of a flying visit to the 'Modern Athens.' The half-mile or so of Edinburgh to the right and left of the Waverley Station is, without exception, unsurpassed for architectural beauty and the picturesque in the Queendom. The view, even from the railway-station alone, is one of exceeding beauty; but it strikes me one sees all there is worth seeing in the mile I have mentioned, as Edinburgh itself is dusty and badly local-boarded. The ride northwards, after leaving Edinburgh, is full of interest. So many historical places of interest pass as it were before one, Sterling, Perth, and other noted spots conjure up the brave Scottish chiefs of old, but in vain do you look for the merest *soupçon* of the national Highland dress.

Unless one is a good sailor, how far better it is to go to Scotland by the fast through express train than go by boat from London, occupying thirty-two hours to Leith, near Edinburgh. I remember once hearing a friend who had left London on the Saturday, had had all day Sunday on board the Leith boat, exclaim: *Sic transit gloria Mundi*; ought to be translated, 'sick *en route*. Monday be glorified!'"

Passing Bridge of Allan, a beautifully situated watering-place, famed, as everyone knows, for its mineral waters, Dunblane was reached. What a charming view one has here of the old Cathedral, dating from—well, I haven't got a guide-book by me, so I can't say—but there is no mistake in saying it is a very fine specimen of Gothic architecture. The town of Dunblane is on the banks of Allan Water. What a magnificent series of wild picturesque views is lost by not branching off to the left at this point, instead of continuing the main line on to Perth! We lose Cambusmore, distinguished by being the place where Sir Walter Scott wrote the 'Lady of the Lake;' Callander at the entrance of one of the main passes to the Highlands, and one of the finest railway rides in the world along the west shore of Loch Lubnaig, with a view of the Braes of Balquhidder, at the foot of which is the famous ' Rob Roy's ' Grave.   We continued our way due north, however, through some very interesting Perthshire scenery, until we reached the famous Tay Bridge, which was crossed very carefully by a single line, when Perth was reached.

As an early train in the morning went to Ballater, about 50 English miles from Aberdeen, as far as the railway route went, I stopped the night at ' Forsyth's ' Temperance Hotel, Aberdeen ; and in the morning arrived at Ballater, which is romantically situated in the Highlands.   There, hiring a trap, I was soon bowling along an excellent road to Balmoral, about eight miles distant from Ballater.   My Jehu was chatty and communicative, pointing out places of interest on the way.

The ride from Aberdeen to Balmoral is most enjoyable, along the banks of the River Dee, passing Banchory and Aboyne.   The hills are very wild and grand.   Morven Hill, near Ballater, being 2,862 feet.   Mount Keen, 3,077 feet.   Lochnagar in Balmoral Forest 3,768 feet, whilst Ben Avon in Glenavon Forest reaches 3,843 feet.   A little to the west you notice Bracriach, and Ben Macdhui, both mountains being over 4,200 feet.

How invigorating the mountain air feels after a city life.   It must be a delightful place to sojourn in during the dog-days, but awfully dull in the winter.   Had I been anything of a botanist, instead of an illusionist, I should have found much to interest, I have no doubt.   After the south vegetation seemed very backward, snow covering the mountains to a great depth.   Passing by Abergeldie, the Prince of Wales' Highland residence, which is separated from the high road by a wide, and I daresay, at times, surging river, over which an ingenious contrivance has been made to draw over, on a rope, the mail bags, &c., we were soon at the gates of Balmoral Castle, where we were challenged by two private policemen beside the gate-keepers.   As I had been expected at 3 a.m., by the Queen's Messenger-train to Ballater, and then on to the Castle, a room was already prepared for me, with fire and every convenience.   A gorgeous footman, in scarlet and gold livery, opened the door as I descended.   Of course, as per usual, when I looked for my card-case it was *non est.*   Did anybody ever find theirs when they most needed it?   Is it not nearly always left in the other coat pocket?   However, I was soon shown into Viscount General Bridport's room, where that gentleman met me, and after a little chat, handed me over to Mr. Heale, the House Steward's tender care.   His kindness and attention I shall not soon forget.   It must have been about eleven o'clock when I arrived, and my entertainment was not to commence till half-past two, so I had plenty of time to make my necessary preparations.

It was in the State Ball-room where I was to perform. Here, Mr. John Brown coming up to me, shook me heartily by the hand, and in his broad Scotch dialect, asked me what he could do for me. 'Anything you want for your arrangements you have only to say the word, you ken, and I'll see that you have it,' said John Brown. 'I suppose,' he said, 'your apparatus is coming up from the station by cart?' 'Not at all,' I replied. 'All the apparatus I use, is contained in that Gladstone bag' 'That's the style!' Brown heartily blurted out. 'Some sense in that. Why the last conjuror we had here, and it's many a long year ago, Anderson, the "Wizard of the North," it was, I remember, brought a van-load of stuff, and it took us half a day or more to rig it up. Anything you need, only give it a name, and I'll see you get it.'

With him, my *deus ex machiná* to assist me, I soon got a table fixed ready for the performance, and a few fur rugs and flowers completed *mise en scène*. Brown seemed rather amused, I thought, at the small quantity of paraphernalia I brought with me. '*Ventre áffame n'a point d'oreilles*,' they say, so after refreshing the inner man with a repast worthy of Lucullus, I was ready for the ordeal, and I ensconced myself behind a screen, a pair of which I had on either side of the table. Presently, the audience entered through a door, in front of which hung heavy tartan-plaid curtains, and picking their way over the highly polished, slippery, oak floor, took their seats. They consisted of members of the Royal Household, Dr. Marshall's family, and, I presume, a few of the local gentry. The silence they kept, seemed to me rather monotonous.

At last, up they all stood, and by that I guessed (and guessed rightly) that Her Majesty was entering the room. I looked for a hole in the screen, but could not find one, so had to imagine what was going on. And is it really possible, I thought to myself, that I am in the same room as the Queen, and am about to address her, and humbug her—for conjuring is nothing else? That expression of Coleridge, 'Its own exceeding great reward,' I thought, applies to my perseverance with a vengeance.

Fortunately, I am not nervous, and a certain conviction an artiste in such a moment has, which may be summarised, as the Americans would say, thusly: 'The perfection of art is to conceal art,' and 'There is not a solitary soul in this room could do what I am about to do' gave me the most perfect nonchalance as I stepped from behind the screen, and bowing low to Her Majesty, who sat on a raised daïs exactly opposite me, with their Royal Highnesses Princesses Louise and Maud of Wales on either side, the late lamented Prince Leopold to the extreme right of her, and Princess Beatrice to the extreme left, whilst the Ladies-in-Waiting sat behind. A gracious inclination of Her Majesty's head was the sign to commence my *séance*.

'I shall have extreme pleasure, I am sure, Your Majesty, Your Royal Highnesses, and ladies and gentlemen, in introducing to your notice, this morning, several feats of high-class conjuring and Oriental magic, feeling convinced that when this *séance* is over, you will all be able to go through everything, I shall have the honour of showing you, as conjuring is *so easy. Any person* can conjure if they only know how.'

In spite of the excitement, I must admit I felt, I could not but feel inwardly amused, as I watched Her Majesty's face as I commenced the first few words of my address. It seemed as much as to say 'What confounded impudence not to commence, "may it please Your Majesty,"' or some other like form, but it changed immediately as I proceeded, and a most pleasant smile settled on her face. My first trick was—taking a silk cloth, and after showing it quite empty standing in the middle of the room, producing from it a huge bouquet of flowers, then bowls of water and gold fish, and tumblers of wine and water, changing, afterwards, the wine to water and water to wine. My first experiment went immensely well, and I saw at once as I bowed to the Queen, at its conclusion, that she was pleased. I next manipulated with cards, and got John Brown to select a card from the pack. He was pretty artful and looked at me as much as to say '*She was no se heelan,*' which is Gaelic for, 'I am not so green,' if I remember rightly. John Brown having selected his card out of the pack, I made the spots leave his card and pass on to a piece of blank paper held in somebody's hand, my favourite *tour de force* with cards.

Viscount General Bridport at this point was sent by the Queen to tell me that anything I required the audience to do for me in the way of assistance to my tricks, the Royal Princesses, or Prince Leopold would only be too pleased to do it.

That put me at my ease at once; I had raised, however, a good laugh at John Brown's expense, when, turning to the Royal Family I remarked—as he selected the card from the pack—'I hope you don't imagine Mr. Brown to be a confederate of mine, you can always, Your Majesty, tell a confederate by his sinister looks, and I am sure that there is nothing of that about Mr. Brown's honest face.'

The Queen laughed heartily at that, and so she did at my cutting remarks about some of her subjects believing in modern 'Spiritualism,' and my comparing them to 'lineal descendants of Balaam's Ass.'

In illustration of the same I used a common slate free from any writing on either side, placing the same on a chair with a piece of chalk underneath it. I took a 'Nuttall's Dictionary,' Warne's Edition, up to one of the Princess of Wales' children and asked her to open the Dictionary at any page she liked, as I was about to command, that the very top or first word on that page, should instantly appear written on the blank slate. She selected the word 'Inkling'. Someone went to the slate, lifted it up, and there sure enough was the word 'Inkling,' clearly and distinctly written on the slate! 'Very clever indeed', remarked the Queen, as I passed by her to receive back the book. I will not trouble my readers with a description of all I did as it seems like egotism, but there was one experiment I cannot help mentioning. Taking a white cambric handkerchief I rolled it up and tied it round with a piece of Turkey red ribbon, and then threw it on to the centre of the floor, where it lay visible to all.

I then gave Prince Leopold a piece of blank paper having some embossed crest on it and asked him to place any three figures he liked on it, then another three—then another three, and three more figures again—then to fold it up.

Taking it from him, I asked: 'Did Your Royal Highness add it up?'

'No, I did not, but I will if you like,' he replied.

'Never mind, Your Highness, I will not trouble you again.

'Will you add it up?' I asked some one amongst the auditory.

It was added up accordingly and I made the exact total appear in letters of blood on the white handkerchief lying on the floor.

I need scarcely say ' it goes without saying,' as our French neighbours have it, this trick went capitally, and the Queen again made a complimentary remark to me when I was near her.

I have performed, I think, to every kind of audience it is possible for a Professional Entertainer to perform before, but I can conscientiously say, I never, in all my life, was made more at ease, or performed before anybody who seemed so thoroughly to enjoy the same, than before Her Most Gracious Majesty the Queen that day.   Apart from being a red-letter day in my eventful life, it will be a day I shall ever look back to as being oneofthe most enjoyable I ever spent.   Besides which, it was my first visit to the ' land o' cakes,' and certainly few could have visited it under more favourable circumstances.

Everyone is familiar with the features of Her Majesty and the Royal Family, so I need not trouble my readers with attempting to describe the same.   I thought I never saw the Queen looking so well as on this, her *Sixtieth* Birthday !

After I had packed up, Mr. Heale showed me the Queen's rooms.   Tartan plaid seemed to prevail everywhere, even to the chair covers.   The drawing-room has a remarkably light, airy appearance, the plaid suite being of a pale colour blending very softly.

Shall I ever forget the beautiful view out of the windows? I can well understand the Queen's preference for Balmoral ! That vista will ever be imprinted on my mind.   Round the room are statues in, I think, Plaster of Paris, or some kind of composition, of the Prince of Wales and his Royal brothers on horseback.   Landseer's picture of the ' Stag at Bay,' hung on the wall, or if it was not the ' Stag at Bay,' it was the stag somewhere.   My visit to this room being *sub rosa*, it was of very short duration, as can be easily imagined, as every foot-step we heard we thought was the Queen herself coming in.

Right royally was I treated at the Castle, and after finishing a bottle of champagne to toast the Queen with, I took my departure about five o'clock that evening.

I could not help laughing to myself at the contrast between my one-horse-chaise at the tower entrance, and the Royal carriage, also at the door, waiting to take the Queen and Princess Beatrice out for a drive.   Through the well-kept grounds we drove, the horse was fresh, the driver ditto, and must I admit the soft impeachment, your humble servant ditto. It might have been the mountain air, but I fancy it was the champagne.

But what a glorious evening it was ! What a sunset you get in these high latitudes ! I shall not forget that ride in a hurry. ' Put a beggar on horseback, and he'll drive '——you know the rest ?

I felt several inches taller and elated up to the seventh heaven, as everything had gone so satisfactorily. There's a great deal in feeling within yourself, if you are an artiste, that your performance has gone down well. Not one *contretemps* had I experienced all day and that was something to be proud of, for, *entre nous*, a conjurer, never mind how careful he may be, is certain at some time or another to make a *faux pas*.

One is struck by the house arrangements of the middle classes in Scotland. People in the large towns live in flats. From the street you enter a dark and, generally speaking, dirty-looking passage, leading to a flight of equally grimy-looking stone steps, these you mount, perhaps, to the height of four or five stories, on each landing are several doors with brass door-plates, bells, knockers, &c., and here reside the people of that particular flat. Every convenience being there, and the poor unfortunate postman having to bring up your letters, his lot is anything but enviable. Amongst the lower classes, instead of an ordinary bedstead standing in the room it is placed in a recess with a door to match the door you enter by. The bedstead reminds one of a bunk on board a ship, and is not at all pleasant to a stranger, besides being decidedly unhealthy.

As a detailed list of each, and every trick I performed might be tedious, I subjoin the Royal programme through which I religiously went, occupying about an hour.

BALMORAL CASTLE,
Saturday, 24th May, 1879.

DR. HOLDEN'S MODERN MAGICAL MARVELS.

Part 1.

EUROPEAN MAGIC.

" Le vin de Chypre,"

Choice Morceaux from the repertoire of advanced Prestidigitation.

" The Ubiquitous Coins of Crœsus,"

" Les Cartes Magnetiques,"

Mystic Calculation, Drawing or Music, Divination of Thought, &c., after the latest physical methods. The *via Media* of the Magic Art, or *cinq Minutes de Spiritisme.*

Part 2.

ORIENTAL MAGIC.
"The Mysterious Cloth of Sed El Manchuc, the Bedouin Marabout;
or, Le foulard Magique,"
A refutation of "Ex nihilo nihil fit."

"Albumazar's Stygian Feat,"
Far eclipsing the Son of Thetis, as Dr. Holden *Styx* at nothing.

"Marvellous Flowers of Barbary,"
(Les fleurs Animées)
" Then will I raise aloft the milk-white rose,
With whose sweet smell the air shall be perfumed."

" Moorish and Egyptian Surprising Wonders."

Concluding with the Sensational Illusion,
" The Blade of Zamalxis."

CHAPTER XXII.

ANYONE being at Glasgow can make a delightful day's trip
down the River Clyde, calling at Greenock and Gourock, two dull,
washed-out, two-hundred-years-behind-the-times-looking places,
then crossing to Dunoon, a perfectly charming little town, proceeding through Loch Long, and calling en route at Kirn and
Blairmore, go as far as Lochgoilhead. I think I never saw more
enjoyable scenery than in these parts, far grander in every respect
than the Rhine and the Dart in Devonshire.

The steamer, 'Edinboro' Castle,' takes the trip daily ; and the
tourist has a couple of hours at Lochgoilhead, a tiny village consisting of half a dozen or so houses and a small hotel. Everything seems very primitive, the only excitement being the arrival
of the steamers and stage coach on its way to and from Inverary.
Dark gloomy mountains rise from the Loch, from whence there
seems no entrance or exit, whilst at times beautiful verdure-
covered hills surround the steamer with pretty villas or estates
scattered about. It must require a good pilot to take a huge
steamer through these parts.

People here seem to have a natural liking for flowers which is
very pleasant to see. Englishmen emigrating to lands where
Flora holds a gayer court, often seem to lose their gentleness
towards flowers. The pedestrian in Cape Town, for instance,
does not step aside lest his foot should crush the spilt camellias.
There are so many camellias.

Nor in Madeira where clothes baskets may be filled with
violets, can the last handful or two at the bottom hope to be
cared for. There are whole wildernesses of violets in Madeira
as there are near Luss, on Loch Lomond.

The woodlands and breaks, hedgerows and lanes, are exquisitely beautiful in their seasons with a prodigal wealth of
wild things, but they here cultivate in their pretty gardens the
flowers which in other countries run riot in waste places. Here,

129   K

every good head of bloom is the reward of patience and almost affectionate care.

A positive tenderness towards the pretty things is thus engendered and there are few who, seeing a very beautiful flower do not check the first impulse to pick it with a thought that it is a pity to do so—this feeling of tenderness prevails not only among the more refined Scotch people, and better educated, but in all classes alike. Indeed it seems to me it is more striking among those who cannot afford to buy the luxury of flowers than among those who have all the treasury of botany at their command.

The fact is a pleasant one. Like the heroine of Jules Sandeau's charming story, Mdlle. de la Seiglière, Luss on Loch Lomond is unconscious of her beauty.

Why do tourists in search of scenery want to visit the Scotch Lochs through? I admit the beauty of the surroundings, but for the same money one can visit foreign parts and I am sure there is more satisfaction in doing the Rhine, and being done in an unknown tongue than in broad Scotch; for 'do' you they certainly will, if they get a chance, in either place, especially in bonny Scotland! I shall be told, I know that I ought to believe in the old axiom of Butler that 'the pleasure is as great of being cheated as to cheat.' But we don't always see things in the proper light, I fear. Abroad, again, you may get as *diablement en colère* as you please over an imposition. There is some satisfaction in that, but in Scotland, if you try it on, you frequently get a Rowland for an Oliver.

It strikes me that the Scotch bear a great resemblance to the Jews, in many ways; and I could not perhaps pay them a greater compliment than by saying so. With the male population the same shrewd look is observable in both their faces; a sort of-take-care-of-number-one-look-certainly, but, at the same time, an expression not noticeable in the generality of Englishmen, viz., a look of conscious superiority over us. I know well it's not a palatable truth, but it most assuredly is so. Take even the little ragged Street Arabs in any large Scotch city or town, watch them for a few minutes, and then say if there is not a manliness and *sang froid* about them perfectly charming.

Ask an outside porter at the railway station how much he wants to carry a basket or box, he could place on his brawny shoulders, just down the street. 'A shilling,' he will answer, and a shilling he will have, and no abatement. In London, a railway porter will do the same job and thank you for a sixpence. The stock-in-trade of a Scotch shoe-black-boy is not extensive, it would go easily into his coat-tail pocket, provided it would only remain there without dropping through ; not like the gorgeous affair that Cockney *confrère* possesses in Whitehall, just before you come to Parliament Street, opposite the War Office, in London. How many years I wonder has that man been there ? He was an institution when I was a lad at school, at dear old Clapham, and on him I used to reckon to smarten me up a bit before I was pre sentable enough to appear before my pater at the Athenæum Club. If such is the case with the lower orders, it is still more observable in the middle-class.

Though I am an Englishman myself, I must say I like to see it, for we are the most egotistical people in the world, without *raison d'être,* that I can see. An Englishman can hold his own anywhere, I admit. I don't for a moment—understand me— uphold the gaunty-gilt-gingerbread look of superiority a Commu- nistic Frenchman puts on ; or the blustering, swaggering look of conceited superiority (if he has a revolver in his pocket) a Repub- lican American puts on ; but does not a ragged, heaven-forsaken Arab of the Desert, with his majestic walk, come up to one's beau ideal of what a man should look like more than those I have just mentioned ? I think so. In a certain degree my remarks apply to the Scotch. To me, they appear decidedly superior to us— in many things—blackguardism included. And what a fine race they are ! What physique ! What an air of independence. It may be, that education has a great deal to do with it—and I should not be at all surprised if such were the case. I have so far, simply touched upon the men. Well the fact is, one must not touch the women at all, or rather not touch upon the subject. With the Scotch women—so with the Jewish—there is a look on the face I like to see. It seems to say; 'I have got so much to do to-day and I'll do it—I am all there. You may look, but do not touch please !'

But here the similarity ends. The former face lacks expres- sion and fire. In fact, I admit I am not qualified to pass an unbiased opinion on the people. *Chacun à son gout !* It would never do if everybody held the same opinion or had the same tastes.

The few remarks I have made apply to the lower and middle classes, and even then there is no rule without an exception. In the higher Scotch circles, as everyone knows, my remarks do not so well apply. There, we find the loveliest women, and the most intelligent women we would ever wish to meet with, while, as for the men, well—it's all the same whether a man be English,

Irish, Scotch, Welsh, Italian, Spanish, French, or German, *if he be* a gentleman.   There can be, but one kind of the species, climate can make no earthly difference—the '*pundonor*' of the Spanish gentleman runs through the blood of all alike who take for their proud motto, ' *Noblesse oblige !* '

Leaving Glasgow at 9.15, p.m in one of the Midland Company's comfortable carriages, the return journey to London seems nothing, as by 8 a.m. the next morning—London—much abused London ('with all thy faults I love thee still') is reached.

It's an immense pity that, in spite of all the excellent arrangements on that line, the traveller has just cause to complain of the practice they have of continually coming round to one's carriage all night long—perhaps just as you get off into a nice nap, and asking for your ticket.   Seven times, if I remember aright, my ticket was examined between Glasgow and London—and bear in mind please, *in the same carriage !* Surely something could be arranged to dispense with so much ticket examining.

CHAPTER XXIII.

NECROMANCY—ROGER BACON—THE ELIXIR OF LIFE—SUPER-
STITIOUS IDEAS—THE CHINESE—SUPERSTITIONS ABOUT BIRDS—
THE SWALLOW—KINDNESS TO ANIMALS A NOBLE QUALITY.

WE may laugh and sneer at those ancient necromantic 'philosophers' we read about; at poor Roger Bacon and the pains he
took to prove the famous Elixir of Life was *aqua regia*, which
now, every schoolboy at all versed in chemistry knows to be gold,
dissolved in nitro-hydro-chloric acid—but are we so very perfect
ourselves? Augustin Nicholas relates, that a poor peasant, who
had been arrested for sorcery, was put to the torture for the purpose of compelling a confession. After enduring a few gentle
agonies the suffering simpleton admitted his guilt, but naïvely
asked his tormentors if it were not possible for one to be a sorcerer
without knowing it! He was immediately and righteously put to
death, and by this instructive example we are taught the folly of
raising irrelevant issues to embarrass the solution of grave and
weighty social problems.

But let us look at home, and bear in mind the proverb about
'Glass-houses and stone throwing.' In many parts of this Queendom, some very strange things are still believed in, according to
the Rev. Thistylton Dyer, in his excellent and comprehensive
work, on 'English Folk Lore,' of which I strongly advise a perusal.
In Yorkshire, a child suffering from whooping-cough is taken to
a neighbouring convent, and given a drink of holy water by the
priest, out of a silver chalice which the little sufferer is forbidden
to touch. By Protestants, as well as Catholic parents, it is considered an excellent remedy, or was until very recently.

In Gloucestershire, a good cure for whooping-cough is a roasted
mouse, eaten by the patient. In some parts of Devonshire,
it is believed that if a child be carried fasting, on a Sunday
morning, into three parishes he will soon get much better.
Whooping-cough is a favourite subject for charms. In Cornwall, a slice of bread and butter or a piece of cake eaten by

133

the patient, and given by a married couple whose names are John and Joan, is considered to be a certain cure. In Yorkshire, owl broth is believed an infallible specific; and in Staffordshire, hanging an empty bottle up—the bottle is an unfailing cure! And yet the School Board flourishes in all the towns and villages in these parts.

It is considered highly unlucky by many to kill a swallow. No doubt this form of absurd superstition has come down to us from the ancients, by whom the swallow was held sacred to their household gods, and therefore preserved. They also honoured it as the harbinger of the Spring, and it is related that the Rhodians had a solemn song to welcome it in. The Germans have a great veneration for the swallow, and its presence on a house is said not only to preserve it from storms and fire, but also from evil.

What a wonderful nation is China—if we only give a moment's attention to it. Let people hold what religion they think proper —for my part, until I find out a purer faith, I incline towards the ancient religion of China. I do not mean Buddhism nor Taonism, nor even Confucian philosophy, but I go back more than twenty centuries B.C. Most interesting would be found a perusal of the ancient Chinese 'Book of Rites,' and the 'Rules of Propriety.' To me, there is something very grand in their conception of that early 'spirit worship' from which all other systems of barbarous worship sprang. I need not here dwell on their idea of meditation, consisting of three days occupied in thinking of a deceased ancestor until his form was actually presented to the mind's eye; and of music in worship, as the means by which spirits and men were brought together, because I am not exactly prepared to endorse all there told us. But, at the same time, the ancient Chinese religion is the oldest dogma I know of, and I respect it on that account more than anything else.

Archæological discoveries convince me that even in England, centuries before the dawn of history, two races existed side by side. The one burned the dead, as all Aryan nations did; the other buried the body whole, but in a contracted posture as the Chinese do to-day, and they, without doubt, were the Turanian race.

To the almost exclusive attention which scholars have hitherto bestowed on the former, our ignorance of the latter is due. Two great factors appear to have been at work in the construction of primitive society in Europe, the earlier was the Turanian ; the latter the Aryan. It is a great pity the Chinese language is so meagre and difficult in its tones and monosyllables ; it reminds one of the same difficulty that poor Frenchman found in learning our language, which he at last gave up in despair, on being informed in reply to a question how two games of *écarté* were going on. 'These two are two to two, and those two are two to two, too.' A recent translation by Dr. Legge of the ancient Chinese native classics, entitled the 'Book of History,' is also well worth a perusal. There is no doubt, for an instant, too much prominence has been given to Aryan studies, to the exclusion of those of the furthest east. Europe and Asia are not two, *but one*, connecting links having been found between the nations of North-Central Asia, and Europe from Manchouria to Lapland. A Turanian race allied to all these nations preceded the Aryan element in Europe, and so accounts for what I have just mentioned. In these thoughts I have just suggested there is a mine well worth working out.

We are too much in the habit of laughing and sneering at the blue-coated, yellow-skinned, pig-tailed, heathen Chinee, and allowing him no claims of brotherhood, a brother perhaps, but not by the same father and mother ! Great as our progress has been, compared to his, and immeasurable as is our advantage over him on the deepest question which affects humanity, we stand in equal ignorance side by side.

The casual reader may imagine these remarks of mine are uncalled for, and many may say that they had better not have been made. Pardon me if I beg to disagree with you. I shall presently have to make some rather cutting remarks on 'Spiritualism,' so that such remarks, coming from one who has just avowed his admiration for the ancient Chinese belief in 'Spirit Worship,' must, I fancy, convince you no bigot is making the assertions here made. The most advanced of modern thinkers can but stand in the face of the Infinite, like old Confucius, the great philosopher of China did, and stretching out his arms exclaim with him : 'There is no man that knows me— there is One alone that knows me, that is Heaven.'

The criterion of finite beings is a striving after *truth* in the sense of the words of the immortal Lessing, ' If God were to hold in His right hand all truth, and in His left the everlasting active desire for truth, though veiled in eternal error, and were to bid me choose, I would humbly grasp His left praying : ' Almighty Father, grant me *this* gift—absolute truth is for Thee alone.'

' It is in this respect that the modern conjurer differs from his ancient craftsman. No conjurer would dare to insult his audience by laying claim to supernatural power now-a-days, because he knows well no one in the auditory would be so ignorant as to believe him. It is to expose imposture, and hold it up to ridicule, I strive after, so let no spiritualist charlatan, or canting humbug expect quarter from me. With us, it is war *à l'outrance*. Looking for a moment at *Miracles*. What is a miracle? According to the nearest Dictionary I can lay my hand on: 'A wonder, a prodigy—in theology, an event or effect contrary to the known laws of nature—a supernatural event.'

According to my common sense—something that has not taken place during this present century, at all events, consequently non-existent, so far as human agency is concerned.

A miracle is a violation of the laws of nature and as a firm and unalterable experience has established these laws, the proof against a miracle from the very nature of the fact, is as entire as any argument from experience can possibly be imagined.

The martin, as well as the swallow, are very often coupled, and, in travelling about, you hear many queer sayings about them.

> ' The martin and the swallow
> Are God Almighty's bow and arrow.'

> ' The robin and the redbreast,
> The martin and the swallow,
> If ye touch one o' their eggs,
> Bad luck will sure to follow.'

By all means, I say, teach children to be kind to the swallow and martin, but not the above-mentioned birds only—to all living birds and creatures alike, if you want to be logical. Religion, inculcating that, and a command to ' do unto others, as you would be done by,' never mind what name it may go by, cannot be far wrong, and can do no one any harm.

Plants have always held a prominent place in Folk-lore, you remember, *n'est-ce-pas* Plutarch's statement, that a few mules, laden with parsley, threw into a complete panic a Greek force on its march against the enemy? As this herb was very largely used in Greece, to bestrew the tombs of the dead, it had acquired an ominous significance, and ' to be in need of parsley,' was a common phrase used to denote those on the point of death. All superstition with regard to parsley has·not yet died away, for, in some parts of Devonshire, it is widely believed that to transplant parsley is to commit a serious offence against the guardian genius who presides over parsley-beds, certain to be punished, either on the offender himself, or some member of his family, within the course of the year. In Hampshire, too, many people will refuse to give any away for fear of some misfortune befalling them, and in the neighbourhood of Cobham, Suffolk, it is believed by many persons, that if parsley-seed be sown on any other day than Good Friday, it will not come double. There are, of course, innumerable stories and legends connected with the rose, which was also largely used by the Greeks for funereal purposes because of the belief that it protected the remains of the deceased. In Wales, to this day, it is customary to plant the white rose on the grave of an unmarried woman ; and a red rose is appropriated to anyone distinguished for benevolence of character.

CHAPTER XXIV.

THE most mischievous kind of humbug I know of is 'Spiritualism,' as practised by paid Media, *i.e.*, people who make their living
out of it, and who stoop at nothing to gain their ends. These
barefaced impostors will pretend to call from the grave—well
perhaps the spirit-form of your poor long-departed-dead-and-gone
mother-in-law! As if we had not had enough of her and to
spare—while alive, poor soul—without troubling us when dead.
It's much too too awfully awful!

Those, who assume a special organ of dreams, which may be
acted upon by the magnetic abstraction of vital energy from one
body and its transferrence to another, are certainly much nearer
to a solution of the vexed question of *bonâ fide* 'Spiritualism' and
'Animal Magnetism.' If, as Dr. Radcliffe says, every muscle-fibre
or nerved-fibre in us is a Leyden jar, provided with a dielectric,
which separates the two kinds of electricity, then much of
the phenomena may be accounted for. As soon as we admit
that our brain may be acted upon by our ganglionic system; that
it may receive impressions from within as well as from without,
I see nothing incredible in the fact that so called ghosts and
spectres have often appeared and still do appear, but only to the
one so situated. Two or more people at the same time have
never yet seen a spirit-form unless the lot of them had been
suffering from D.T. Shakespeare, who made many a ghost
'revisit the glimpses of the moon, to make night hideous,' has
clearly touched upon the 'Spirit Question' in Macbeth, when he
or Bacon makes the ambitious Thane exclaim :—

> 'Is this a dagger which I see before me,
> The handle toward my hand? Come, let me clutch thee !
> I have thee not, and yet I see thee still.
> Art thou not, fatal vision, sensible
> To feeling as to sight? or art thou but
> A dagger of the mind, a false creation,
> Proceeding from the heat-oppressed brain ?'

This last question might have served as an answer to all
spiritualistic manifestations, if people would only study Shakespeare, not for mere amusement as a powerful poet, but also as

a deep philosopher, who gave us in his works a whole system of psychological truths. Let us adopt some simple means to cure society of this mental and bodily disease; let there be a Royal Commission sent out to investigate the spiritual phenomena of our spiritualistic publicans from a scientific point of view. We have Commissioners in Lunacy, Commissioners to inquire into the vegetable and animal condition of water, to test whether food be fit or unfit for human consumption; and Royal Commissioners in Agriculture; why should we not also have Commissioners to look after the working of 'Psychic Force?' Yet these Spiritualists are allowed to go their way.

Those who have had time to occupy themselves with a historical survey of psychology, know that Thomasius made an end to witchcraft as soon as he ceased to believe in it.

Let us courageously face the mysterious Spirits of our times and they must vanish. It is a mis-directed charity of society which allows those to be imposed upon whose deranged nervous system makes them an easy prey to spiritual charlatans. Nobody can doubt that there is a propelling, and lifting force in us. Our muscles possess the power of expansion and contraction; still we are not allowed to expand our arms with contracted fists and to propel them towards the faces of our neighbours. The police would take cognizance of such a mechanical experiment, and fine or imprison us. But as soon as our intellect is concerned, spiritualistic quacks of every kind are allowed to play upon other human beings, as if they were but wooden instruments. These Spiritualists pretend to know all our psychical stops, they deem themselves authorised to pluck out the very heart of our life-mystery, to sound every one from his 'lowest note to the top of his compass of vitality' Why so? Because 'we think less of man, than of flutes, and pipes and drums.'

We may spread mental disease in the form of hallucinations, spectral visions, or spiritual manifestations, because we like to enjoy our freedom and to make fools of ourselves. The electric and magnetic forces with which we are endowed have been attributed, by Dr. Gassner to the Evil Spirit; our modern Spiritualists use the same spirit only in another form; with them it is an accommodating spiritual servant of some Medium. These 'Media' arrogate to themselves infallible powers; they know the general condition of all the other worlds of the universe, except our own, and for half-a-crown, ten-and-six, or a guinea, will hear, and cause others to hear, the harmony of the spheres resounding in front parlours and back drawing-rooms; they are perfectly acquainted with all the occurrences of the Spiritual Kingdom of ghosts and spectres, but can rarely speak Latin, though this advantage was enjoyed by Father Gassner and his spiritual famulus, who, at least, had the merit of being scholars.

But if we abhor Commissioners, let us at least have the Schoolmaster, not 'abroad,' as the saying goes, but 'at home.' Let us not be altogether only technical, but let us consider that we are spirit as well as matter. That we are bound to study our psychical construction 'goes without saying.' For spirit and matter are in everlasting causal connection. 'As there can be no bile without a liver,' 'there are no thoughts without a brain.' I heard once of a very efficacious remedy for all spiritual phenomena.

An English physician was called in at a ladies' school, where one hysterical girl infected many others with hysteria, this malady being, as many other psychic derangements are infectious. After he had in vain tried various remedies, he one day observed to the mistress, in the hearing of the patients, that there remained but one chance of effecting a cure ; the application of a *red-hot* iron to the spine to quiet the nervous system. Strange to say the red-hot iron was never applied, and the hysterical attacks ceased as if by magic.

A similar instance occurred in a large school near Cologne, where the revival mania, encouraged by a bigoted head-master, had infected some weak-minded students. But the Government soon cooled the religious excitement, remembering that much mischief had been done by one James Böhme, in the year 1612. A Commissioner was sent out to inspect the schools. The boys were assembled, and the Commissioner, after many irrelevant questions, at last touched upon the religious fervour of the students with the remark that he had heard with regret that they were afflicted with visions of holy, and unholy personages, and that if this should continue the school would have to be closed as a haunted place ; the chief visionaries would be altogether expelled, and the head-master dismissed. The effect of this admonition was perfectly miraculous. Not one single revival took place any more. Remedies of this description might be profitably applied in treating the cases of our own Spiritualists, who, according to their own ideas, 'never tell a lie.' With regard to that historical interview between the transgressing little George Washington and his aggrieved parent, I have always considered the confessed inability of the former to tell a lie, a most unfortunate moral pecu*liar*ity. Had he been able, I have no doubt

he would have executed a piece of matchless mendacity that might have stood as a model for all future generations of Spiritualists :—
'A slippery and subtle knave ; a finder out of occasions, that has an eye can stamp and counterfeit advantages.'—*Othello*.

The appearance of a Spirit's hand in a semi-dark room is one of their special phenomena. Let me explain how this is performed :—While sitting round a table the Medium fastens to his boot a wax hand, which is attached to an elastic band, so that at pleasure it may fly up the legs of his ' ditto dittos,' or be slipped down again when needed. Some Media use an india-rubba or gutta-percha hand ; in either case the effect is the same—very striking. Only a small portion of the hand is made to appear at the edge of the table. It requires a man with long legs, and the more athletic he is the better for the success of the manifestation—save the mark ! It seems that certain people have a singular superstition to the effect that if a baby afflicted with—or afflicting—the whooping-cough, shall kiss the back of a jackass, it—or the whooping-cough—will experience immediate relief. If the disease and the superstition shall ever walk hand in hand through Southampton Row, W.C., the Editor of a certain paper, not a hundred miles from there, will have a golden opportunity to receive many a chaste salute.

The same Editor has lately shown a remarkable instance of self-possession. He owns a mule.

'Spiritualism,' as an imposture, is the more shameful because it trades on grief. From small beginnings and an obscure propaganda it now impudently assumes the dignity of a religion. ' Professors ' live by it, indulging themselves in idleness and luxury at the expense of public credulity. There are, at the West-end of London, private houses where every sort of spiritualistic trickery goes on from day to day, and where dupes in a good rank of life are eased of their cash in return for interviews with supposititious ghosts. The audacious quacks, who make believe to recall the dead, not content with a personal connection of well-to-do simpletons, preach 'Spiritualism' as an evangel, describing the details of an after-life in Heaven, and affecting an intimacy with the unknowable, which should excite contemptuous laughter but for its back-ground of mischief. The victims of the spiritualist craze are more to be pitied than the slaves to opium. For while the one may leave to the sufferer intermittent flashes of reason, the other clouds the mind completely and perpetually with a curtain of fallacies hung upon the most daring of all modern forms of imposture.

Exposure cannot silence nor disgrace suppress the professional spiritualist. Driven with contumely from one place he settles in another, still further to unhinge weak minds, and in many instances to sow the seeds of insanity. What will most strike the visitor to the wards of a mad-house, is the number of patients afflicted with 'voices.' The unhappy creatures, often weak in body, and always with poorly-nourished brains, cherish the pitiable fancy that voices from another world continually sound in their ears. That, however, is but a single item of the evils fostered by the encouragement of 'Spiritualism.' Persons of sensitive brain, bowed down with grief and yearning after loved ones taken hence, are apt to be persuaded that the spirits of their dead return to them in some shadowy shape, and at the paid call of the spiritualist impostor. Thus the pure sentiment of natural sorrow is cheated of its dues, and the noblest longings of the human heart are made the mock of jugglery. The influence of this disgraceful trade in lies is peculiarly dangerous in a so-called age of reason like the present. Just as in a religious period the majority accept the dogmas of faith without inquiry, so in a condition of wide-spread scepticism unbelief itself becomes crystallised into a creed, which the unthinking adopt because it is the fashion. History and tradition of civilised and savage races, however, agree in recording that the gross sum of humanity, cultured and uncultured, will hold to some hope beyond the portals of the grave where stands : "The shadow cloak'd from head to foot, Who keeps the keys of all the creeds." Where recognised religions fail an imposture-like 'Spiritualism' steps in, and for the greed of gain pretends to impart the secrets of the Spirit-world—pretends to call back the souls of the dead from where we may hope, but cannot know, they dwell. Working behind the veil of secrecy and in the dark, it is not often that these mountebanks are exposed. When, however, such good fortune does reward inquiry, the wider the publicity given to the information, the greater is the prospect of warning the weak-minded against the evils of this dangerous and growing form of rascality.

Forsaking generalities for the firm ground of fact, we have to deal with a remarkable exposure of pretended 'Spiritualism,' which were it not for the natural credulity of mankind, should strike a fatal blow at this insidious superstition. Sir George R. Sitwell and Herr Carl von Buch, F.C.S., wrote a letter in which they detail their experience of the results of experiments into so-called 'Spiritualism.' Being anxious to put its pretensions to the proof, they sought the advice of a person 'eminent' in the art, craft, creed, or whatever it be, and by him were recommended to attend certain meetings at an influential Institution, at which, they were assured, the *séances* were the most genuine in England and held under strict test conditions. On the occasion of their first visit no manifestations took place, probably because the inquirers themselves tied the Medium. At the next *séance* which they attended, the Chairman of the company assembled, himself an officer of the Institution, directed the tying process, and this time a 'spirit' did appear, in the form of a pretended ghost of a female child, aged twelve years, and answering to the name of 'Marie.' Looking intently at the messenger, assuming to come from beyond the boundaries of another world, the inquirers spied what seemed to be a corset beneath the diaphanous robes of ghosthood, and, doubting whether spirits wore stays, they redoubled their attentions, and ultimately came to the conclusion that, judged by voice and manner, 'Marie' was no other than the professional Medium herself. Influenced by the true scientific spirit these gentlemen were not content with the result of a single experiment, but made a third visit of inquiry, this time accompanied by Mr. John C. Fell, engineer, and his wife. Once more 'Marie' appeared. These four independent and credible witnesses heard audible sounds of undressing behind a curtain, and were shocked at the levity of 'Marie's' behaviour and conversation. It is certainly not surprising that suspicion, already on the alert, should be confirmed by a display of volatility so inconsistent with the assumed character of the 'appearance.' Determined to make a still closer acquaintance with the vivacious and apparently youthful ghost, one of the four darted forward and laid hold of 'Marie' by the wrist. According to the argument by analogy, the possession of the wrist postulates the attachment of a material body, and proves to demonstration that 'Marie' is a common cheat. When one of the party had laid hold of the 'spirit' another drew aside the curtains and discovered the Medium's chair empty, and with the knot of the rope slipped, while, to make assurance doubly sure, the stockings, boots, and other discarded garments of the Medium lay about in ungraceful confusion.

According to the report of Sir George Sitwell and Herr Carl von Buch, the objects named were handed round among the strangers and friends present to make certain of their identity. It is almost needless to add that an official connected with the show, hastened to put the company in total darkness, or that the persons belonging to the Institution took refuge in recrimination and abuse. Sir George Sitwell, Herr von Buch, and Mr. Fell put their case fairly and temperately before the public when they said, that leaving general conclusions on 'Spiritualism' to others, they claimed to have proved that in a Society recommended to them as the first of its kind in England, the Medium has been publicly detected in the fraud of personation. When certain other famous Media, whose names are familiar to the public, at different times found London no longer suited to the object which they had in view, the Metropolis knew them no more ; and should 'Marie' find Bloomsbury untenable that ingenious but disingenuous materialised wraith, like the 'uncouth swain' in 'Lycidas,' may probably flit to-morrow to 'fresh woods and pastures new.'

If it were possible to credit the *ex-parte* announcements of professional Spiritualists, it might be worth while to establish regular communication—a sort of ghostly postal system—between the material and the immaterial worlds, and, were such an innovation desirable, persons fitted, by pretension, for the office of postmen in space would, doubtless, be forthcoming. Indeed, the exceptional cleverness of advertisers who seek patrons from among the readers of Spiritualist prints can only be realised by the study of that form of literature. It would seem to be possible to purchase a series of papers and essays 'by individuals now in spirit life.' It is, however, to be regretted that the advertisement announcing this remarkable work does not explicitly state whether the authors produced their 'copy' before leaving this, or sent it on from another place. It is, likewise, consolatory to know that for the small sum of one penny we may obtain the portrait of a notorious 'appearance' sketched by an artist 'who saw him materialise in daylight.' There exist and flourish, so it would appear, healing as well as trance Mediums ; and there would seem to be but a narrow line of demarcation between the spiritual, the medical clairvoyant, and the professional astrologist. A lady undertakes to cure all classes of disease for one guinea if provided with a lock of the patient's hair, a specimen of his handwriting, and two leading symptoms. Persons afflicted with anxious doubts on the diverse subjects of business, marriage, and absent friends may have their minds set at rest for a half-crown's worth of postage stamps. At a comparatively small outlay the public are invited to read all about life beyond the grave, 'described by a spirit through a writing medium,' and a fashionable tailor retails garments of the best quality, 'at special prices to Spiritualists.' It by no means follows that all these people are impostors. Some may be self-deceived, others may seek to advertise their wares in this manner simply as a matter of business. As a question of public policy it is open to discussion whether a professed spiritualist discovered in the commission of a palpable fraud should not be proceeded against by the Public Prosecutor. Scarcely a week passes in which some ignorant hag is not brought before the magistrates and convicted of imposing on servant-girls and pretending to tell their fortunes by occult means. The mischief arising from pretended communications with the 'Spirit World' cannot well be over-estimated; and if, for the sake of argument, it were allowed that some so-called Spiritualists really and honestly believe themselves to be possessed of the powers which they assume, they should be among the first to encourage prosecutions such as I have indicated.

Apropos of the latest craze of Society, 'Amateur Palmistry,' you can hardly now find any social gathering, from a wedding breakfast to a picnic, at which some lady or gentleman does not profess the occult art or science; and as curiosity is quite as prevalent a social curse as ever it was, of course you have, in your turn, to surrender your hand for investigation. Let me at once admit that the requisite manipulations of one's hand by a fair experimenter are not altogether unpleasant to the *corpus vile*, and one does not mind hearing a little harmless nonsense about 'lines of life,' 'mounts of Jupiter and Mercury,' 'stars,' 'crosses,' and the like; but I do not like to be told that my finger-tips are 'quarrelsome,' and when the young lady gravely raises her eyes to mine and says, 'You have twice betrayed a trusting heart, and once it was through avarice,' I feel positively uncomfortable. Especially annoying is it to have one's wife come up just in time to hear, 'From first to last your career has been, and will be dominated by the influence of three women!' Worst of all you are expected to admit that there may be something in all this, and that the Sibyl has certainly made some startling hits. If you pooh-pooh it, everyone at once concludes that you resent being told bitter home-truths.

The palmist of the clubs has no redeeming features. His touch is unpleasant, and he does not strive to say what he can in your favour. On the contrary, I believe that, under cover of his pretended art, he delights in a disagreeable plainness of speech, for which under ordinary circumstances one would kick him. On the other hand, I have heard him butter some of my friends in a manner wholly contemptible.

CHAPTER XXV

FORTUNE-TELLING BY CARDS—A SPANISH SUPERSTITION—
THOUGHT-READING—ITS FALLACY AND ABSURDITY—A FEW
COMMON-SENSE OBSERVATIONS—CURIOUS INSTANCES WITH
REGARD TO THE SO-CALLED 'SECOND SIGHT.'

TELLING fortunes by cards, and lucky and unlucky numbers is
another very popular belief. In southern Italy where the game
of *Loto* is much indulged in by all classes, from the Phelebian,
down to the Lazonori, the latter superstition is very patent; and
the reasons given very absurd. I remember once, at Naples, being
told by a priest that No. 4 was his lucky number, and he
accounted for it by reminding me, not only did the ancients
venerate that number, on account of it representing the perfect
square; but that the Deity in nearly all the modern languages
was spelt with four letters.

DEUS	...	... *Latin*	SYRÉ	...	... *Persian*
Θεος	...	... *Greek*	GOTT	...	... *German*
AVDI	...	... *Turkish*	DIOS	...	... *Spanish*
ILAH	...	... *Arabic*	DIEU	...	... *French*
TEWT	...	... *Celtic*			

There is a stupid Spanish superstition that it is unlucky to
touch a dead or drowning person, which no doubt accounted
for the death of poor Miss Probyn, who was drowned under the
very eyes of her friend Lady Sebright at Biarritz, only a short
time ago, whilst a hulking, ignorant Spanish fisherman, who
was on the spot with his boat, rendered no assistance until a
wave dashed the lifeless body on to the beach at Lady Sebright's
feet.

My readers may remember in my last papers I made reference
to the belief in the supernatural power of some men indulged in
by our poor benighted brothers (save the mark) in South Africa.
There is some excuse possibly for them, poor wretches, as they
know no better, but what can we think when we see in this
country, and America, people well up in the social scale, lend-

146

ing themselves to about the most arrant impositions evei introduced.

I refer to 'Thought Reading!' As if any man, woman, or child, on the face of the earth, could read what you or I thought of. Say, the day before you had seen a Magic Lantern Entertainment and from amongst the various pictures you selected one of those pictures representing, let us say, a greasy-looking individual in furs, looking like ''Arry,' of the East Whitechapel Amateur Company in 'Called Back,' with one of his eyes on an Aurora Borealis and the other on an old knacker of a Rein-deer-scene-Iceland. Does any sane man believe that the 'Thought Reader' can tell what we are thinking of? We think ourselves so very superior to everybody else, so immaculate, in fact, in everything, that to an observant foreigner we must really at times seem a paradox. Of course I, as a Magician, ought to be the last man in the world to object to it you say. Still, I cannot help thinking at times, Carlyle was not far wrong when he said the population of this country was fifty millions—mostly fools! Have you not, ovei and over again, noticed people walk right out in the road, and get covered with mud, sooner than pass under a ladder? They refuse to sit down to table if thirteen are to be the number. Would I? Try me!

I like a liar—a thoroughly conscientious, industrious, and ingenious liar. Not your ordinary prevaricator who skirts along the coast of truth, keeping ever within sight of the headlands and promontories of probability—whose excursions are limited to short fair-weather reaches into the ocean of imagination, and who paddles for port as if Beelzebub himself were after him whenever a capful of wind threatens a storm of exposure, but a bold, sea-going liar, who spurns a continent, striking out for the blue water, with his eyes fixed upon the horizon of boundless mendacity; therefore, whenever I meet a professional Thought Reader now, my hat is at half-mast in token of profound esteem and conscious inferiority.

Common-sense is, of course, against the attempt to see through brick walls, but many people are superior to common-sense, and are not to be deterred by its dictates from encouraging the endeavour by the sacrifice of time and money, and by applause. Scientific men, philosophers, and theologians are all at one with common sense in this matter; but this is to some minds only another reason why they should persist in their experiments. Not much encouragement is obtained even from the Seers. Even that heterodox one, Swedenborg, whom dealers in mysteries are fond of quoting without reading, who claimed that he had been on the other side of most brick walls, and could describe the scenery beyond, does not really give much satisfaction to those who wish to see through on their own account. He, however, does not venture to approach the brick wall of the future, and is very vigorous in denouncing all attempts at converse with the departed as a disorderly delusion which leads to insanity—a warning which has found abundant confirmation since his day. Rossetti, in his 'Aspecta Medusa,' has the fine idea that one's eyes should not know any forbidden thing itself, but that its 'shadow upon life' should be enough for us; and certainly the shadow seen by friends brooding upon the lives of those who have given themselves up to penetrating this last-mentioned brick wall is, in all conscience, dark enough. A more unhealthy-looking and generally 'unfit' lot of human beings than a number of ardent Spiritualists in *séance* assembled, it would be difficult to find out of a lunatic asylum, and if a tree is to be known by its fruits, that tree is certainly one that cumbers the ground. Disordered, nervous systems, shattered mental powers, and incapacity for healthy life and work are the sole rewards of the devotees of this particular fine art, as anyone can testify who has had the misery of their friendship.

One turns with pleasure, however, from the crazes of 'Spiritualism' to the follies of 'Thought Reading,' as a doctor might turn from a case of *delirium tremens* to one of hettlerash. The latter is a comparative innocuous amusement, and its outcome is not likely to be very serious. It will, no doubt, ultimately, after the proverbial nine days' wonder is over, develop into a form of pastime for evening parties in the winter, to be brought forward when a hostess is at a loss for something wherewith to entertain her guests. And if young ladies are to have their thoughts guessed, and young men are allowed to guess them, I can conceive that it will become a very popular pastime indeed. The privilege of placing his hand on the forehead of a fair 'subject,' and the propinquity which the experiment necessitates, will not come amiss to susceptible youths, nor will ingenuous maidens, whose innocent thoughts might, of course, be read by anybody be averse to so scientific an excuse for flirtation. Beyond this sphere, however, I do not expect to hear much about 'Thought Reading' or Amateur Palmistry.

There is a connection between the three brick walls I have mentioned, the endeavour to see into the future—to talk with the departed—and to penetrate into the minds of the living: they are all attempts to subject the human mind to influences which it is obviously not intended to bear or cope with. The philosophical reason, if anyone wants it, why Thought Reading is a brick wall, is the same reason which shows that foretelling the future, and intercourse with the dead, are brick walls; and is simply this, that if these things were not brick walls, men might possibly continue to exist but they would cease to exist as men, because their freedom of mind would be gone. The knowledge of the future, the control of the departed, and the influence of other men's secret thoughts, would be to them a Gorgon's head which would deprive them of the liberty of thinking and acting for themselves. The reason is in the very nature of things.

There is, of course, a great difference between the dabbler and the devotee. The man who takes up 'Thought Reading' to-day as a fashionable craze, and, perhaps, rhododendron growing to-morrow—if that happens in its turn to be fashionable—is not likely to do himself or anybody else much harm. And there is this also to be said. If a man will spend his time in intently looking upon a brick wall, he will note a score of facts in connection with that wall which escape the eye of him who only looks as he runs by. The colour and texture of the brick, its interstices, and the particular bond in which the wall is laid, will all be revealed to him; and in this sense—but in this sense only —it must be allowed that he sees further into a brick wall than does the other man. He will know a great deal more about the brick wall than the man to whom it is a yellow primrose—I beg pardon—a brick wall—'and nothing more!'

So the present pursuit of Thought Reading, no doubt, will bring to light many useful facts in regard to mental operations. We may, therefore, rest content to let the gazer gaze as long as he likes, and make all the notes he can; but when he starts up in ecstasy and tells us that he has at last seen through the wall, we are bound to tell him that the phenomenon is subjective, and advise him in the kindest possible manner to go and get his head shaved.

A person gravely informs the world that at the burning of the Archiepiscopal Palace at Bourges, among other valuable manuscripts destroyed, was the original death-warrant of Jesus Christ, signed at Jerusalem by one Capel, and dated A.U.C. 783. Not only so, but he kindly favours us with a literal translation of it.

One cannot help warming up to a man who can lie like that! Talk about the 'Emma Mine Swindle,' or the 'Glasgow Bank Directors' Fraud!' Compared with this tremendous fib, they are as but the stilly whisper of a hearthstone cricket to the shrill trumpeting of a wounded elephant—the piping of a sick cocksparrow to the brazen clang of a donkey in love! I have endeavoured to expose silly superstition in these pages. It is so degrading, so utterly absurd, that the only wonder to me is, that an educated man can ever confess to being superstitious! Have I succeeded?

If, gentle reader, I have convinced you (as I honestly believe myself), there is truth in nothing *supernatural*, and that those teachers who would teach you otherwise, have, as a reason, that it is their living to propagate these doctrines, that it is a matter of pounds, shillings and pence to them to make the ignorant believe the nonsense they teach them—then, I say, my efforts have not been in vain.

' SECOND SIGHT.'

Among the numerous crotchets which have, at one time or another, excited popular interest and demanded the attention of even our learned men, may be reckoned 'Second Sight.' Indeed, no less a person than Dr. Johnson was so favourably impressed with the plausibility of this notion that after, in the course of his travels, giving the subject full inquiry, he confessed that he never could 'advance his curiosity to conviction, but came away at last only willing to believe.' Sir Walter Scott, too, went so far as to say that 'if force of evidence could authorise us to believe facts inconsistent with the general laws of nature, enough might be produced in favour of the existence of 'Second Sight.' When we recollect how all history and tradition abound in instances of this belief, oftentimes apparently resting on evidence beyond impeachment, it is not surprising that it has numbered among its adherents advocates of most schools of thought. Although, too, of late years the theory of 'Second Sight' has not been so widely preached as formerly, yet it must not be supposed that, on this account, the stories urged in support of it are less numerous, or that it has ceased to be regarded as great a mystery as in days gone by.

In defining 'Second Sight' as a singular faculty 'of seeing an otherwise invisible object without any previous means used by the person that beholds it for that end,' we are at once confronted by the well-known axiom that 'a man cannot be in two places at once'—a rule with which it is difficult to reconcile such statements as those recorded by Pennant, of a gentleman of the Hebrides, said to have the gift of foreseeing visitors in time to get ready for them, or the anecdote which tells how St. Ambrose fell into a comatose state while celebrating the Mass at Milan, and on his recovery asserted that he had been present at St. Martin's funeral at Tours, where it was afterwards declared that he had been seen. It must be remembered, however, that believers in the theory of 'Second Sight' base their faith not so much on metaphysical definitions as on the evidence of daily experience, it being of immaterial importance to them how impossible a certain doctrine may seem, provided it only has the testimony of actual witnesses in its favour. In spite, therefore, of all argument against the so-called Second Sight as contrary to every natural law, it is urged, on the other hand, that visions coinciding with real facts and events occurring at a distance—often thousands of miles away—are beheld by persons possessing this remarkable faculty. Thus Collins, in his ode on the 'Popular Superstitions of the Highlands,' has the following allusion to this notion :—

> 'To monarchs dear, some hundred miles astray,
>   Oft have they seen Fate give the fatal blow !
>   The seer, in Skye, shrieked as the blood did flow,
>   When headless Charles warm on the scaffold lay.'

In 1652, a Scottish lawyer, Sir George Mackenzie, afterwards Lord Tarbat, when driven to the Highlands by fear of the Government of Cromwell, made very extensive inquiries concerning this supposed supernatural faculty, and wrote an elaborate account of its manifestations to the celebrated Robert Boyle, published in the correspondence of Samuel Pepys. Aubrey, too, the famous antiquarian, devoted considerable attention to the subject, and in the year 1863 appeared the treatise of 'Theophilus Insularum,' with about one hundred cases gathered from various sources. From the numerous narratives recorded of this belief, it appears to have had a specially strong footing in Scotland. In the year 1799, a traveller, writing of the peasants of Kirkcudbrightshire, relates that 'it is common among them to fancy that they see the wraiths of persons dying which will be visible to one and not to others present with him.' Within these last twenty years it was hardly possible to meet with any person who had not seen many wraiths and ghosts in the course of his experience. Indeed, we are told that many of the Highlanders gained a lucrative livelihood by enlightening their neighbours on matters revealed to them through 'Second Sight;' and it is not many years ago since a man lived at Blackpool who possessed, as he pretended, of this faculty, was visited by persons from all parts anxious of gaining information about absent friends. One of the best accounts of this superstition, as it prevailed in the Highlands has been bequeathed by Dr. Johnson in his 'Journey to the Hebrides :'—'A man on a journey, far from home, falls from a horse ; another, who is perhaps at work about the house, sees him bleeding on the ground, commonly with a landscape of the place where the accident befalls him. Another seer, driving home his cattle, or wandering in idleness, or musing in the sunshine, is suddenly surprised by the appearance of a bridal ceremony or funeral procession, and counts the mourners or attendants, of whom, if he knows them, he relates the names ; if he knows them not he can describe the dresses.

'Things distant are seen at the instant when they happen.' This belief, too, it may be added, has not been confined to our own country, curious traces of it being found among savage tribes. Thus Captain Jonathan Carver obtained from a Cree medicine-man a correct prophecy of the arrival of a canoe with news the following day at noon ; and we are further told how when Mr. Mason Brown was travelling with two *voyageurs* on the Coppermine River, he was met by Indians of the very band he was seeking, these having been despatched by their medicine-man, who, on being interrogated, affirmed that 'he saw them coming, and heard them talk on their journey.' Mr. Jamieson, referring to its existence in Scotland, says : 'Whether it was communicated to the inhabitants by the northern nations who so long had possession of it, I shall not pretend to determine ; but traces of the same wonderful faculty may be found among the Scandinavians.' In recent years one of the most interesting instances of so-called 'Second Sight' occurred in connection with the death of Mr. George Smith, the well-known Assyriologist. This eminent scholar died at Aleppo on the 19th of August, 1876, about six o'clock in the afternoon. Curious to say, on the same day, and at about the same time, as Dr. Delitzsch—a friend and fellow-worker of Mr. Smith's—was passing within a stone's-throw of the house in which he had lived whilst in London, he suddenly heard his own name uttered aloud in 'a most piercing cry.' which a contemporary record of the time said 'thrilled him to the marrow.' The fact impressed Dr. Delitzsch so much that he looked at his watch, made a note of the hour, and recorded the fact in his pocket-book, this being one of the many straightforward and unimpeachable coincidences which, even to an opponent of the theory, is difficult to explain.

Again, persons gifted with the faculty of 'Second Sight' are said, not only to know particular events at a distance precisely at the same moment as they happen, but also to have a fore-knowledge of them before they take place, for—

> 'As the sun,
> Ere it is risen, sometimes paints its image
> In the atmosphere, so often do the spirits
> Of great events stride on before the events,
> And in to-day already walks to-morrow.'

A Scottish seer, for instance, is said to have foretold the unhappy career of Charles I., and another the violent death of Villiers, Duke of Buckingham. Mr. Tylor, in his 'Primitive Culture,' relates the case of a Shetland lady, who affirmed how, some years ago, she and a girl leading her pony recognised the familiar figure of one Peter Sutherland, who they knew to be at the time in ill-health in Edinburgh; he turned a corner and they saw him no more, but next week came the news of his sudden death. It appears that coming events are mostly forecasted by various symbolic omens which generally take the form of spectral exhibitions. Thus a phantom shroud seen in the morning on a living person is said to betoken his death in the course of that day; but if seen late in the evening no particular time is indicated, further than that it will take place within the year. If, too, the shroud does not cover the whole body, the fulfilment of the vision may be expected at some distant period. Waldron, in his 'Description of the Isle of Man,' alluding to 'Second Sight,' tells us how, 'before any person dies the procession of a funeral is acted by a sort of beings which, for that end, render themselves visible;' and we are further told how the people of St. Kilda used to be haunted by their own spectral wraiths, certain forerunners of the impending death, visions of this kind having been denominated by the ancient Gaels as 'Shadow Sight.'

In my various entertainments I make a special feature of 'Second Sight,' and manage to produce most wonderful effects; but cannot help thinking of what Cicero said about one augur meeting another, whenever I meet a brother professional 'Second-sightest!' *verb. sap.*

CHAPTER XXVI,

EXPLANATION OF A FEW EASY EXPERIMENTS IN MAGIC PRO BONO PUBLICO.

THE Art of Magic is one of the oldest sciences we have. Ever since ' Wild in Wood the Noble Savage Ran'—Humbug in some form or another has existed, and always will exist. Was it not Dean Milman, who said he believed in ' the immortality of Humbug?' I do not for one moment gentle reader, mean to say that the mere perusal of these pages will make you a perfect full-blown Necromancer!

As Tyndall says :—'All great things come slowly to birth!' Copernicus pondered his great work for thirty-three years ;—. Newton for nearly twenty years kept the idea of gravitation before his mind ; for twenty years also he dwelt upon his discovery of fluxions ; the late Mr. Darwin, the greatest naturalist of our time—and perhaps of all time—for two and twenty years pondered on the problem of the origin of species. So, to become a really successful Magician, years and years of arduous study must be devoted *con amore* to the Art before one can hope to write *Vici !*

I wish, in these pages to explain to the reader a number of interesting experiments, which, performed amongst a circle of acquantances or a small audience will cause much wonderment. The old style of Conjuring is now out of date altogether, the less apparatus you have the more you are thought of. For that reason I here confine myself to simple natural Magic—not Stage Experiments requring an outlay of hundreds of pounds.

Several startling tricks can be performed by the merest tyro, after perusing these pages, at a very nominal outlay. The endeavour of the writer being to enable his readers to perform, say before a few friends at an evening party, a Punch, a Smoking Concert, or Penny Readings; he will select from his extensive *repertoire* the easiest and at the same time the most effective ones.

154

THE DEMON COIN.

Smear a little soap, (or virgin wax mixed with Venice turpentine and melted together) over one side of a florin, five franc piece, dollar, or penny, and place it behind the door, or under a plate, a glass or anywhere in the room you like ; say behind a picture, stuck to the wall paper, unseen, of course, by anyone present. Now, you must have a round piece of metal or one of the above mentioned coins very carefully sewn up in one corner of your pocket-handkerchief by laying another piece of the same pattern over the disc or coin, and then sewing it over, so that when the handkerchief is opened it is utterly impossible to detect anything suspicious about it. Unless these instructions are carried out, it stands to reason, someone present would notice the peculiarity of the corner of your handkerchief.

Now for the *modus operandi !* Take a coin from your pocket, or borrow one of the same value as the one you have 'planted' (if I may be permitted to use the word), and showing it to those present, remark that you have the wonderful power of making money fly. 'Nothing very wonderful about that,' someone may very possibly remark, 'my wife can do that with a vengeance !'

'Pardon me, I did not mean what you mean, this is what I would demonstrate.'

'I place this coin in the centre of my pocket-handkerchief. You feel it do you not? Hold it firmly—so. Sure you have it? One, two—three ! 'Abracadabra Arabi Pasha Pass,' which is Gum Arabic for 'Vanish,' and lo ! the coin has passed from where it was, right through the closed door ! Open the door—please—and there it is stuck fast to the other side !'

You have guessed, of course, how it was done, but not so your audience. As you cover the coin you slip it either down your sleeve, or on to your knees, if you happen to be sitting down, and get the prepared corner just under the centre, thus, whoever, holds the handkerchief naturally mistakes for the coin. Catch hold of one of the other corners—whisk it quickly away—and there you are—don't you know ?

'THE WIZARD'S POCKET-HANDKERCHIEF.'

This is made by getting two silk handkerchiefs, of a dark pattern, exactly the same pattern, and joining them together at the edges so that when held up they look like *one* handkerchief. In the very centre of one of them you cut a slit, and hem round its edges. Let the slit be large enough to slip an egg or a large watch in it. You will perceive that if you now take either of the above articles, or a card, or in fact anything not too large, and covering the prepared handkerchief over it, at the same time slipping whatever it is inside the slit a few inches or so, you may safely pretend to mysteriously vanish it by catching hold of one corner and jerking the handkerchief away, taking care, of course, to keep the slit towards you. It really appears, if you are quick enough and take care to put your handkerchief in your pocket at once—it really appears, I say—as if by some uncanny process you had caused the disappearance of whatever article you are performing with.

'HINTS ON CONJURING.'

Never perform a trick over twice. Do not of course say you cannot do so, but make up any little joke you like, such as: 'This is *the* one day in the week I dare not do so, now had it been yesterday, I would have repeated the trick with pleasure. Always bear this in mind: Your audience follow your eyes. So if you want them to believe you have something in your empty hand, pocket-handkerchief or whatnot, look intently there and there only, until you have managed to get rid of what you wish to. *Directly*, lay claim to no supernatural power whatever; if you have amongst your audience any educated people nothing shows so much bad taste. Without patter, or perhaps I should say, appropriate remarks, tricks go for very little. A successful Wizard is not a man who performs to perfection sleight-of-hand, or Oxford-Street-Toy-Shop-Mechanical-Tricks, but a man gifted by education and travel able to cope with all he may come in contact with, and never at a loss with some happy *repartee*. In short to be a successful Wizard, you must not only be a consummate actor but an artiste in every acceptation of the term. In England such men may be counted by one's fingers on one hand, and then there may possibly be a vacancy. You see, I insist very strongly on this point. In time, you will arrange your little by-play and remarks to each trick you perform. A golden secret is: *Imagine you are really what you pretend to be*, viz., a Magician—and a disciple of Zoroaster himself. At the same time bear in mind that nothing is so annoying to your audience as a domineering, half-and-half-sort-of-style. Try your best to find the happy medium natural style, and if you intend to take a course of lessons, be most careful whom you study under.

There are so-called Professors of the Magic Art, who pretend to give lessons, who evidently have mistaken their vocation, and appear more at their ease dabbling with the Three-card Trick on a suburban race-course than murdering the Queen's English and trying to teach the young idea how to shoot, or rather 'conjure' in Oxford Street! Give such people a wide berth.

There ought to be no such word as *fail* in a Magician's vocabulary, test everything before you perform, and if at all shaky, get new lines, silk, or whatnot; don't trust to chance, and expect no pity from your audience; neither give nor take it. Was it not Talleyrand who remarked: 'There is something not altogether displeasing in the misfortunes of our best friends'? Practise your tricks before a looking-glass, and be as hypercritical as you can with yourself. Even when you fancy yourself perfect—every time you have any spare moments—practise. You cannot have too much of it. I never let a day pass without trying over a palm or two. I hope these few hints may prove of some little service to my reader. Never expose a trick by showing how it is done. Your audience expect to be humbugged. I never knew an *artiste* yet who publicly did so. A man must be beneath contempt who would so degrade the art.

THE TRICK OF TRICKS.

You take a seat, and then borrow a walking-stick, or an umbrella, or even perform with the poker. Pretend to mesmerise the article passing the hands over it in the orthodox style, and at last it will be apparently under your influence, so much so that you can make it stand upright or incline to the front at command. This really marvellous trick is simplicity itself. Take a needle and sew a piece of silk twist (Tailor's Twist it is called) from knee to knee, eight inches in length will suffice, fasten off both ends with a strong knot. It is not visible to the company, and you can walk about with it on your 'ditto-dittos' till ready.

You will at once perceive, that, opening out your legs will make the silk taut, so much so, that placing, say the poker against the silk, and, of course, nearest to you, it must of necessity stand upright, slack it, and the poker bends forwards. There is the whole secret in a few words.

'THE GREAT INDIAN SAND TRICK.'

I well remember once, at Benares, being mystified over this very illusion, and paying a handsome sum for the secret. The performer takes a bowl of water, and a bowl of sand, and asks anyone present to take a handful of the sand, and throw it in the water, and bring the sand out of the water dry! Someone tries, and, naturally enough, fails. The performer, however, accomplishes the feat with ease, and this is the simple method. Before performing this trick, get a new frying-pan, fill it half full of silver sand (which has been previously well washed and dried in an oven), and when warm stir the sand with a sterine or wax candle, stir it well until the whole of the sand has been mixed thoroughly with the wax candle, and then let it dry and cool. Place it in a dish or bowl, or anything you have handy, and get your hand full of ordinary unprepared sand. This you hand to someone to insert in the water. The audience think it is a fair sample of the prepared sand, which will be found to come out of the water quite dry, for the simple reason that it is coated, as it were, with the wax, and so the water has no effect on it, whilst the genuine sand melts away.

'THE ENCHANTED SEGAR.'

Borrow a tall hat, and a segar or cigarette, of anyone present. Place it on the crown of the hat and it will stand upright, and bend about as commanded. Explanation :—To the end of a black-lead pencil fix a strong needle. Conceal it in your hand, or, better still, slip it in the lining of the hat. The moment you borrow the hat, push it (the needle) through the crown of the same and stick the segar on it. It will then move about as required. Your hand being inside the hat conceals any movement you make. You might, for instance, remark :—'To accomplish this experiment, you see I have only to draw an imaginary line from here to here, *i.e.* from the segar to the glasses, and it is but a narrow line that separates the sublime from the ridiculous,' as someone somewhere remarks :—' Do you see that imaginary line, Madam ?' 'No.' '*Ne moi non plus,*' still you know we must draw the line somewhere.

CHAPTER XXVII.

WEATHER SUPERSTITIONS.

MANY people are so foolish as to believe in weather superstitions. In our changeable climate, forty days reckoned anywhere in the year are likely to afford a supply of rain. The St. Swithin legend is, that when the holy man died in 868, after holding the Bishopric of Winchester for eleven years, he was buried, according to his own desire, in the open churchyard— a sensible protest against intramural interment. After he was canonized, the monks intended to move his body in solemn procession, and inter it in the choir. This the Saint resented with floods of rain for forty days, and thus caused the design to be abandoned. Legends with mystical numbers of days in them are of doubtful authenticity. The number forty became one of the favourites from its occurrence in the Bible, and if Noah's Flood had been occasioned by a shorter rain, St. Swithin would no doubt, have been satisfied with the smaller quantity. As a matter of experience, many rainy days are found to occur as summer gradually passes into autumn ; and whether the 15th or the 26th of July is wet or dry, the chances are about the same, and St. Swithin's votaries keep their faith intact whether the clouds confirm or contradict the prophecy. On the Continent, Swithin is not a weather Saint, but the popular desire for connecting weather changes with such a personage is gratified by taking St. Médard, whose day is now on the 8th of June. When the Romish Church reformed the Calendar, I do not know if all the Saints were moved on, but the date mentioned is the starting-point for the imaginary forty days of rain, or fine, as the case may be. Popular rhymes refer to each Saint ; a Scotch one says :—

> 'St. Swithin's Day, gif ye do rain.
> For forty days it will remain ;
> St. Swithin's Day, an ye be fair,
> For forty days 'twill rain na mair.'

The first lines of a French rhyme say :—

> ' St. Médard pluvious,
>   Forty days dangerous.'

The Germans have a similar verse, but the accident of *tag* (day) and *naoh* (after) making a rhyme-like gingle, caused their proverb to refer to six weeks instead of forty days. Another German verse makes the weather on St. Médard's Day the rule for succeeding days till that moon ends. An Austrian proverb says :—

> ' If St. Médard is wet,
>   Much rain you will get.'

Other Saints are supposed to influence the rainfall; amongst them are Peter, Paul, Barnaby, and Gervais. The last Saint has the merit of occasionally converting Swithin from his watery intentions, and a French proverb may be rendered—

> ' If St. Gervais is fine,
>   St. Swithin may shine.'

This day is the 19th of June. Peter and Paul take thirty instead of forty days under their control. Their rhyme says :—

> ' Peter and Paul pluvious,
>   Thirty days dangerous.'

A reference to Cruden's ' Concondance ' will show that many remarkable thirties occur in the Bible besides Judas's thirty pieces of silver. St. Barnaby acts like Gervais, but begins his work earlier, on the 11th of June. A French verse has it :—

> ' If St. Médard gives a soak,
>   You will surely want your cloak ;
>   If 'tis fine on Barnaby Day,
>   Then at home your cloak may stay.'

Antiquaries have not traced the origin of St. Médard's claims as a weather Saint. He was Bishop of Noyon, and of Tournay, and died in 545. He is credited with having established the Rosary of Salency, a prize for virtue to be given to the most deserving maiden— *la Rosière.* In England, it is considered unlucky by the peasantry to gather apples before St. Swithin has baptised them, and certainly there is a probability of their being very sour. Swithin has quite supplanted Médard in modern English memory, but Chaucer, without mentioning his name, then no doubt well-known, wrote :—

> ' If on the eighth of June it rain,
>   It foretells a wet harvest men sain.'

The 1st of July is dedicated to a swarm of Saints—Rumbolt, Simeon, and several more—and Chaucer said :—

> ' If the first of July be rainy weather,
> 'Twill rain more or less for four weeks together,'

which is a prudent prophecy, having a due regard to uncertainties. The 2nd of July was dedicated by Pope Urban VI. to the celebration of the visit of the Virgin Mary to the mother of St. John the Baptist, and rain on this day was supposed to predict forty days of wet. St. John the Baptist has his day on June 24, and an old proverb quoted by Dr. Forster repeats the forty days' rain notion, and adds 'certain harm to nuts,' which prolonged wet at that time is likely to cause, and to other crops also. Our forefathers had, or fancied they had, so much assistance from the Saints in prognosticating the weather, that they ought seldom to have been wrong ; but there were exhibitions of doubt and infidelity at various periods, and in 1697 the author of 'Poor Robin's Almanack,' quoted by Dr. Forster, put into it the following poem, which must have been thought as bad by the priests then as some of the things lately said by Huxley, Darwin, or Herbert Spencer have been pronounced :—

> ' In this month is St. Swithin's Day,
> On which if that it rain they say
> Full forty days after it will,
> Or more or less, some rain distill.
> This Swithin was a Saint, I trow,
> And Winchester's Bishop also,
> Who in his time did many a feat,
> As Popish legends do repeat.
> A woman having broke her eggs
> By stumbling at another's legs,
> For which she made a woeful cry,
> St. Swithin chanced for to come by,
> Who made them all as sound, or more,
> Than ever that they were before.
> Better it is to rise betime
> And to make hay when the sun do shine ;
> Than to believe in tales and lies
> Which idle monks and friars devise.'

M. A. Lancaster, writing in *Ciel et Terre* on Médard as a ' Weather Saint,' supplies the verses relating to him I have cited, and observes that over the greater part of Europe Spring is the driest season, and that after a prolonged absence of rain a few wet days attract a good deal of attention. In any changeable climate the statistical method will not do much to correct a popular belief.

M

At Brussels, for example, from 1833 to 1882, M. Lancaster finds Médard had twenty-eight of his days rainy, and twenty-two without rain. After the rainy Saint's day the average of those years gave 20.4 of days on which rain fell, and on the contrary occasions there were 18.1 days of rainfall. Thus the Saint's claims to be a 'weather prophet' had a little the best of the figures ; but if, instead of taking an average, some 'infidel' person looked to the facts of each one of the fifty years, in no case would he find the forty days' wet or fine follow as they should have done. In England, while the other Saints have been forgotten, Swithin is still remembered, perhaps on account of a popular, though certainly not authentic story, that he wept for forty days on account of a severe beating administered to him by a termagant wife. The faith in St. Swithin as a 'weather prophet' is fast declining in this unbelieving age, and in another generation may become extinct. Arguing against a popular superstition is of no avail—perhaps, even, it strengthens the credulity ; but there is a quiet and scarcely noticed filtration of knowledge from the intelligent and inquiring few through the credulous many, that gradually undermines foolish notions. Prophecy-makers have this advantage—that the cases, if any, of their success, produce a strong and abiding impression upon ordinary mortals, while their failures are soon forgotten.

CHAPTER XXVIII.

'SPIRITUALISM'—AN EXPOSE OF THE IMPOSTURE—HEAR BOTH
SIDES OF THE QUESTION—A REMARKABLE INCIDENT WITH RE-
GARD TO SO-CALLED 'SPIRITUALISM'—'THE FLOATING TABLE'
— 'SPIRIT RAPPING'— THE SPIRITUALIST MUSICAL BOX —
'INVISIBLE WRITING.'

ALLOW me now, if I am not boring you too much, to touch on a
different subject, viz., 'Spiritualism,' and after reading the same,
if you feel so inclined, you will be able, I make so bold as to say,
to fill up a very considerable portion of an evening's entertainment by performing the different feats here mentioned.

If, according to the Jesuite teaching, 'the end sanctifies the
means,' then I submit, one has little difficulty in dealing with
such a subject as 'Spiritualism,' as it is right outside the bounds
of theology and, *par consequence*, no sensitive mind can feel hurt
at any remarks, I may make, and to cope with such a subject as
this they must be to the point believe me. Were it otherwise, I
would be the last person in all the world to take up the subject
for I respect, equally, everyone's religious belief. I think I hear
someone say : 'Mr. So-and-So believes in it, and he has a sensitive mind, and is a good, a very good man—and would do
nothing wrong on any account. Don't be quite so sure about
that, if you please, and don't judge always by appearances. Such
dear, good, worthy, pure-minded souls, to my certain knowledge
have turned out very queer fish 'ere now—not that Mr. So-and-
So may do the same—oh dear me, no !

Such being the case, it suggested itself to me that I could
find nothing more in my line than the exposé of this doctrine.
What do they say, 'Set a thief to catch a thief,' don't they?

Now I believe in always hearing both sides of a question.
I never forget an old African proverb I once heard during my
professional tour through the Dark Continent, which translated
ran, 'An one-sided story is always right. Ear, hear the other
side before you decide.'

163

I hear the Spiritualists say, 'Expose it? *Cui bono? Cui bono*, indeed? Not much, I fear me—still I will now plunge like 'Homer' *in medias res*. Let's hear what they have to say for the defence. Says one of them :—

'I tied up an accordion with tape, binding it round and round, and sealing it with wax, and my crest (*tête d'un rossignol d'Arcade*), so that it was impossible to play it. I placed it on the Medium's knees and a committee handcuffed his hands behind his back. The lights were lowered and yet that accordion played, as did also a guitar which was placed out of reach of the Medium. Marvellous to say that guitar floated over our heads !!! Who but Spirits could produce such manifestations? 'My dear sir, you are as much mistaken as a Sporting prophet. As I don't believe in ' beautiful myths,' I will hasten to answer you, *I* could and so could *you*! Procure a small tube, place it in the valve-hole of the accordion, breathe and blow into it alternately, and then, by fingering the keys, you will be able to produce precisely the same effect.

A telescopic-rod extending several feet, is concealed about the Medium's person, who fixes to it the guitar, in which is a musical box with a small piece of writing paper so placed as to touch the steel, or vibrating tongues of the box and you will find this closely imitates the well-known twang of the 'light guitar.'

If 'Balmain's Phosphor Paint' is covered over one side of a tambourine previously exposed to the day-light, and this is fixed to the end of the telescopic-rod, and shaken over the heads of the audience it is immediately put down to Spirit agency. The same with an old glove with a wet sponge inside. Outside you smear it over with oil of cloves and phosphorus, and then fasten it on the rod, and then we have the *Spirit Hand*. Or 'another way' as Mrs. Glasse would say : 'use Phosphorus, melted gently in oil of cloves, and then rubbed over the instrument you mean to float.' But use very great care. Let me ask you—did you ever know one single—now only *one*—I don't want you to strain yourselves too much—one single instance where any *good* came of this belief in Spirit Power? If I paused until the Greek Kalends I should not get an affirmative reply. On the other hand—did you ever know any *ill* come of it? If you don't, I do. 'Spiritualism' is like Macbeth's dagger 'there's nothing in it.' Such being the case, am I to remain silent for fear, forsooth, of saying something that might offend someone who seems to forget we are in the enlightened Nineteenth Century and not in the Dark Ages? How apparently educated people believe such rubbish caps the climax. On this subject, I am come to no rash conclusions.

For years I have watched its spread, attended its *séances* and tried my level best in vain attempts to find one redeeming point in its favour.

I am reminded of a very touching incident which took place not a hundred miles from Southampton Row, London. The daughter of a much respected widow of a leading Spirit Medium just before she died, exclaimed, 'Papa, take hold of my hand and help me across!' Her father had died two months before. Did she see his 'spirit-form'? There is not the slightest doubt of it, say the Spiritualists. But, I ask, with all due respect, were those the exact words she made use of? Is it not far more probable that what the poor child said was, '*Papa, take hold of my hand, and I will help you out of that?*'

Mankind are constantly starting at events which they consider extraordinary. But a philosopher acknowledges only one miracle. Let us, if we can, coolly and philosophically look at the subject before us and we may then possibly 'pluck the flower safely from the nettle danger.' Either it is true, every mortal word, or marvellous manifestation you have ever heard of, or, on the other hand, it is a tissue of wicked lies from beginning to the end. There's no medium—I will admit none— You see, I am not like the Spiritualists!

I think I hear someone present muttering, *sotto voce*: 'The floating table is a marvellous manifestation! It actually floats round the room just where the Medium wills it to go! Nothing shall ever convince me but what this is a genuine manifestation! My own table, Sir! If it had been a prepared one I might—mind I only say I *might*—have been sceptical. But to see that dear good Mr. So-and-So the, Medium, after harmonising the influences with a hymn forced to follow that table whither it listeth,' first up one side of the room and then the other—enough to convince anyone, Sir—except a thick-headed Conjurer—Sir, I don't believe you would believe anything."

I should certainly not, my easily beguiled Spiritualist, believe in table floating. Here's the very thing that would lift the table round the room. Look—a movable steel rod to draw out from your sleeve and so made to grip under the edge of the table and then fly back when done with by means of an elastic band. It is generally attempted with a confederate, who has another of these articles up his or her sleeve, but where the table is a light one, one is quite sufficient I find.

'Spirit Rapping' is frequently performed by the aid of electro-magnetism, but more often by far simpler methods. The magnet is enclosed in a little mahogany box, and can be readily fixed in any required position, passing the wire down the leg of the table, then under the carpet to wherever the assistant is concealed. Now be good enough not to misunderstand what I say. I am not here dealing with Animal Magnetism, but with 'spirit-forms' who are said to have appeared materially to human beings, here on this earth we inhabit. I will not even go so far as to say, that you have *not* seen what you honestly believed to be a spirit. A man in a fit of *delirium tremens* has been known to have seen, what he thought, any amount of them. You have possibly seen Charles Warner in 'Drink.' The play by Charles Reed, I mean. But what does that prove? Neither he nor you really saw a spirit. It was simply imagination, and if more than one of you saw what you thought to be a 'spirit-form,' there was evidently a stronger will-force, or odylic-power present than your own. Many people believe in will-force—look at the Grand Old Man at Westminster, for instance. You say, '*How about the spirit raps we heard?*' In reply, will you allow me to ask you a most pertinent question before I answer you. 'Where is your keeper?'

My poor silly, misguided imbecile, haven't you got sufficient sense in your poor cracked head to know that an immaterial being, that which you call a 'spirit form' has no bones to its incorporeal knuckles or toes to rap with, and that they are not allowed to bring material walking-sticks or umbrellas with them. You surely don't mean to say, now that you come to think of it, that those raps you heard were caused by 'spirit power?' No, of course not. But do you remember being told by that good dear soul, Mr. So-and-So, that they were? Yes, you do. Does it not strike you very forcibly that if you are gammoned over one little thing in this doctrine, that the chances are you have been done so in many? No? I expected such an answer. Thanks! Don't concede too much, or I fear me you won't have a leg to stand on before we get half way through.

When I tell you that everything Spiritualists have done, have been done by the Profession to which I have the honour to belong. What does that prove? 'Nothing at all,' you say, and might add very likely, 'Possibly you are a Medium yourself, and don't know it.'

There are *some* people in this world with whom it is a mere waste of time to argue any given subject, for it leads to nothing in the end. I can say this much. I certainly do not mean to argue with Spiritualists, for I have too deep a sympathy for their affliction, poor creatures. Let us hope and trust they will be cured by degrees—not too sudden—for if they saw what sorry idiots they made of themselves, it might be quite too utterly too much for their nerves, and they might collapse altogether. Would there were a few more men like Prince Rudolph, of Austria, about to expose their shams.

'How?' you ask, 'does the Medium free himself after being tied up by the committee?' Nothing in the world is easier—when you know how. The rope-tying feat is beneath our notice. It is done at every fair and often at street corners.

Some Media permit themselves, you say, to be tied by one of the audience. Well, in this case, the Medium inflates his body, and sits in such a position that all his muscles and limbs are distended. When he resumes his normal position the ropes become loose and he releases himself.

To get out of the handcuffs, you have a duplicate key attached to an elastic band get-at-able behind your back. When tied with braid or strips of linen, a slip-knot on one wrist is bound to be there. It matters not how you tie up the Medium's wrists ; so that while talking, before the lights are lowered, he has only to ease the knot, and is·free in an instant, and back again in another instant.

At the end of the telescopic tube, I have previously mentioned, you may fix a trumpet or whistle, and by blowing through the tube sound can be evolved, and when the tube is floated about the dark room a discordant band of Spiritualistic music appear to the materially and physically benighted audience to be in the room à la Wagner. The floating in the air is done with a lay figure, got up to resemble the Medium.

The bulls-eye lantern in the hands of an assistant is so worked that a change is effected reminding one of the scenes so artistically worked out by Mr. Henry Irving in the 'Lyons Mail.'

'How about the Spiritual Musical-box?' you ask. 'Simple in the extreme,' I answer. An oblong piece of plate-glass is suspended by means of four cords hanging from the ceiling, and on this slab is fixed the Musical-box, which plays and stops at command. 'But how?' you ask. In the box is put a balance-lever, which, when the slab is in the slightest degree tilted, arrests the fly-fan and so stops the machinery. When you give the command, the slab is made level, and, the fly-fan being released off, the machinery starts, and plays the time. When you want it to stop the cord on either side is slightly pulled, the balance-lever falls, the fly-fan is arrested, and, of course, the music finishes.

Having, I hope, shown you the fallacy of 'Spiritualistic Rapping,' there still remains the 'Invisible Writing' manifestation I am reminded. True; I had almost forgo tten that, and yet I ought not to have done so, considering I was the inventor of a conjuring trick closely allied to the same, viz., 'The Slate Trick.' Though I don't believe in raps, I do in chalk; so, by-the-bye, does my Writing-spirit, Miss Jennie Sarah Ann Jones, related on her mother's side to Joe King, the great Spiritualist—pardon me, I am not joking, it is an historical fact! Whenever I require a message I call on Miss Jones, and, on blank slates (Welsh ones preferred), I get written what I require. There's a sort of grim irony in the fact, *entre nous*, that, when alive, Miss Jones kept a milk-shop near Burton Crescent, and died of milk-fever; not, of course, that that has anything to do with chalk! As I make a point of never exposing a conjuring trick of my own invention, I must be excused from stating how this is effected. If you come often enough and see my performances, you will possibly find it out. The writing by Spirits on the ceiling is done by means of the telescopic-rod, chalk being rubbed on the Medium's head to make the sitters believe it was done with his head. Now comes a poser from some infuriated believer. 'In my own room, my own family, only, being present—well, with the sole exception of Mr. So-and-So—I wrote the maiden-name of my great-grandmother's cousin's wasJherwoman! I placed it—folded up—under a volume of Dr. Samuel Kinn's 'Moses and Geology,' which is heavy—I mean a heavy book.

'The lights were all turned out, we were all sitting round the table, and, yet Mr. So-and-So was able to tell me the name I wrote. Mind without the lights; being turned up—but in pitch darkness—what do you think of that? You and your miserable, weak milk-and-water-jokes about Jones and the chalk, I'm a Welshman myself Sir, and theres not a dishonest man amongst us, Sir, and we are all George Washingtons and never tell a lie. Bah! I thought I should give you a clencher!!'

'It's a good thing something did not leak out during the time the room was in darkness,' I answer. If Mr. So-and-So had in his pocket a phial containing phosphorus and oil of cloves all he had to do was to take quietly the paper, open it under the table cloth, then open the cork of the phial from which a blue flame would be emitted quite sufficient to read the name, or even tell the exact hour and second a watch was previously stopped at, whilst none present could see the slightest light.

I have, however, slightly improved this method. Cut a round

piece of 'Balmaines Phosphorescent Card and fix it inside your hat lining and you can see to read distinctly by it, of course being mindful to keep the opening of the hat away from the audience. They say 'There's a silver lining to the darkest cloud.'

Be careful that yours does not show in this case, however, or this excellent trick would be exposed.

Did it ever strike you, how illogical these people are? Grant for one moment the bare possibility of a Spirit appearing here below. That means that you, a good angel soaring in heavenly bliss above, are to come down into a back parlour, let at 10s. a week-gas-and-coal-extra in Bloomsbury, or elsewhere, at the beck and call of a souless beer-imbibing-radical-money-grasping-Spirit-Medium, to play tambourines, or a cornet, the only instrument whilst alive that you could perhaps play being a barrel-organ. Why, it is rank blasphemy! to use the mildest term!

Of course it would not be quite so hard on you if you had to take an upward journey. The change then from 197° in the shade to the stuffy back parlour, might be an agreeable change!

And yet, I have heard these people say that this is a grand sublime religion which enobles them! *De gustibus non est disputandum.* There *must* be in this belief some attraction, or it stands to reason we should not hear of so many converts. One has not to look very far to find the same.

Tell me. Is there a man of honour who would allow any dear relative, of the opposite sex, to sit in a dark room with these paid Media men? If you answer yes—I say—and I don't intend to eat my words, you are a disgrace to the name of Englishman, and I don't envy you your feelings. Were a daughter, or sister of mine to attend one of these *séances*, after I had duly warned her of the danger she ran, I would never allow her to enter my doors again. I have challenged these people over and over again in every part of the world—almost everywhere I have visited—to show me a 'spirit-form' under any conditions they like—*but in my own room*—and with this *proviso*, viz., that I am allowed to put a bullet through the Spirit's head, which would, one would think, be quite immaterial, but they have always failed to see it in that light, and seemed to think it very material. Well—possibly there is something in that!

In conclusion, I can only say, that, whatever remarks I have made are fully justified. I firmly believe that many good people have got somewhat mixed up in their ideas. They confound 'Spiritualism' with that grand, undeveloped yet, mystery, 'Animal

Magnetism.' They have only to give this subject a very short, deep thinking over, asking themselves, are they rational human beings—endowed with one spark of logic in their brains—or must they hereafter be put down as lineal descendants of Balaam's Ass.

And now, gentle reader, I hurry to write *Finis*, as I fear I have bored you long enough with my *cacoethes scribendi!* If, however, these pages prove of value to any future Bohemian who may wish to carve out his future alone and unaided, I shall be doubly rewarded. Let him, however, also read Gaboriau. He is at least suggestive, and as he is an author much studied by Prince Bismarck, he will, at the worst, lose his time in good society. One cannot be altogether certain about anything, and I have a great horror of being dogmatic, but this I can say, if one takes for his motto, *Noblesse oblige*, remembering that a gentleman should live chivalrously and lovingly to God, and the King, and his lady, not attending to the little wants and totally forgetting the great and only real ones—that man will have little to reproach himself with when *finis* indeed arrives. Nothing can be nobler than honour, love, and faith, and I have always striven to command my ways upon that rule. It is not only written in all noble histories, but in every man's heart, if he will take care to read. *Palmam qui meruit ferat.*

www.ingramcontent.com/pod-product-compliance
Lightning Source LLC
Chambersburg PA
CBHW022355020726
47500CB00002B/294